This didn't have to be demons from hell.

Easing the clip back into the grip, I gently worked the slide to chanber a round and leaned back in my chair. Might be pure coincidence that a visitor came exactly at midnight and fog blanketed the city. Hey, anything was possible. I tightened my grip on the Glock, disengaging the safety. *Then again . . .*

The footsteps thumping along the hallway stopped right outside my door. There was a short pause, and then somebody politely knocked twice.

"Excuse me, I saw the light under your door," a soft feminine voice said. "May I use your bathroom?" She sounded sweet and southern. Pure corn pone and hominy grits. A delicate flower of the South. "The one in the lobby is broken, and I really have to pee something fierce. Please?"

"Just a sec," I answered cheerfully, aiming at chest level where the heart would be on a human being. *Yeah, she was from the South, all right. Straight down south. Near the core of the planet.* Hell.

—From "Falling like Gentle Rain" by Nick Pollotta

UNDER COVER OF DARKNESS

EDITED BY

Julie E. Czerneda
and Jana Paniccia

DAW BOOKS, INC.
DONALD A. WOLLHEIM, FOUNDER
375 Hudson Street, New York, NY 10014

ELIZABETH R. WOLLHEIM
SHEILA E. GILBERT
PUBLISHERS
http://www.dawbooks.com

First Printing, February 2007
1 2 3 4 5 6 7 8 9

DAW TRADEMARK REGISTERED
U.S. PAT. OFF. AND FOREIGN COUNTRIES
—MARCA REGISTRADA
HECHO EN U.S.A.

PRINTED IN THE U.S.A.

ACKNOWLEDGMENTS

Introduction © 2007 by Julie E. Czerneda and Jana Paniccia

The Scoria © 2007 by Doranna Durgin

The Gatherers' Guild © 2007 by Larry Niven

Kyri's Gauntlet © 2007 by Darwin A. Garrison

Falling Like the Gentle Rain © 2007 by Nick Pollotta

The Things Everyone Knows © 2007 by Tanya Huff

The Invisible Order © 2007 by Paul Crilley

Borrowed Time © 2007 by Stephen Kotowych

Shadow of the Scimitar © 2007 by Janet Deaver-Pack

The Good Samaritan © 2007 by Amanda Bloss Maloney

Seeking the Master © 2007 by Esther M. Friesner

When I Look to the Sky © 2007 by Russell Davis

The Sundering Star © 2007 by Janny Wurts

The Exile's Path © 2007 by Jihane Noskateb

The Dancer at the Red Door © 2007 by Douglas Smith

Table of Contents

INTRODUCTION

Julie E. Czerneda and Jana Paniccia

THERE IS A world beyond the one we know.

Whispers reveal paths to its location. Symbols decorate its lintels. Handshakes gain entry into its domain.

A domain of power—where oath-bound men and women hold the keys to tantalizing knowledge, astonishing magic, and unparalleled authority. Under cover of darkness they live out their lives as reflections of ordinary citizens, even while working to shape the course of human destiny.

We debate their motives. We debate their influence. We debate their *very* existence. Yet what do we really know without belonging ourselves?

What of those few who *do* step through the veil shrouding our world from that hidden one? What cause sparks their desire, leads them to knock on that unseen door, to accept the responsibility of knowing the truths most of us can only imagine?

This is the premise we gave our talented group of authors: journey beyond the whispers, the rumors, and the hearsay . . . delve into the realities of those who become a part of the secrets and those who live and die to keep them.

We hope you enjoy the results as much as we have.

THE SCORIA

Doranna Durgin

Scoria: The refuse from the reduction of metal ores.

"ALLEKSA! ALLEKSA!"

Voices raised in joy, in a rare daring.

Galetia twisted from her sentry spot and raised her own hands high, flashing fingers open and closed in the approval of their kind. "*Alleksa!*" she shouted down into the bowl of the arena ruin, a midnight darkness spotted with tiny ground fires and fire spinners on the move. A spontaneous, whirling circle closed around the central dark spot that held Alleksa.

Hidden here outside the city, only the Scoria celebrated the night.

And only the Scoria celebrated surviving the coming of age that the citties took for granted. Alleksa proved more blessed yet . . . she would not only survive, she would thrive. Everyone saw the signs—the flashes of change without fever, without shakes, without chills. The ripples of ethereal *otherness* across her face, without the rash that so often came with such a strong turning.

3

She would be one of their strongest.

She might even live through to adulthood, protected by this secret gathering of the abandoned, the discarded . . . those both lost and found. Each year, more infants were plucked to the safety of loving arms. Each year, more youngsters lived through the change.

But, oh, the authorities had begun to suspect. There were too many of them now—too many who survived exposure on the rugged ceremonial hillside so steep, so treacherous, even those who left vulnerable infants to perish sometimes fell to their own deaths. For all Galetia knew, her own father had met that fate. She felt no regret at the thought. He'd seen those brief, newborn signs of who she was—of *what* she was—and he'd abandoned her. In spite of him, she'd lived. In spite of them all, she'd grown. And now, with barely eighteen years claimed, she was one of the elders of the Scoria, almost ready to attempt full integration into the copper-spawned city.

From within the city she could observe . . . she could send warnings to the Scoria. They had to be more careful than ever these days if they even hoped to survive. For it was the Scoria come-of-age that those in city had feared all along.

Galetia had come of age a handful of years earlier, and had exchanged her hunter-gatherer duties for those of the watch, employing her new facilities to protect those younger. Thanks to the change and new affinities with the animals of her world . . . she could see in the dark, perceive an amazing range of sounds, manage a sense of smell above all others . . . and more. Owl, bat, fierce iron-hided rhino . . . her instant ability to connect with the animals she encountered, to borrow from them, had outmatched any of the other Scoria before her. Her ability to connect with her fellow elders had created a level of communication the Scoria had never before experienced.

Until Alleksa. Alleksa would certainly surpass her . . . Alleksa, if she gained wisdom to match her innate ability, would almost certainly lead the Scoria into a new era. All the elders spoke of it, having seen the signs in the gangly young woman. All the elders were determined to lead Alleksa to that wisdom.

Galetia hadn't yet decided if Alleksa herself had that same determination.

Didn't matter, not tonight. Tonight was for the celebration—the certainty of the younger's survival. The Scoria filled the arena, lithe, immature bodies whirling fire pots on pilfered chains, dancing in a frenzy only the constant fear of annihilation could so freely bring to the surface. The crumbling arena held them in safety, hiding them . . . nurturing them.

This old arena, long abandoned, held a deep warren of burrows beneath the stone structure of the steep seating rows. Half the oval arena lay destroyed by a long-ago mud slide. The other half had withstood the onslaught of mud and trees, and the debris piled high against the outer wall. Over the years the Scoria had extended their burrows through that architecture of trees and natural mortar; they'd dug deep into the hill, stealing stone bones from the crumbled arena to shore up their dwellings. They kept vigil on the hillsides, they ran a nursery as efficiently as any city nanny, and they made daring nighttime raids for supplies the rugged, spare surrounding hills and ridges couldn't provide. They stayed hidden from city eyes, their outrunners and elders always alert.

'Ware!

Denye's voice came to her inner self, a voice she heard only within. An inner ear for which the citties feared her, feared them all.

Dive? she asked him. To sound the dive would send the youngers scurrying for their burrows, dousing their lights and clearing the arena faster than any cittie could imagine. To sound the retreat would send them bolting for distant, ready caves—but they hoped never to make that run.

Too late for dive.

That shook her. Too late? Had someone managed to come so close unperceived?

Only if they'd meant to. If they knew to stay concealed.

That shook her more deeply yet, a hard fist clenching around her insides. After all this time, did someone suspect? Did someone hunt them?

Can't—

Denye's voice cut short, interrupted by another of the elders in a focused call that Galetia couldn't hear. Didn't matter. She understood. Denye wasn't in a position to stop the intruder without giving them away—or worse, without killing the cittie.

And that was the strongest of their rules. No killing the citties; no hurting them. Not even in self-defense. Those things would only draw attention to the arena.

As something else already had.

Galetia glanced down into the arena, taking an instant to open wide, both arms spread in reception, both hands opening and closing in unconscious hand flashing as she did what no cittie could ever do—that which made the Scoria pity them all, and never regret who they were. She drank in their joy, their exultation. *Alleksa!!* they shouted, as loud in their unspoken celebration as in their spoken.

And then she whirled into the darkness, leaping familiar architecture with the surety of the hill goats, bounding cityside with the confident abandon of her *otherness*, knowing her face held the overlay of the changes and her eyes had gone huge and wild. She circled downwind of the crooked footpath that had once been a heavily traveled road and almost instantly picked up the scent—a single man. He wore an expensive scent overlain with dank, nervous sweat and he oiled his hair, and it was enough to tell her more than he'd ever suspect.

Merchant. Thought much of himself. Had an important patron.

And there was no good reason for him to be here. No good reason for anyone to be here—not on this road, not at this time of night. Not ever. He'd heard something; he'd guessed something. And he looked to impress his patron with information of unique importance.

Galetia ran a parallel path uphill of the one the man traveled. None of the Scoria ever used it; they hoped for it to grow over. They kept idle explorers away, fostering the belief that the arena had become a nest of cabra dens—using the carefully relocated carcasses of actual cabra kills to do it. They developed a cabra team, those who could most influence the big cats and who practiced guiding them—herding them. Taking them to staked-out prey, until the cabras came to associate the herding with the pleasant coincidence of food, and resisted less and less.

Only a fool would come out here at night. And a fool could be easily fooled.

She eased in so close she could smell nothing else, could hear his rapid breathing, could even feel the warmth of his body radiating into the night, a body perfectly visible to her in the scant moonlight he used to navigate. "*Rrrrrr-chk-chk-CHK!*"

Only one thing made that noise.

The man gasped, freezing so abruptly he stumbled in his tracks.

"*Rrrrrr-chk-chk-CHK!*" She brushed her hand through

the dried grasses of autumn, a rustling so faint she wasn't sure the man would even hear.

He heard. The stink of his sweat increased; his breathing all but stopped.

"*Rrrrrr!*"

"Goddess!" he gasped, and turned on his heel, bolting back down the path in the moonlit darkness, even though running from a cabra only guaranteed that the cabra would leap to pursue.

A *real* cabra.

Galetia laughed into the darkness and bounded back to join the celebration.

Alleksa did not noticeably crave wisdom.

Made restless by the onset of the change, made wily with the new skills that came and went like the breaking of a young man's voice, she slipped away from her outmatched vigil sitters to run in the hills, to sit along the ridges with the breeze lifting her thick ragged hair, to crawl through the interlaced branches of the north slope bittertree woods. She took her sling and brought back small game; she took bow and arrow and brought back a yearling deer. But she couldn't slip Galetia off her trail. Galetia ghosted her, the only one whose skills ran nearly as deep as Alleksa's would—but did not, not quite yet. Galetia tried to reach her mind, found it polished and impenetrable . . . kept trying anyway. And unseen, she followed Alleksa as the younger ran the ridges closer and closer to the city, gaining enough ground to look down into that crowded collection of homes and grand official buildings and the colorful awnings and brightly painted stalls of the marketplace.

Galetia did not have to touch her mind to know her thoughts. Once the youngers had mastered the change, they became elders. And the elders were allowed into the city. There they used their skills to steal much-needed supplies, took odd jobs to earn coin for the group, and learned the skills the citties knew. They learned to blend in . . . to pick up bits and pieces of information, sometimes even to hear when someone's newborn had shown glimpses of *otherness* in those few precious hours before it subsided, hidden until the change.

Then the Scoria knew to send someone to the hillside, to snatch the baby from the certain death that waited.

All the Scoria obsessed about their first encounter with the city. With the citties themselves. And Alleksa, a girl raised with lessons of mistrust that had never quite taken, now driven by the changes, barely sane at that . . .

Galetia caught her, once, on the verge of descending the hill to creep in the backside of the city. She stood at the edge of an outcrop, hidden by a sentinel of stone. Her features had gone fey with the change, her expression determined.

And Galetia, atop that stone sentinel with Alleksa none the wiser, spoke sharply, with intent to startle. "Lose your change-phase halfway down, and you die. No plain old younger can make that slope. No cittie."

Startle Alleksa did, with those first few words. She leaped back into the darkest shadows of the rocks, looking for Galetia with a mix of guilt and insanity. "You!" she said. "You shouldn't be able—no one should be able—"

"Too true." Galetia swung her legs over the side of the sentinel and leaped down, as light on her feet as the stealthy cabra she'd imitated only a few nights earlier. "Ought to say something to you, that."

Alleksa's pretty face closed up in stubborn denial. Her lips, pouty baby lips, pursed. "Give me a few days," she said. "You won't be able to do it anymore."

"Longer than a few days," Galetia said. "You know that. Longer yet, before you have the control to be safe among the citties. And even then you go out with someone." She smiled, much as a cabra might smile. "Probably me, from the looks of things."

Alleksa turned her back with a flounce of offense and stalked back into the garden of rocks between which the citties believed no man nor woman walked.

And they'd be right. Such places were for the Scoria alone.

Galetia understood. They *all* understood, all the elders. The change made you that way—took away your common sense as it altered your body, inflating emotions from joy to anger to carefree abandon, all in the space of a conversation. And the elders knew no one had been through a change so great as Alleksa's, not and expected to live. They spoke to her, but they did not punish her. They turned the entire Scoria underground into a watch network, and if the youngers couldn't reach the elders through silent communication, they could still pass the word from one to another with amazing swiftness. They confined her to her section of the warrens, and they ran regular head counts.

When they came up short, it was Galetia's job to track her down. She wore herself thin, maintaining her duties along with her new responsibilities to Alleksa, and so the elders pulled her from those duties. She rested as she could, waiting for the call . . . knowing that at the end of the trail she'd find Alleksa with eyes fever-bright, the change flaring through her body, and no more sense than the goddess had given a mud mite. "It will pass," she told Alleksa—told herself, if truth be told. "It will pass, and one day you'll wake and wonder that it ever was. That you were ever other than you.

"You don't know that," Alleksa told her, fierce with the natural inner ire of the small bak-bak squirrel that lived in the lower hills. The changes took her more deeply these days, and showed no signs of letting up. "None of you know that. There's never been one like me. You don't know that it'll *ever* end." And the tenacity of the bak-bak left her in a rush, turning her back into a younger who sobbed with frustration and followed meekly as Galetia returned her to the warrens.

And Galetia knew she was right.

"Two more babies this week," reported Rurie, the elder only a year younger than Galetia. "Looking good for their survival."

"Two more," echoed Kisa, stroking her stomach as if she could imagine bearing babies herself one day.

It happened, sometimes. But they took pains to keep it from happening here in the warren, knowing their space was precious and their expansion room nonexistent.

Bodhan shook his head, running his hands over the veil of long, knotted rivergrass hanging at the uneven, rounded wall. Their tally system—of supplies, of warren space, of the Scoria themselves. "The grass is becoming unbalanced."

"We cannot leave them to die," Kisa said, flaring as though any of them had or even would suggest it. They only looked at her. "They are our own kind. Our *only* kind."

"We will all die if we cannot balance things," Bodhan said. He had a skill with the tallies, and for details.

That's when they looked at Galetia. All of them. Elders with the weight of the warrens on still-young shoulders. Elders facing their mortality, their inevitable expansion, and their limitations. They looked at her, and

Rurie said, "Watch Alleksa. She's the one who can change things. Who can find us a new home . . . or teach the citties to leave us this one even if they learn we're here."

Watch Alleksa. Keep her safe. Keep her away from the citties.

Galetia said, "I will."

She's been seen, Bodhan told Galetia, calling from as far away as the city. Stone houses, cobbled streets . . . cittie lives were surrounded by stone, and copper. Bodhan was an occasional day laborer there, and he had, aside from his practical skills, a knack for culling gossip.

Although this particular gossip hadn't needed any culling; it came freely. *It's all they talk about. The wild girl, lurking in the hills. How did she get there? How does she survive? That she's one of their castoffs is evident to them. They merely argue over which wild animal took her as its own, snatching her off the hill.*

An entire community of wild animals, that's which one. A community grown over generations until it was finally outgrowing its allotted territory. A community grown strong enough to keep even Alleksa alive.

If they were lucky.

It's going to take more than luck now, Bodhan said, picking up on Galetia's not-so-subtle thoughts. *Now they're looking for her. And in looking for her—*

He didn't need to finish. In looking for Alleksa, they would find the Scoria. All of them.

The interruptive babble in her mind started all at once.

Galetia! She's—

I can't find—

And one inner voice from the city silenced them all, horrified into an inner shout—*Goddess, she's HERE!*

Galetia bolted to her feet, scattering the littlest youngers who had been practicing knots and roping, clustered around her cross-legged work position. Even those youngers, still blind to inner voice, understood the import of her reaction. "Is it Alleksa?" they asked, all at once and half of them still lisping. Nothing more than ordinary children in these years before the change. "Is she in the city?"

They were too young to comprehend the nature of the development, or what it could mean to their survival in these next few years. Not so the other elders, the new elders who only went into the city with an escort and trainer and who had still heard every word of the babble and the emotions behind it. A new elder burst into the warren, her eyes wild. "I'll take them," she said, meaning the children who crowded Galetia, their knotwork forgotten and dropped to unravel on the floor. "Find her! Save her!"

Her outer voice generated an echo of inner voices. *Find her! Save her!*

And what they really meant was *save US!*

Galetia ran from the warren. She ran out into the arena, waved ahead by a sentry who signaled the all-clear. She bounded up the stepped seating with borrowed grace, not wasting her time wondering how Alleksa had gotten past them all. She'd been in the change phase and she'd done it; she'd been in the change and she'd made it into the city, endowed with all the speed and cunning of every animal that had ever wanted to go unseen. But while the change was upon her, she was vulnerable to detection as cursed . . . and when the change left her, she'd be vulnerable to the citties.

Save us!

Galetia fell into a steady, rangy trot, wolflike in endurance, and in economy of movement. She hadn't bothered to change into cittie clothes—the knee pants that ballooned to huge proportions; the fine-woven blousy top with droopy, fashionable sleeves that only got in the way. She wore the clothes of the hunter-warrior the citties had made of her: rough-woven knee-length trous, leather leg-bells loosely covering her lower legs and strapped tight at the bottom to keep away the mud ticks and root leeches, and worn leather ankle-shoes stolen from someone's back stoop. Atop she wore the season's half-cape and hood over an indeterminate muddle of a shirt.

Not girl's clothing. But neither was her short-cropped hair meant for a girl, and she hardly moved like a cittie girl, stumbling in too-short box-toed shoes or getting tangled in an excess of material at her knees. And if her breasts this past year had become impossible to ignore, the indeterminate muddle of a shirt and half-cape obscured them well enough for a first glance, maybe well enough for a second.

Or whatever it took to get Alleksa out of the city and away.

She cannot stay, Galetia told the others, her inner voice steady even as she panted evenly for breath, running along the old city path that none of them ever used. *I will take her away. To the caves, perhaps. To the lake—*

So far? they asked her. But no one protested. They did nothing but beat at her in a constant pummeling of escaping thoughts, using the web of thought that Galetia herself had once stabilized. Their worry, their anger at Alleksa, their understanding . . . every one of them had been through the change. Every one of them had been driven to stupidity and danger along the way. They knew the stakes here. What Alleksa could do for them . . . what she could do *to* them if allowed.

With voices in her head and panting in her ears, Galetia almost missed the signs. Someone else coming toward her, twisting through the trees at a steady walk and perceptible at a distance only because of Galetia's hawk-imbued vision. She leaped from the trail, loping uphill with every intent to skirt the interloper.

With her first step, she realized her mistake—that the crooked trees thinned, leaving her exposed to a man clothed in hunting garments much like hers. The hunter gave a shout, lifting one hand to point, the other whirling a tangler weapon of leather and stone—and though Galetia leaped farther uphill, the man anticipated her move and flung his tangler directly into her new path.

Leather wrapped around her legs, tripping her; the stones smacked against her shins, a white-hot pain that numbed her legs. Galetia fell, and she could not help but tumble down the hill. Only by grabbing a spindly, warped tree trunk did she keep herself from landing at his feet. Already she reached for her flint knife to free herself, and already she flung her mind wide open to the elders, letting them see. Letting them know. Making sure they understood if another was needed.

In the background conversation, she heard snatches of Bodhan's report, his efforts to send others to find and shadow Alleksa within the city. For only Galetia could handle her one on one, and only because Alleksa could not yet rely on herself.

Because if she could, she wouldn't be in the throes of the change. She wouldn't be in the city, drawn by curiosity, driven by the warped sense of reality that came with the change.

But Galetia was long past that stage, and she had far too much experience with citties to be cowed by a man who had no concept of her true strength and speed, or of the adeptness with which she'd learned to lie. "Are you crazed?" she sputtered, sparing him only a swift glare as she tackled the confining leather with her knife, ignoring the pained shout of protest from the hunter. "These are cabra hills! Take me down, will you, when I'm already running for my life?"

"Here, now!" the man said, gesturing at her knife and ignoring her words. "Unwrap 'em, like!"

"No call for it," Galetia insisted, sawing all the harder at the leather as the man broke from the trail to come after his precious tangler. If he got that close, he'd see she was no boy. He'd think of Alleksa and he'd start to wonder. "Take what comes to you, then."

"It was a mistake, that's all. I'm not hunting cabra or deer today."

Alleksa. The man hunted Alleksa, with no idea that she'd already gone to the city.

Galetia ripped the tangler free of her throbbing legs and threw it at the hunter. She put strength behind it, and the rocks thudded into his chest, knocking him hard enough to stumble and fall. "Another day, we'd have words over the pain you've caused. Today, I'm getting out of cabra turf." And even leaping up on unsteady legs, she quickly put herself out of his range. She pulled the doors to her mind closed, enough to nurse her pain in privacy—but not so much she didn't hear the cabra team head out.

For there *were* cabras in these hills. And the team would find one, guide it to the right place at the right time.

She had warned the cittie. He hadn't heeded her, and now he would discover the truth of her words.

And the Scoria, long reviled simply for what they might possibly grow up to be, would finally deserve the fears they inspired.

* * *

Galetia hoped the movement of the run would ease her legs, keep the swelling down and the blood moving.

She'd been wrong.

Let me look for her, Bodhan told her, sensing her difficulty through even the small inner window Galetia had left open. *I can get away from this crew—*

A crew on an important work site, pulling down the remains of a damaged building—a city-owned building, with a jaded and experienced work crew who took their conduit of inside information for granted. And for what would he lose that connection? The opportunity to watch Alleksa evading him.

And she would. Bodhan, for all his skill with the number grasses and detailed projects, could not keep up with Alleksa—and could not hold her without drawing attention. Galetia could do both.

I should have been watching her. Never mind that a handful of others *had* been watching her, and let her slip away. Or that Galetia had needs—to sleep, to eat, to rest her mind in time with the children. She was the only one who could have stopped this.

By goddess, she'd stop it now.

Bodhan perceived her answer, flashing her unspoken acceptance. But he added, *If you need me . . .*

She wouldn't.

She slowed on the outer edges of the city, coming into it through little-used alleyways left only to the bold. Noxious, dangerous . . . they reflected none of the city's stolid splendor, the magnificent buildings, the streets that were bright both day and night with their tall cedar-oil lamps, the gentle drift of those out walking simply for the purpose of being seen. This was an area of skulkers and wounded and those who barely survived—along with those who made it hard to survive. But Galetia settled into her cabra's stalk, her eyes confident, her gaze quick, and her sling ready in her hand. No one bothered her—everyone here knew the difference between predator and prey, even if this particular predator wasn't as graceful as she ought to have been.

Two rows of buildings separated this section of ragged homes and the glory of the city—warehouses, storage rooms, and a line of stables and livestock shelters for the animals not allowed in the city proper. Galetia paused between two buildings, finding a quiet spot beside a struggling tuft of grasses. This close, she would be able to sense Alleksa directly, her familiarity with Alleksa's touch honed by weeks of close proximity and endless hours of searching. Even if she were in a change phase, Alleksa couldn't hide herself; she could only close herself off.

The deep, welcome scent of water, a burbling splash, delightful fine spray against hot skin . . .

She wasn't even closing herself off. She was too far immersed in what she'd found . . . and no wonder. The ever-flowing central city fountain was a delight to the senses, even for those without quite so many senses to delight. Sun sparkling off water, coins glinting from the glass mosaic of the fountain floor—all copper, all thrown in thanks to the copper ore mining that kept this city prosperous. The giggling and singing of the water as it splashed from one tiered saucer to the next, spraying the air with a mist so fine that rainbows often surrounded the fountain itself.

Once she'd seen it, Alleksa wouldn't have been able to resist, driven by her changes and a mind not quite sane in the middle of it all.

Galetia opened her eyes, found herself so quickly grown stiff that she dared not rest any longer. Following Alleksa's simple, profound sensory exhilaration, she moved through the streets as quickly as she could without drawing attention to herself. In the background of her mind, the elders encouraged her, a support tinged with desperation. *Save her. Save us.*

Alleksa stood at the fountain, arms outstretched as if greeting ecstasy. Those around her—servants of the affluent, carrying errand baskets and private messages and responsibility—gave her wide berth, for the most part pretending they saw nothing at all. Children—running those same errands, or simply tagging along with their parent—had no such compulsion. They pointed, asking questions. They laughed at Alleksa's bemused expression, her eyes half-lidded, a smile curving her lips. They laughed at her rough clothing, at the scanty nature of it in spite of the taste of fall in the air.

In the warrens, she would have been plenty warm. Here in the bright sunshine, her skin looked pale, her hair washed out, her face bleached of color aside from the spots on her cheeks and lips that looked too full, too mature on that thin face. Here, she was attracting attention. Soon enough the wrong person would see her . . . someone who was determined to do something about this spectacle.

Alleksa, Galetia whispered, making her way around the edge of the small square within which the fountain sat. She had little hope that Alleksa could or would hear her, but it would be best for them all if she did, if she could pull herself away from that which so delighted her beleaguered mind. *You are not safe. Come to me.*

Alleksa's body gave a little shiver of denial. She turned her pale face to the sun. On it shimmered the signs of change, clear for all to see. Shadows chasing across her skin, sparks of iridescence and hints of color.

So be it.

Lower legs aching, pounding with the pain of too

much swollen bruising inside skin too small to hold it all, Galetia did not waste any time. Not with Alleksa's change out there for the whole of the city to see—not when some of them had already gasped and drawn back, forgetting to pretend they saw nothing at all. Galetia strode to the fountain, shaking off the grim fear of those who perceived the situation through her thoughts. All these years they'd stayed hidden . . . and now they tee-tered on the verge of exposure, betrayed by the strength of the change in which they'd so recently placed their hopes.

Galetia did nothing more than put her hand on Allek-sa's arm, her voice almost hidden in the song of the fountain as she said, "*Now.*"

Too late— Bodhan's inner voice whispered into her mind, so close that she jerked around to find him at the edge of the square, having come in spite of her injunc-tion against it.

Scoria voices wailed in silence, filling her head in re-sponse to what Bodhan now showed her from his better vantage point. The constables, striding into the other side of the square with truncheons to hand, their faces holding fear beyond what any mere adolescent girl could inspire. They'd heard. Even now Galetia heard the mur-murs through Bodhan's ears, where through her own she heard only the sweet fountain. *Her face! Did you see her face?* and *It's her! It's the girl from the high ground. She's one of the cursed!*

Cursed . . . cursed . . . cursed . . .

Galetia's fingers dug into soft skin. Alleksa's eyes wid-ened, bemused by the change, by the fountain, by Gal-etia's presence. She did not try to break away; even fey, she had long learned she could not evade Galetia. But the constables rounded the end of the long fountain, and Galetia needed more than that. She needed *Alleksa*, returned to her senses—shedding the change, or *using* it. With the constables bearing down on them, she needed cooperation . . . she needed *help*. To do this on her own . . .

She could. Hurt, profoundly frightened for her own, for the future of the Scoria—Galetia could still do it.

But not without giving away just how much the citties had to fear.

She reached out to Alleksa, unable to imagine failure. She wrapped herself around that embattled mind, blanketing it, scrabbling against that smooth, polished surface that was Alleksa. And then she found her grip and she *wrenched*—

Alleksa's eyes opened wider yet as the change drained from her face, as she twisted to look over her shoulder and her eyes finally took in more than just the mesmerizing fountain. Her mouth opened, those lips rounded to say everything that showed so clearly on her face, in her mind. *Oh! I'm so sorry! I didn't mean to—I didn't know—!*

"Go to Bodhan," Galetia said, more roughly than she meant to as she pulled Alleksa away from the very grasp of the constables, trading places . . . shoving Alleksa hard enough to make her gasp, to send her reeling toward the crowd. Standing in the way with sad defiance—only an instant of it before she twisted her expression in a jeer and brought the change to the surface, deliberately flashing *otherness* within the very reach of the constables. *Decoy.*

We're away!

She saw it on the faces of the constables—their realization that Alleksa was gone, their fury. They leaped for her, and Galetia slid out of reach, calling on all that frightened the citties to forge her own escape. No more than Alleksa could she be caught here, proving the very existence of her kind. If she made her way clear of the city, running out toward the mines and foundries, running nowhere near her beloved warrens . . .

Once she lost any pursuit, she could rest . . . she could make her way below the city and across the ridges to the fall-back warrens. Just as would Bodhan, escorting Alleksa changed . . . Alleksa in control. Alleksa who reached out to her now, full of gratitude and sorrow. *I am whole, thanks to you*, she said. *We will be safe; we will lead them far away when they follow.*

Perhaps Alleksa would be the one to escort Bodhan.

Galetia spun away from the constables, reaching deep for the change, unable to truly overcome her wounded legs. Her hood fell away to reveal her touched features, to draw another gasp from the crowd. "Cursed!" they cried, several voices as one. And again—"Cursed!"

No, blessed! She ran along the edge of the fountain, balancing on its narrow lip as the constables splashed awkwardly into the deep water, trying to cut her off. The elders spoke to her as one, a wash of pride and support and extra determination, although Galetia needed none. Alleksa and Bodhan were safe, and the Scoria had time to abandon the warrens, concealing them to start the waiting. Waiting to return . . . waiting until Alleksa's strength could lead them to a new way of life. Galetia would have laughed out loud . . . had something not quite abruptly slammed into her ribs. *Between* her ribs.

She had only a glimpse—the hunter, returned from the arena trail alone, bruised and battered and bleeding. Her hands clutched cold bone handle, cold copper, quivering deep in her side.

She splashed backward into the water, sinking into its crisp grasp, eyes full of wet sparkle and light and the amazingly dark plume of her own blood.

Sinking. Numbed and sinking and unable to fight it.

No! Inner voices exploded into the sudden silence of water muffling her ears, crying out in communal agony. *No!*

But it was Alleksa's voice that broke in to override them all. Cool, as soothing as the water. The ache in Galetia's lungs became as nothing; the spear of fire in her side faded away. *We are here*, Alleksa said, suddenly old for her years. *We are with you. And you will always be with us.*

For the Scoria were never alone. The Scoria, dregs of this thriving city, took care of their own.

And when Alleksa returned, the city would understand.

Galetia did, and she smiled into the fading sparkle and light.

Doranna Durgin was born writing (instead of kicking, she scribbled on the womb) and never quit, although it took some time for the world to understand what she was up to. She grew up attached to college-rule notebooks and resisted all attempts at separation. Eventually she got a college degree (Wildlife Illustration) and had grand adventures on horseback in the Appalachians before turning full-time writer and ending up in the Southwestern high country with her laptop, dogs, horse, and uncontrollable imagination.

Doranna writes eclectically and across genres, with backlist in fantasy, tie-in, SF/F anthologies, a mystery, and romance. You can find a complete bibliography at www.doranna.net, along with scoops about new projects, lots of silly photos, and contact info. And just for kicks, Connery Beagle has a LiveJournal (connerybeagle) presenting his unique view of life—drop by and say hello!

THE GATHERERS' GUILD

Larry Niven

FROM A FEW hundred feet up in the moonless Northern California night, the restaurant was invisible. A redwood forest ran up a mountain, with no work of humanity in sight. I followed the pale light of my GPS indicator down, trusting it knew what it was doing.

I'm a Gatherer, but my branch is Sales Tax. I'd never yet seen Gregor's, a favorite hangout of the IRS elite.

A shadowy mass sank past me, too fast, no lights. I veered, not bothering to curse. Too many idiots already fly cars. I dread the day taxpayers find out they can fly. Flight belts are much safer for the people below—but several hundred million flying taxpayers would still be too dangerous, and Jeez, what if they got cars?

I was below the treetops now, surrounded by trunks. Below me, the car mushed out on silent fans, then settled on a lawn. I glimpsed light in a narrow line: windows showing below the restaurant's roof. I edged toward it, easing around a redwood's thick trunk.

Blocked by the redwood, I saw light flaring around the trunk's curve on both sides.

Somehow, I instantly accepted that Gregor's had exploded. I eased forward against the tree as the sound blasted me. It slapped me against the bark. I hung for a moment, dazed.

Gregor's burned. I saw the car catch fire, too. I eased to the ground and crawled into some bushes to watch.

Maybe fifteen people ran, staggered, and crawled out of Gregor's. Guards came running from the forest to help them. I couldn't guess how many were left inside. I didn't see Marion. I feared she was still inside, and I feared to go and look.

"Mel," Woody said, "Why didn't you try to help?"

I started to answer, but Christine came into the room. Woody's wife is a taxpayer. We held off while she poured coffee from the secret fields on Mount Hood. "Breakfast in fifteen minutes. I called room service," she said.

After Christine left, Woody added meager splashes of century-old Hawaiian rum.

"I didn't want to push my luck," I told him. "Friday the thirteenth, and Gregor's was burning. I was afraid to help. They were all IRS people. They'd have taken me for the bomber."

It was still dawn, not office hours yet. I'd come to Woody's penthouse apartment in Portland for refuge.

Woody said, "We'll give it to the media as a mob hit. Now tell me what you were doing there in the first place."

"I had a date."

"At an IRS site?"

"Marion Nye is IRS, or was." I swallowed. I hadn't really faced it: Marion could be dead. I hadn't seen her emerge from Gregor's. "She's mid level in Creative

Math. We met last May at the gathering in Jamaica, and went on to her villa in Spain. It wasn't espionage, Woody. Just sex."

"You should have told us."

"You'd have had me spying on her."

"Oh, I might like to ask her about that Beverly Hills thing—"

"Hell, I'm still deciding how serious we . . . are. Spy on each other or get married? I wanted to see what her friends were like. Woody, what's it like, married to a taxpayer?"

He shrugged. "I have to keep a few secrets. She never wonders how I can afford this place, and she doesn't know about the Hawaii house. She just thinks I make wonderful coffee."

I laughed.

Woody was looking at his four-foot-by-six-foot computer monitor. He said, "Okay. There were three dead in the blast. Eleven injured. Marion Nye is in the secret hospital in Portland."

"Good! How is she?"

"Stable, it says. So that gives us anywhere between five and eight suspicious deaths, all IRS, all within the last two months, and nobody knows who's doing it. It's driving the IRS crazy. They could start bombing *us*."

"Could it *be* us?"

Woody didn't answer. The top levels at Sales Tax don't tell us everything.

"What if we could solve this ourselves?" I asked.

Woody's lips pursed. "First you'd have to find out who's doing the killing. Then it has to be someone that isn't us. We don't know that yet. Then you have to make the IRS believe it. You like mysteries?"

I grinned.

Room service appeared. We stopped to eat, and made

conversation for Christine's benefit, before we settled in
for some computer work.

Eloise Stern had drowned. That was seven weeks ago at
"June in Jamaica," mid-June 2005, when the upper ranks
of all the United States tax gathering bureaus met for
four weeks of riotous excess. If the Jamaican police had
done a proper autopsy, they'd have found her lungs
filled with champagne from the swimming pool.

Fourth of July: Harry Greene had been poisoned.
Woody stared. "Poison? Doesn't the IRS have garnetine?"

Garnetine is an inoculation against most poisons. I
said, "No, that's just ours, just Sales Tax. One day we'll
trade garnetine to them for something we need."

"Damn office politics." He read on. Washington DC
police found Greene's death puzzling. Stomach contents:
both beluga and salmon caviar, with onion and chives
and chopped egg as condiments. Odd things to find in a
government employee earning $80,000 a year and spend-
ing the night alone.

Three might have been ringers, but they'd died very
close together. Jane Hennessey was descending Everest
when she'd had a stroke. Samuel Jefferson and Keki
Tomomato had died within days of each other, both
from heart attacks or strokes, no autopsies yet: the only
deaths ever recorded (except that their presence never
would be recorded) aboard the International Space Station. All in July, 2005.

"Too many strokes," Woody said.

I said, "Coincidence happens. Strokes happen when
the oxygen's thin."

He said, "Say Jefferson and Tomomato pulled rank:
that would get them up to the Space Station without
training. Their hearts stopped all by themselves. Hennessey's probably did, too."

"Yeah." Why murder her on the way *down* from Everest? Why wait?

"Which leaves *five* killings and not many suspects. We're looking for an organization, right? No single person could do all that."

I nodded. I was keeping half an eye on Woody's computer screen. We might be getting more word of Marion.

"What have we got for suspects? There's Sales Tax, that's us. There's Hidden Tax. There's the IRS itself; it might be some kind of internal war. They've got the power and the dominance games, too. We'd like it to be Hidden Tax, because if it's internal IRS, we won't know which side to talk to. What do you know about Hidden Tax?"

"They're pretty secretive."

Woody sipped coffee, waiting me out.

"Oh, all right. They're ungodly rich, even compared to the rest of us. They were a fringe group once, a branch of Revenue when it was just one branch, until they put the country on a silver money basis. First silver, then just paper. There isn't any real money anymore. They can get all the wealth they need by printing it. *We* have to play numbers games."

"Where's their motive? Why would they bomb a restaurant, or poison people? Hidden Tax were the ones who took *all* the gold away—"

"Roosevelt era. Before you were born."

"And then let the taxpayers play with it again years later! They didn't need it! What would they have to gain from a few murders?"

"What do any of us have to gain? Rich people don't fight each other. They've got too much to protect."

"And yet wars happen."

"Woody, there are other suspects. What if Congress—"

Woody snorted. "Congress. The Army. The President. Mel, those people are all chosen for mathematical illiteracy. They can't tell a million from a billion. When they pay eight thousand bucks for a hammer, where do they think the money goes?"

"Maybe it's Customs Collection," I suggested.

"They're too small."

"It turns them mean. Jealousy." I stood up. "I need to see Marion."

"I'll come with you. After that, we've got better search programs at the office. Let's see if the victims had anything in common."

Marion was awake. We had to shout; the blast had left her a little deaf.

"I wasn't that close," she told us. "I was watching the entrance for you, Mel. I saw him come in."

"Who?"

"Don't know. He didn't look like one of us. He looked like a backpacker."

"Backpacker? The guards should have got him."

"Yeah. The maître d' stopped him, and then boom." She tried to wave her hands, then let them fall.

Woody said, "Marion? Is IRS serious about Bev Hills?"

She smiled wearily. "Beverly Hills belongs to Sales Tax. Playing tourist there isn't a hassle. Of course that's just me talking. Mel, I'm tired."

I kissed her and started to leave.

"He had a funny T-shirt logo," she said. "A propeller with too many blades."

The hypersonic subway from Oregon into Washington, DC, ends at the tenth subbasement of the Watergate. Security was a hassle; it has been ever since Nixon's CREEP squad tried to burgle our secrets. The elevator took us down to the forty-second.

Down the hall they were questioning a huckster. We listened for a few seconds.

These days there are programs to keep track of sales tax. The only judgment a merchant needs involves where to apply it. This Martin Massoglia was a dealer at conventions, a traveling show, and that left him more chance to make mistakes.

Glyer is a huge man, a mountain looming over the little huckster. Massoglia looked bravely up at him. "Doesn't it strike you as crazy, turning every shopkeeper and restaurateur into a tax collector? We're not all math whizzes like you guys. We only want to buy and sell."

Mike Glyer belly-laughed. "Internal Revenue turns every citizen in the country into an accountant, and jails him if he won't play. Is *that* unfair?"

Massoglia said, "Yeah!" and Mike chortled. Woody and I kept walking. We'd heard the argument too often.

Gatherers, tax collectors, have to be good with numbers. We get more than our share of mathematical genius. Woody was a little worried about putting our programs to work in the office computers. Someone might notice.

"Tell them it's a game," I said. "Maybe even get them involved."

"I'm running just these five victims," Woody said.

I got us coffee at the hidden pot, avoiding the coffee we keep for taxpayers.

"They were all married," Woody said. "In fact, they were all married to taxpayers."

"Mean anything?"

"Let's see if . . ." He typed. By and by he said, "Last two months, four suspicious deaths in Sales Tax, two married—but not to taxpayers—and two singles. Harry Tanner just disappeared."

"Maybe they all cheated?"

"Let's see if Tanner had a significant other . . . okay, he dated some. Mel, do you remember Grace Wembley?"

"Sure." She worked here. We'd shared dinner twice. She also dated taxpayers, though; she hung out in the better bars. Then— "She was mugged. Poor damn Grace."

"She always talked her head off. I never knew how you could stand it." He was typing. "And she dated Harry."

I said, "See if any of the victims was considered a Security risk."

Of nine possible deaths by foul play, seven were considered Security risks. "Maybe they talked to the other Gatherer clans. Or even to taxpayers," Woody said. "That could be bad, couldn't it? What happens to Security risks in the IRS?"

"Or here in Sales Tax? Nobody quite knows. Woody, let's see how far back this goes."

It must have started slow. The first disappearance that fit the pattern was in autumn of 1978. Then nothing for four years. Then it started building up, deaths and disappearances.

The hair stood up on the back of my neck. There were dozens. "Five on Independence Day, various years. That mean anything?"

Woody said, "Yeah, that was the other thing they had in common. July fourth, and lots more on the thirteenth of every month. It's two different messages, Mel, and that's why the program didn't catch it."

"What's it mean? Bad luck? And . . . independence."

A long silence ensued. Then Woody asked, "Have you ever listened to old Monroe Kennedy?"

"I try not to."

"He's over a hundred twenty. In his day the Gatherers were sure that no tax should ever go over twenty percent. You could double—and triple-tax them, but if any tax went over double-tithe we'd all be found hanging from lampposts."

"Obviously he was wrong. Your point?"

"They fixed it by taxing smaller groups. Any one group might want someone else's taxes to go up instead of his. Graduated income tax, it's called, and property tax increases. It's worked for years, decades, but how long can it last?"

"In California . . ."

"What?"

The memory wouldn't come.

We wandered back to the room where Glyer was still hassling Massoglia. We watched for a bit. They'd shot him with a truth drug. Veritas isn't proprietary; all of the tax agencies have it. Massoglia was babbling all his secrets, if he had any.

Office work can be entertaining at the IRS. They bring in famous writers and singers for audits and get them to dance through hoops, perform or lecture or autograph. Here, it's too much like work.

"Marion's backpacker," Woody whispered, "must have been carrying a bomb. We've got no protection at all against a suicide bomber. How'd he get there? He didn't come in the Director's flight car. He couldn't have walked in, could he?"

I said, "Flight belt."

"Did you see any other fliers?"

"No. I got to dinner a little late."

"If he'd walked in, the guards would have stopped him. Hey." He pointed as Glyer puffed a mist into Massoglia's face. The dealer would go home with no notion of where he'd spent the last six hours.

"Amneserol. Give a guard a little less than the standard dose, he'll lose an hour's memory of hanging out in the woods."

I nodded. "He'd still have to come in with a flight belt. We'll find it ditched somewhere."

Woody didn't answer.

Woody left after work. In an hour and a bit he'd be back in Portland with his wife.

I called the secret hospital, but Marion was asleep. I decided to stay in Washington. I booked a room in the Watergate, the part above ground, then went to the Smithsonian. I'd get them to open the back rooms. They've got more stuff stored than most taxpayers would believe.

I stopped in the gem display rooms to look at a gorgeous footbath-sized chunk of malachite. The legend said that it had been given to Spiro Agnew when he was Nixon's Vice President. I looked around . . . and she was looking over my shoulder. Pretty, middle-aged, curly brown hair.

"I love malachite," she said. She was wearing a T-shirt under an open jacket. The shirt bore a symbol like a propeller with too many blades.

I said, "So do I." I'd been thinking about pulling rank on the Smithsonian clerks. Sometimes they'll let a tax man go home with something.

She said, "It's too heavy to carry and too big to stick under my suit jacket, and we'd need a distraction."

"Have dinner with me, and we'll come up with a plan."

She looked me over. "Okay. I'm Winnifred. Have you got a car?"

"No."

"I do."

*   *   *

Back in the Watergate, I got us drinks from the minibar—miserably poor stuff—and ordered a room service dinner. We talked a little. I spun the usual tale, not hiding that I was a tax man. But Winnifred, I thought, was being evasive.

Presently a waiter knocked. Winnifred stood briskly and went to the door. I was startled enough to remain seated. I was feeling the liquor, too.

She signed the check and got rid of the waiter. "I've given you a Mickey," she said.

She must have used a lot. I was feeling the effects despite the garnetine. I stayed seated. "That symbol," I asked, waving my arm wildly, letting the words slur. "What's it mean?"

"Prop Thirteen. Aren't you out yet? Proposition Thirteen was the law they passed in California in nineteen seventy-eight, that dropped property taxes back to normal levels and kept them there. We use it as a symbol for— Why am I saying this?"

"I put a little something in your drink, too."

She broke into a delighted smile. "I knew it!" she crowed. "You bastards have got an actual, working truth serum, just like in the pulps! How long does it last?"

I grinned at her. "It's permanent. Can you imagine what would happen if that ever got loose among the taxpayers?"

"Congress first. Then the Supreme Court." Winnifred was beginning to babble. "There's nothing in the Constitution about abortions and evolution and, and, they bloody well knew it. Then give it to the media. Then—" She lost some of her smile. "Everybody. How could you stop? Bomb the rivers in the Muslim countries with truth stuff so the ones who can read can't lie about what's in the Koran."

Damn, I was thinking of hiring her! I liked the way she thought. But— "Winnifred, what were you going to do with me?"

"Hang you from a lamppost."

"No." Even during the interbureau wars, we never hanged a tax man in public. It's far too likely to start a trend. "The others, you never did that."

"It's time."

"You'll see weapons you never dreamed of," I said. We glared at each other. "How did you set off that explosion in Oregon?"

"Our man hiked in with a bomb. Sequoia National Park, after all, and you don't have to stick to the trails. He had an amnesia drug we got off an IRS man, for the guards."

"How did you talk him into it?"

Her face screwed up in hatred. "*You* did. He lost everything to taxes."

"And the others? Drowning, poison—"

"And strokes! The Customs people have something that will cause a stroke a few days after you take it. You people have endless miracles, Mel, some evil, some wonderful. Why not share?"

"Not enough to go around," I told her.

"We . . . not *we* . . . *you* went to the Moon in 1969, and built a base, and stayed. Where do you launch from?"

"The Saturns launch from Kennedy, at a base that's supposed to be closed. Closed to us, too," I said bitterly. "Nobody gets to Lyndon Base but IRS people."

"And the freeway system under Beverly Hills, and the Caspian lakes full of beluga sturgeon—and then you put luxury taxes on food. How can you justify it?"

I sighed. "Winnifred, have you ever read the newsletter they put out just for funeral directors? 'The bereaved have a deep need to spend more money than they can afford. It ameliorates their grief.' Or listen to anything the nurse and teacher unions tell themselves. It's just incredibly easy for anyone to believe he deserves more than he's getting. What if you did get to keep all you make? What would you spend it on? Look what you buy with it now!"

She glared. "We'll take you down. You can't keep drowning us in paper forever." With Veritas in her, she had to mean it.

"I'm sorry, Winnifred." I got up, and she got up, but I was faster.

I was looking out at the dawn when she woke. She sat bolt upright in bed and stared at me. "Oh, God, who are you? I don't remember anything."

"We were picked up by a flying saucer and got to know each other that way. How about breakfast?"

Puzzled look. I said, "Kidding. It was the Smithsonian."

She left cheerful. We'd exchanged phone numbers. She thought I was an accountant for Wachovia.

And I took the elevator down to Minus Forty-Two.

She hadn't known as many names as I'd have liked. Even so, when I turned my list of the Prop Thirteen Gang over to Woody, we'd have something to trade with IRS. Maybe I'll see the Moon before I die.

Larry Niven has written science fiction and fantasy at every length, and weirder stuff, too. He lives with his wife of thirty-six years, Marilyn, in Chatsworth, California, the home of the winds.

KYRI'S GAUNTLET

Darwin A. Garrison

KYRI TRELLAN CLOSED her eyes and leaned back against the warm plastic of the air supply duct, breathing out a long sigh and trying to let go of the nervous knot in her stomach.

The end of supply duct four had become her hidden sanctuary less than a day after she had arrived on Crossroad Station. Here, far above the hustle and bustle of the freight and passenger decks, she could find a cool breeze and a measure of quiet. The scents of flowers and food plants arriving with the freshly recycled air from hydroponics soothed her nerves. When she closed her eyes, she could imagine herself laying on her favorite grassy hill on Escaflow, listening to the birds in the maples.

"They should be on this one," said a soft, childlike voice inside her mind. She felt the tickle of tiny claws against the skin between her breasts as Eperr, her bonded Nlyx, stirred and began to climb up to his "lookout." She opened her eyes and glanced down in time to see his tiny, hamsterlike nose and twitching whiskers poke out of the button loop in her blue coveralls to peer

through the grate at the end of the duct. Kyri smiled in spite of her nerves.

"Ever the optimist, eh?" she asked out loud as she turned her head to watch the *Merlin's Pride* drifting toward docking clamp number seven. Her spot at the end of the duct also provided a spectacular view of the three-story-tall transplast panels that converted the hulking freighters into glittering technologic koi floating within the infinite black aquarium of space.

"Well, it is the last ship in from the jump point and they did say they would be coming on this needle." Kyri shook her head and thanked fate once again that Nlyx could only interface directly with the speech centers of human minds, although the empathic abilities of her gengineered companion could complicate things at times. She hoped that he would write off her doubts about their possible "alliance" to her overall worry.

"You need a bit of skepticism, Eperr," she suggested gently as she rolled onto her hip to watch the freighter's final approach to the ring. "You're too trusting at times." The lessons of Escaflow had been burned into the soul of the Coven, if not the childlike Nlyx.

Eperr's empathy colored his next thought-words with a tinge of righteous indignation. *"I'm not a child anymore. I know not to blab about the gauntlet to them."*

A brilliant red light flashed to life above the *Merlin's* air lock, accompanied by an intermittent siren. Between the claxon calls, a vaguely feminine synthesized voice called out, "Ship arriving, stand clear." Stevedores three levels down from the duct shook themselves from their waiting positions, to man a bewildering array of loaders and haulers. Kyri watched the choreography of commerce swing into action as the main cargo hold opened up to the dock. Beyond the transplast, a slender gangway swung through the vacuum to align itself with the passenger hatch.

"I'm not worried about 'blab,' Eperr," she told the Nlyx as she extended a finger to scratch the feather-soft fur of his head. "There are just far too many ways this charade could go wrong. The last thing we need right now is to expose ourselves to people like them." She lifted her finger from his head and gestured through the grate toward a pair of "special" customs officers in their new black-and-silver uniforms. The two swaggered up the loading ramp to meet the hand-wringing master of the *Merlin's Pride*. She did not envy the ship owner the bribes he was going to have to pay.

"But this was your *idea!"* protested Eperr. Kyri sighed. That was the problem bonding with Nlyx: they lost all objectivity where their "partners" were concerned.

"Yes, I know," she whispered as passengers began moving down the gangway and into the station, "but it seems a lot more dangerous in the doing."

The Coven had survived by being "dead" and staying invisible to the internal security bureaus that the Oligarchy had corrupted prior to seizing power in the Senate. Their home had burned so that they could survive. No matter how clear their course seemed, she still could not help but question if what she was doing would prove to be the right thing in the end.

Kyri had a clear view of customs desk and old Thanus' bald pate. Although the Oligarchy had moved quickly after their coup to replace key people in the bureaucracy, they certainly did not have enough resources to take all the grunt positions as well. So, not only had Thanus kept his job and his faded uniform of gray with its dark blue seams, but Kyri and her friends had kept their gateway on and off the station. That relationship, along with a couple of carefully placed bribes, made sure her "guests" would be assured of getting through customs without undue "New" Senatorial scrutiny.

She leaned back against the wall and watched idly as the inevitable queue built up in front of Thanus' station. The first couple through the turnstiles carried a baby wrapped in a partially opened enviro-cradle. As well, they were lugging more carryon items than a small infantry platoon. Kyri almost laughed at Thanus' rigid posture of dismay as they began setting parcels on his rickety inspection table. Next in line was a man wearing a black pinstripe jumpsuit, carrying nothing more than a handheld data assistant. Thanus waved him through perfunctorily. After that, a portly woman with a massive bleached hairdo and a bright red synth-silk dress two sizes too small for any single dimension on her body swayed up to the table. Kyri laughed as the woman twisted and swayed in an apparent effort to get Thanus to look down the front of her dress. The old man was not having any of that, though, and made her empty the contents of every bag she carried.

As the now-disheveled woman stomped away from the table, Kyri's "guests" appeared at the turnstile. Legionnaires. There was no mistaking the pair, a man and a woman, despite their civilian clothing and discreet clothes and hairstyles. Although the angle was poor, she still estimated that they towered over Thanus by at least twelve centimeters each.

"Eperr? Can you give me a read on Thanus? I think he may be losing his grip."

Tiny, tickling movements stirred beneath her shirt as Eperr readjusted the aim of his nose.

"Hm," said Eperr noncommittally. *"Yeah. Okay. He's . . . he's confused. Little off where he expected to be. Nervous. No panic yet, though."*

Kyri let out a sigh of relief. "Thank goodness for that, at least. What about the Legionnaires?"

"The two big ones there at the table? Is that them? Wound tight. Kind of cold on one hand and hot on the

other. Sort of like explosives waiting for a detonator, I'd say."

"Oh, rapture. Let's hope nothing sets them off."

She and Eperr watched as the two soldiers presented their papers to Thanus, who took them with only the slightest nervous shake of his hand. They placed their small bags on the table and opened them while the clerk checked and stamped their documents. A few words were exchanged back and forth, broken by a pause to allow Thanus to clear his throat, after which the old man waved them through with one hand while beckoning to the next person in line with the other.

"Time to move, then," Kyri whispered to Eperr as she shifted back away from the grate to scurry down the duct. The first step was complete. How had one of her friends put it in their planning sessions? Something about how to eat a vat of bovine protein . . . *one bite at a time* . . . that was it. She grabbed the side rails of an access ladder and slid down to the maintenance hatch at the base of the feeder duct. With a twist of the dogging lever, she pushed open the reinforced door just a crack. The Legionnaires walked by the open end of the service corridor, sticking out in the general flow of humanity along the main causeway. She slipped out of the side passage and into the crowd, trailing the pair while doing her best to remain anonymous in the human herd.

Eperr's empathy proved instrumental in tracking the two once he had their mental "flavor." Their charges proved quite adept at ghosting down random corridors and between various bits and pieces of dock equipment and detritus. Without the Nlyx, Kyri certainly would have given herself away trying to keep them in sight. Even so, by the end of the hour, she was forced to think beyond tracking the pair into anticipating their actions.

"These two have had some training," she muttered as she threaded her way between two scuffed fork-walkers. This tertiary corridor would allow her to arrive at the designated hostel ahead of her charges.

"You would know," Eperr agreed enthusiastically.

"Hush," she said as she squeezed the loop of her shirt closed in front of the Nlyx as she peered around a corner. "I never completed the courses. I know just enough to understand how stupid I am." A muffled feeling of sulking floated across her consciousness as she stepped out from an access hatch that offered an excellent view of the hostel entrance. Kyri leaned back into the shadows left by a strategically inoperable light fixture and considered her insight.

She let out a sigh of resignation. She had expected military intelligence and had even planned for it. Still, after seeing how well they practiced their craft, she felt another twinge of panic. The threads of the plan started to feel slippery in her mind.

"Quit worrying," Eperr chided her. *"You'll give me an ulcer."*

"You? What about me?"

"Your stomach is bigger."

"What the hell does that have to do with it?"

"You can tolerate more stress. A poor, tiny creature like me has a lot less surface area to spread worry around in. My mother always said . . ."

"Your mother tried to eat you when you were ten days old."

A haughty psychic sniff filled her mind. *"I bonded more in ten days than you did in ten years. Anyway, she said . . ."*

"Hsst!" Kyri warned him, thankfully breaking off his trip down memory lane, which was a shorter walk for the two-year-old Nlyx than it was for Kyri. "They're here."

The two Legionnaires appeared from the left of the opening, glanced at the entrance of the hostel, then back at each other. With a nod, the man walked into the portal. The woman slipped to the left out of Kyri's sight.

"What are they doing?" the Nlyx pleaded, squirming in his pocket and climbing up to his "porthole" in Kyri's blouse.

Kyri shifted down the corridor a bit to hide behind some empty foam crates. "I think they're being careful."

The two coconspirators sat in nervous silence, watching the far door of the hostel. After five tense minutes, the male Legionnaire left the building and turned right, the same direction his female companion had gone.

"Do you want to follow them?" Eperr suggested eagerly. His enthusiasm for playing spy was starting to get on Kyri's nerves. So, rather than answer him immediately, she squashed herself against the wall.

"Can you still feel them?"

"Oh, yes. They're not far away at all. I could probably track them all the way across the station now."

"Then we'll just stay here for a bit."

The gray color of disappointment floated across her link with Eperr, but she was not about to give in to his sulking.

"Take it easy," she muttered as she stretched out her legs. "This isn't about having fun, you know." She became aware of Eperr's faint rodent smell mixed with the lingering aroma of partially rotten cabbage coming from a crate, which did not go well with the scent of burned rubber coming across her link with the Nlyx.

"Spoilsport."

"Let's relax a bit and see what they do," she temporized as she pulled her dock hat out of her pants pocket and set it over her eyes. "We've until mid-third watch before the meeting."

*   *   *

In the end, what the Legionnaires "did" was "nothing." Kyri actually managed to get some sleep between the watch chimes right up to the appointed rendezvous time. Her chrono buzzed her wrist five minutes before the appointment, warning enough to wipe the sleep from her eyes, clear her throat, and wake the Nlyx.

"Can't a guy get more than ten minutes of shut-eye in a row around here?" he griped as she gently rubbed him awake.

"Try three hours, you lump," she chuckled. "Besides, if you need to go, I'd like you to do it now rather than in my bra." By the time the one-minute warning buzzed silently against her left wrist, they were both awake and ready to face the next "bite" of the mission. Kyri straightened up from behind the crates, stretched out her kinks, and walked into the main corridor.

She spotted the male Legionnaire sitting in the bistro next to the hostel almost immediately. His business clothes and height set him apart from the normal station-side professional crowd that frequented the place. As Kyri followed an indirect path toward him, she subvocalized a request to Eperr.

"Where's the woman?" she asked.

"She's in the other hostel across the corridor and concentrating very hard."

Kyri risked a glance upward and saw the outline of a face in one of the second-floor windows, slightly distorted by a boxy shape that rested next to one cheek. She felt a shudder as she realized that the woman no doubt had a sniper weapon of some kind trained in the direction of the table that Kyri was about to approach.

"You're worrying again," Eperr observed in an acid tone.

"She's got a gun."

"Of course she's got a gun," the Nlyx replied with an empathic eye roll. *"Spies tend to be rather cautious when plotting treason."*

Kyri felt a flush bloom on her cheeks. "If it was simply treason," she snapped, "you and I wouldn't be involved." She felt Eperr cringe from the venom in her words and felt guilty.

"I'm sorry," she said in the best "soothing" voice she could manage subvocally while trying to put her worry out of her mind. *"I shouldn't let the past get to me."* A feeling of acceptance flowed from her tiny companion, and Kyri felt her confidence swell as she stepped into the tiny shop, her fretting left behind now that the wait was over.

The busy mid-shift dinner hour had filled the small dining room. Kyri first moved to the corner bar and ordered her favorite pineapple-kiwi mixer, which allowed her to scan the people sitting in the room. None of them appeared to be paying either the Legionnaire or her much mind. Sipping at the juice, she strolled to the soldier's table and slipped into the opposite seat. If her appearance surprised the man, he gave no sign.

"You're right on time," he said in a conversational tone. Kyri shifted slightly, looking directly at the window where his partner was no doubt watching through her scope.

"The woman is surprised . . . and now she's worrying," said the Nlyx. Kyri let the ghost of a smile cross her lips.

"You're on time as well," Kyri said without looking away from the window.

The man nodded once. "When is the meeting?"

Kyri turned back to look the man in the eye, then downed her juice. "Right now," she said in the coldest tone she could manage. She stood up from the table and began working her way through the crowd without looking back, another smile crossing her lips as she heard a muffled curse followed by apologies as the large man tried to keep up with her.

"The woman is moving, too," Eperr warned as she stepped into the main corridor.

"Good," she muttered. The second "bite" of her meal had gone down just as smoothly as the first, but plenty of protein waited in the vat. "Let the others know we're coming."

At first, she walked to the side corridor that she had used to watch the hostel. Once she was out of the general flow of traffic, though, she ran to the hatch and into the tertiary tube beyond. Eperr kept up a running dialogue as she jogged from access tube to access tube, helping Kyri keep track of the Legionnaires even as she slipped in and out of the tight spaces. She had to make it hard enough to be convincing, but not so hard that she lost them. Twice she had to backtrack and allow first the man, then the woman, to catch a glimpse of her as she rounded a corner.

Her route took them coreward through the conical station, farther and farther from the central docks at the rim. The corridors began to lose the polished look of the more "public" areas. Graffiti tags appeared, along with broken machinery and various kinds of garbage. Kyri even had to jump over a sweat-stained stimjunkie who was sleeping off a hit in the middle of an accessway.

At long last, panting hard and with sweat plastering her hair to her head, she entered the tube that led to the storage bay they had found for the meeting. She sprinted to the corroded hatch and put both hands on opposite sides of the lock wheel.

"They're almost here," Eperr warned as Kyri's strain-

ing finally broke the wheel free with its characteristic high-pitched squeal. A half turn was all it took before she was able to shoulder the hatch open, its hinges protesting the whole way.

She stepped over the jamb and dashed into the shadows toward the back of the room where she could watch both the door she had just entered by and the side exit that led to the derelict front office. Fitful light from adjacent rooms cast the warehouse area into patches of black and dim yellow. Kyri brushed back a sopping strand of her raven hair behind her left ear and tried to control her breathing.

"This is so *exciting!"* Eperr crooned as he stuck his nose out of the loop. *"It's just like being in a* Max Vel *thriller vid."*

"You watch . . . too much . . . vid," gasped Kyri between breaths. Her heartrate slowed, but beads of sweat still flowed down her face and neck. "Besides . . . have you ever . . . seen him sweat?"

"Um . . . no, not really. I wonder if his Nlyx has to put up with a sweaty bra pocket?"

Kyri's transient urge to smash her small companion flat evaporated as the male Legionnaire peeked around the edge of the hatch.

"Is that both of them?" she subvocalized.

"Yes, although the woman is hanging back a bit."

The man slipped through the open hatch and moved to a bit of shadow on the right. Long seconds filled with soft footsteps crept by until another shadow crossed the opening. Kyri took a deep breath and stepped forward into a puddle of yellow light where she had placed a small foot switch.

"You both might as well come in," she called. "We know you're there."

The man's tall figure stepped out of the shadows and

into another square block of reflected light. He turned his head and muttered into his collar, and then the woman stepped through the hatch to join him.

"Kyri Trellan?" the male Legionnaire asked. Kyri raised her head and tried to look as impressive as possible.

"I am."

The Legionnaire looked at his female partner, who nodded in affirmation. He turned back to Kyri.

"Good. I am Commander Velk, Third Expeditionary. This is my aide, Lieutenant Kobe."

Kyri nodded in acknowledgment. "Welcome to Crossroad Station, Commander, Lieutenant. You've come a long way to chase a rumor."

"Hardly a rumor," Kobe interjected, her clear voice almost musical with some faint, colonial accent. "We have been trying to crack the Coven Project for years."

Kyri snorted. "Given what happened on Backtrack, perhaps you should have concentrated your efforts elsewhere." Although she had spoken without overt sarcasm, the mirrored flinches her words elicited on both the commander and lieutenant's faces told her almost as much as Eperr's empathy.

"Hindsight," Commander Velk said after a brief pause, "is a merciless teacher, and we have had all too many lessons of late."

"Speaking of rumor," Kyri broke in, "word on the docks is that First and Second Expeditionary magically disappeared. Neat trick, if it's true." This time, instead of flinches, she received faint smiles.

"Like the commander said," Kobe admitted, "we have learned many lessons."

Kyri nodded. The Oligarchy had been using the Senate to teach all sorts of "lessons," and not just to the fiercely independent Legionnaires.

"So," she said, spreading her hands, "here we are. You wanted to speak to us, so . . . talk."

"Do you speak for all the members of the Project?"

Crossing her arms, Kyri gave the commander a cold stare. "I was elected leader, but I hardly need to speak for them." She stepped on the floor switch. Light fixtures attached to catwalks and walls hummed to life, and the Legionnaires gasped in surprise. Kyri felt a satisfied smile quirking at her lips . . .

. . . Because she knew that behind her the teenaged host of the Coven had silently emerged from the shadows.

"Here is the Coven, Legionnaires," Kyri said as she stepped forward. "Now speak your minds."

"They didn't show up on my scan," muttered Kobe, obviously thunderstruck. Velk hissed through his teeth at her, and the lieutenant visibly stiffened.

"That's very impressive," the commander allowed as he stepped forward to meet Kyri. "You must understand that we had no idea of your abilities or training. In fact, we weren't even sure you'd escaped."

"Obviously," Kyri agreed sardonically and felt a little thrill as the muscles in Velk's jaw clenched.

"Look," he said, a little irritation leaking through his control. "We don't have to play power games with each other. With the Senate putting out bounties on every Legionnaire and continuing to sniff for hints of the Coven, the obvious action is to join forces and begin working against the oligarchic puppet masters writing the legislation."

Kyri sighed. "You don't ask for much, do you? The Coven is completely safe so long as we remain hidden. The moment we throw in our lot with you, we expose ourselves to far greater risk. We can disappear into humanity. You cannot."

"But what the Senate did to you . . ." Kobe began, but Kyri held up a hand, stopping her outburst.

"That is the past. We not only survived, but we triumphed and disappeared. All that's left of our eugenics tanks are the charred ruins of Escaflow. Can you say the same of the modification facilities on Sol?"

"You can't like what you're seeing," protested the commander, his temper rising. "They murdered an entire planetary population to take down the Fourth. We sacrificed most of the Third to save First and Second along with their ships. We didn't come through all this just so you could keep hiding!"

"And what shall we do, soldier?" Kyri answered him coolly. "You have two and a tenth bloodied Legions left. The colonies are already in shambles, and you'd be hard pressed to recruit from the inner worlds where the Oligarchy holds Senatorial sway. For our part, most of the Coven is fifteen standard years old like myself or younger. Most of us have yet to begin to reproduce, let alone raise families. What you see is what we are."

Velk clenched his fists and drew them together before his chin. "You can't just give up without a fight!"

"We can if it means we will survive."

As Velk opened his mouth to reply, Kyri subvocalized a single word to Eperr.

"Now."

Doors along the catwalk and to the sides of the warehousing space slammed open as shock troops in Senatorial black and silver charged in. An amplified voice boomed into the storage bay.

"Halt! You are all under arrest by Senate decree! Lay down your arms and surrender!"

For a heartbeat, shock froze everything. Kyri stared hard at the commander and the lieutenant.

"Kobe!" the commander yelled as he reached inside his jacket and began running, "Get them out of here!"

Before Kyri could turn her head, the lieutenant had grabbed her about the waist and lifted her into a carry position. The soldier spun around and yelled back over her shoulder to the impassive ranks of the Coven.

"Come on, you kids!" she called in a firm command voice. "Follow me!" With that she charged toward the door through which she, the commander, and Kyri had all entered the warehouse.

The commander's gun spat fire at the gathered Senatorial troops. Pulsor fire answered in kind and began to dance on the floor around the Legionnaire and his lieutenant. Troops fell before the commander's accurate fire, but others shuffled to throw off his aim and allow for reinforcements to join them on the floor and catwalk. A burst of rounds stitched the floor beneath Kobe's feet and she stumbled, hurling Kyri toward the door as she fell.

"Run!" the Legionnaire screamed at Kyri before she rolled onto her back, adding her own return fire to the commander's.

Kyri staggered to her feet and brushed at her clothes. *"Are you okay?"* she subvocalized to Eperr.

"Whee!" he answered brightly. *"That was cool!"* Kyri snorted and walked back to the lieutenant.

"What the hell are you doing?" the woman yelled when she saw Kyri approaching. "Get out!"

Kyri raised her hand and made a gesture in the air. She let her mind flow through Eperr to calm the panic flowing through the Legionnaire.

"Be still," she said softly as Kobe's eyes lost focus. "You are safe and your part in this play is done." The woman sagged to the floor and slept.

Kyri looked up and watched as the commander continued to try and dodge the hail of illusory blaster fire he saw pouring in his direction. An imaginary hit took him in the leg and he fell, but he wobbled back to his feet and lurched behind a transit crate, firing all the way. Another shot took him in the shoulder and he spun to the floor. Once again, he forced himself back up, grasping his small gray energy pistol in the opposite hand.

"How much more are we going to put him through?" asked the Nlyx. Behind Velk, the members of the Coven seemed to be evaporating and reappearing as some left the link and others joined. Maintaining the illusion between stars was taxing, but the rotation kept the image fluid, up to and including tricking the commander and lieutenant into believing that they had actually fired their weapons.

"Only one thing left to do, Eperr," she said softly. With that, she asked him to bring out her own creation.

A young female Coven member ran in front of the commander, obviously confused and shaken. Through the Nlyx, Kyri could feel Velk's shock and panic. The man staggered up from behind his pitiful cover and grabbed the child, rolling her into his embrace as dozens of pulsor shots sank home in his now-exposed back.

"Enough," she sent to the Coven through Eperr as she stepped forward. The host of Senatorial troops began to evaporate as the avatars of the Coven disappeared from the warehouse.

"Peace," she said as she neared the agonized Legionnaire, "and rest. Safe. You are safe." She saw Velk's pain disappear as his body relaxed into a trancelike slumber.

She knelt down next to the commander and rolled him onto his back. Up close and with the sweat of effort covering his face, she could now see the spiderweb trace of old scars on his face, hands, and arms.

"Here is one who has suffered much, Eperr," she said softly. "Let's see what he can tell us."

She let her fingertips drift to the soldier's temple and focused her mind through Eperr's, seeking the man's memories. From his early days as a proud volunteer, through training and thence to deployment, she walked the path of his life. As he traveled between the stars, she followed, fighting by his side across the worlds of man. She saw him always trying to hold back the dangers outside the colonies, still striving to do the right thing after witnessing selfish expediency so many times.

Then came the betrayal.

His rage and tears became her rage and tears. The skies burned above as Senatorial ships bombarded their own troops, the Legion too independent to be trusted by the oligarchic conspirators. She saw harried rearguard actions, desperate suicide charges of orbital ships, and finally the panicked flight into the Dark Cluster with the First and Second Legions . . . she witnessed and felt it all.

Kyri came back to herself and reached up to touch the tears flowing down her face. She had seen their plans and hopes, and knew them to be like her own. The commander's eyes flickered open, his eyes finding her teary ones.

"Are we dead?" he asked, soft and confused. Kyri laughed through a sob and scrubbed at her eyes with the back of her hand.

"No, Commander, you're not dead," she confided as she reached out to brush his hair aside, "and neither am I."

"What . . ." he began, but Kyri quickly put a finger on his lips to silence him.

"Illusion, Commander, and an example of our power combined." She put her hands behind his shoulder and guided him into a sitting position. "I am the only member of the Coven physically present on this station." His gaze snapped to Kobe's prone form, and he tried to struggle to his feet.

"No, wait," Kyri said as she held his shoulder. "She's only sleeping." Velk turned back to her, confusion once more taking root in his eyes. She chuckled.

"I'd like you to meet someone." She held out her left hand before the loop in her blouse and Eperr scurried into her palm.

"A hamster?" the Legionnaire asked, nonplussed.

"Hiya!" Eperr greeted them both with a little wave.

"A . . . talking hamster?"

"Hey!" protested Eperr as Kyri chuckled.

"A NLYX," Kyri offered, "Neurologic Linkage Experiment. An engineered symbiote and the secret of the Coven's power. We are never a single person, but always two. And more. The linkage, along with the ability to cast illusion and plumb memories, means the Coven can act as one. More than enough for the Senate to sentence us to death."

"It's not a hamster?"

Kyri smiled and shook her head. "No. But that is neither here nor there. You wanted an alliance and you shall have it."

He stared in disbelief. "You had to torture us to do that?"

"Not torture . . . test," Kyri said flatly. "A trip through a mental gauntlet to gauge your true self. Although we may seem young to you, we are not so silly as to trust even an enemy of an enemy by their word alone. We wanted to take your measure, and now we have it. Your actions speak louder than all the rhetoric of the Senate."

She reached out and took the commander's right arm, clasping his wrist.

"You have made your pact with the shadows and gained friends and spies across the human sphere, as well as instantaneous ship-to-ship communication once you add a Coven member to each ship's company. The Senate has called us outlaws and pirates, but mankind has never seen corsairs such as we shall be. Together we'll turn their treachery back on them and take back the inner worlds."

"*Pirates?*" exclaimed Eperr as he scampered up onto their rapidly warming clasp. "*I can do pirates! I saw a vid once.*" He stood up on his haunches and brandished a tiny fist. "*Arr!*"

Author, heavy truck engineer, and model airplane designer Darwin A. Garrison lives in Fort Wayne, Indiana, with his wife, three children, and various pets. Notable among the nonhuman inhabitants is a hamster, Butter Cup, who steadfastly refuses to utter a single word. She does, however, twitch her nose in a most knowing manner.

Darwin began writing during high school after he started receiving books from the Science Fiction Book Club. He published one story in a college journal before giving up writing in favor of completing his engineering education.

After many years in industry, Darwin again took up the word processor in 2002 out of desperation to do something that made sense. Although originally started as a creative outlet, the response from local friends encouraged him to show his stories to a wider venue via the web. The responses from a variety of readers there encouraged him to focus on learning the tools of the SF/F trade in earnest.

Any success he experiences is entirely due to the

patient efforts and support of his friends and mentors in the writing community. As for those worthies, you know who you are, so consider yourselves hugged.

FALLING LIKE THE GENTLE RAIN

Nick Pollotta

JUST AS THE OLD church clock started to chime midnight, the moon was suddenly blanketed by thick clouds and there came the sound of heavy footsteps outside my office. *Oh, no, they had finally found me!*

Moving fast, I silently opened the top drawer to my desk and pulled out a Glock .357 Magnum. The checkered grip filled my palm like the handshake of an old friend, firm and reassuring. Dropping the clip, I quickly checked the load inside. Lead dumdum, silver bullets, and US Army armor-piercing rounds. Not much, but it was the best I had. But then, in spite of what the movies show, private investigators rarely use a gun. Especially ones that specialize in corporate espionage. No damn dirty divorce work for me. Love betrayed, weeping and screaming, widows and orphans . . . no way. I was trying to keep my soul clean, ever since I took possession of the Key.

Easing the clip back into the grip, I gently worked the slide to chamber a round and leaned back in my chair. This didn't have to be demons from hell. Might be pure coincidence that a visitor came exactly at midnight and fog blanketed the city. Hey, anything was possible. I tightened my grip on the Glock, disengaging the safety. *Then again . . .*

The footsteps thumping along the hallway stopped right outside my door. There was a short pause, and then somebody politely knocked twice.

"Excuse me, I saw the light under your door," a soft feminine voice said. "May I use your bathroom?" She sounded sweet and southern. Pure corn pone and hominy grits. A delicate flower of the South. "The one in the lobby is broken, and I really have to pee something fierce. Please?"

"Just a sec," I answered cheerfully, aiming at chest level where the heart would be on a human being. *Yeah, she was from the South, all right. Straight down south. Near the core of the planet.*

Two thousand years ago, King Solomon himself had built a temple to keep the Key safe from the wrong hands. Inhuman hands. The Crusades in the Middle Ages—just a cover story for the Knights Templar to get it back after being stolen by a traitor in our ranks. William Shakespeare wore it around his neck in a leather pouch for safekeeping, which is why all of his hair fell out so young. Mozart died from touching it with a bare finger, and Beethoven went stone deaf from doing the exact same thing, trying to prove it wasn't really dangerous. George Washington wanted to use it to help his troops in the American Revolution, but Ben Franklin gave it to Paul Revere to hide somewhere safe until the fighting was over. The key he tied to that famous kite was merely a decoy to throw pursuers off the trail.

Finally, Jules Verne devised a way to keep it safe— wrap it in soft lead foil—and Oscar Wilde pretended to be a homosexual and went to jail rather than divulge that secret. Nikola Tesla tried to destroy the Key and was driven insane. Jack Benny was badly scared just from looking at it in the moonlight, while Louie Armstrong and Colonel Sanders flatly refused to believe it could possibly exist. John Glenn wanted to cast it into space, but Wally Schirra talked him out of it. Presidents, congressman, and generals kept it hidden in Fort Knox for decades, but when that location became known to the others, the Key was given to me.

For over two millennia, my brother Freemasons had fought, lied, cheated, stolen, and died, to keep the Key from the unholy hands of our enemies. Some of them even took the blame for crimes they had not committed and been sent to jail for life, or executed, just to keep any official investigations from going further and discovering the possible existence of the Key. And, more importantly, what it unlocked.

Now, I have the bedamned thing sown into my leather belt, and somehow, They had found me, were knocking on my office door, coming to get me, *kill me*, and take away the Key of Solomon to unlock That Which Should Never Be Opened.

"Come in," I said smoothly, taking the Glock in a two-handed grip and holding my breath. *Steady now, easy does it, don't want to shoot a civilian. . . .*

In a thundering explosion, the door was blown off the hinges, a maelstrom of smoke and splinters buffeting me hard. Blindly, I triggered the Glock, blasting the big Magnum rounds at the shadowy figures gliding through the burning remains of the door.

One was hit and fell, flashing into ash. Another staggered backward, clutching a withering arm that pumped yellow blood. But the rest pulled out sawed-off shotguns and discharged a volley of steel flechettes, the fiery barrage tearing my desk apart until only the Lexan military plastic shell underneath remained. That caught them by surprise, and I used the confusion to kill two more of the demons. *To achieve success, plan for failure. And, brother, did I ever plan.*

Firing twice more at their misshapen heads, I rose and kicked aside my chair, then dove through the closed window. The shattering glass sounded like the end of the world, and searing pain slashed along my back and legs as I fell five stories toward the misty waters of the Chicago River.

Holding my breath, and praying that I didn't smack into a boat, I hit the water hard, losing a shoe as I just scraped past a concrete pylon, missing a grisly death by a scant inch. *Hand grenades and horseshoes.* Dark things rushed at my face from the murky depths—old cars, shopping carts, union officials—but I stayed calm and tried to holster my gun before flailing my arms and swimming for the surface. *Follow the bubbles, hot shot. Always follow the bubbles!*

But even as I started heading upward, big things with too many arms dropped into the water alongside me. Fueled by adrenaline, I tried to swim faster, but clawed hands reached out to rip at my clothing and flesh, pulling me down, away from the light, down to the muddy bottom and a slow death by suffocation.

Glowing eyes filled the darkness, and blood began to cloud the water. Red blood. *My blood.*

Reaching desperately into my jacket, I fumbled for the cigar tube I had carried since the day I became the Guardian. My predecessor had carried it for fifty years without ever using it, as had the man before him. The ancient steel was oily beneath my fingers, but I managed to pop the top and a tiny vial floated upward. Gnarled hands snatched for it, but I was there first and crushed it in my fist.

The contents of Christian Holy Oil, blessed kosher salt, and Moslem Holy Water mixed freely and then dissolved into the Chicago River to spread outward like a healing balm, clearing the dirty water to crystal clarity. Choking and burning, the things slithered away from me, seeking refuge in the Stygian mud below, bottom feeders seeking their natural habitat.

Now free, I moved for the surface, concentrating on the task, not the goal. My lungs were nearly bursting. I was burning for air, tiny bubbles squeezing out from my clenched lips, sips of life leaving me behind. But I had to ignore that. Get past the pain. There was only swimming, nothing else in the world mattered but the movement of my arms and legs. Keep swimming, keep going. *Move with a purpose, Freemason!*

Erupting from the expanding pool of clean water like a dolphin on steroids, I splashed about, pulling in a ragged lungful of fresh sweet air, almost reeling from the rush of oxygen.

As my head cleared, I swam out of sight beneath a wooden pier, and clawed my back onto the brick-lined shore. I was exhausted, but could not stop. Had to keep moving. Get away from here and find someplace to hide. Steal a car and drive out of town.

Glancing across the river, I saw Them standing in the smashed window frame of the office building. Human shapes with nightmare eyes that watched me hatefully, desperate to follow, but knowing to do so would burn them to the bone, or whatever demons had. *Chitin?* Could be. Lord knows, they always bugged me.

A swirling cloud covered the moon for a single heartbeat, and when it returned, they were gone. Instinctively, I went for my gun and found only empty leather. Damn! Must have lost my Glock in the river. Time to boogie.

Dripping wet, I stumbled for the street and headed

downtown. I needed help, and fast. There was a Free-mason lodge only a few blocks away. One of the main reasons I had chosen an office overlooking the smelly Chicago River.

The night was warm in spite of the unnatural fog and my clothing was almost dry by the time I found a police car parked at the curb, the two police officers inside sipping steaming cups of coffee. Smoothing back my damp hair and straightening my ragged clothing, I tried to look more like the loser in a bar fight, than the winner in a battle against demons.

"Excuse me, officers?" I asked hesitantly, stopping a few feet away. *Never rush toward the police.*

"Well, well, and what do we have here?" the younger cop drawled in a voice heavy with contempt.

The older cop watched me closely, then dismissed me as harmless. "Been drinking and fell in the river, buddy?" he demanded, defying me to question his authority.

"Actually, no," I started, but was interrupted by the sound of the car door opening.

"Keep your hands in sight, asshole," the young cop demanded, placing his Styrofoam cup on the hood and pulling a set of stainless steel handcuffs into sight. "The locals don't like drunks wandering the streets and bothering the tourists. A night in the tank will do you the world of good."

And get me killed. With no choice, I spoke a Word of Power.

The younger cop wrinkled his face in confusion, but the older cop did an abrupt change of attitude.

"Hold it, rookie," he commanded, climbing from the vehicle. "I know this man."

"You do?" the policeman asked sounding confused.

"Sure." Reaching out, he took my hand and we shook, exchanging grips and signs. The grips were familiar, but different. Not a Freemason, but FOP, Fraternal Order of Police. Our secret division of law enforcement agencies. Good enough.

"What do you need, Brother?" the older cop asked softly. The fog flowed along the city street making the few pedestrians shadowy figures.

"A weapon," I said, pressing the signet ring on my hand into his palm one last time.

"Done," the man replied, sliding the Heckler Koch 9mm automatic from his holster and passing it over. Along with two spare clips from his equipment belt.

"Many thanks," I sighed, tucking the mortal weapon into my clothing and out of sight.

The younger cop was flabbergasted. "You . . . you gave him your gun?" he gasped, a hand instinctively going for his own weapon. "Just what the fuck is going on here?"

"Ask the desk sergeant," the older cop said. Then he glanced over a shoulder and barked. "I said ask the sarge, kid!"

"Yes, sir," the rookie replied sullenly, shuffling back to the car and reaching for the hand mike clipped to the dashboard.

"New guy," the older cop said in apology.

"No problem," I replied, checking the clip, and working the slide. Even from a Brother, I always check a new weapon. We've had traitors before in the Freemasons, sad to say.

"Got a BTK?" he asked, pulling a small volume from his shirt pocket.

I shook my head, uncaring if it was a Christian Bible, Torah, or the Koran. There were many rooms in His mansion. The Freemasons accepted good men and women of any faith. "I'm not fighting a vampire," I laughed, exhaustion giving my words a slightly hysterical tone. "Although it sure would be nice."

"Oh, demons again," the officer said, not posing it as a question. Reaching into a pocket, he pulled out a butane lighter and shoved it into my hand.

Now that I gladly accepted. A crucifix was the symbol of the Redeemer, the forgiver of our sins. That didn't do a lot of damage to hellspawn, in spite of what the movies say. On the other hand, monsters always ran from fire. That was the symbol of the Creator. "*Let there be light.*" "*And a hand of fire moved across the mountain . . .*" "*A column of fire led the Israelites out of Egypt . . .*" "*Reverently, Moses approached the burning bush . . .*" Fire was the sign of the One, The Creator, Great Architect of the Universe, She Who Must be Obeyed, the Big Cheese. Monsters were unable to stand the pain of His light. Back in my office had been a sealed ziplock bag containing a BTK soaked in gasoline. Nothing made hellspawn run like the fiery light of a burning holy book! But I never had a chance to use it, more's the pity. And there was no going back now.

Thanking the Brother of my sister organization in the name of the Father, I moved off into the fog, keeping a close watch on the shadows, making sure they weren't keeping a close watch on me. Somebody moved in a dark alleyway, and I pulled the HK 9 mm. As they moved away, I holstered the gun, and went to hitch up my belt—there was only the empty cloth loops of the damp pants. Frantically, I checked again, but my belt was gone. But who . . . how . . . ? *Inhuman hands clawing at fabric and flesh* . . .

Spitting out a forbidden Word, the sidewalk under my feet cracked. They had it! The demons had the Key! If Satan knew where the Lock-Of-All-Locks was located, then Armageddon may have already started. A cold sweat broke over my body, and I started running along the foggy sidewalk, checking the cars parked at the curb.

No time to waste. I had to get to the nearest Freemason lodge and spread the word fast.

Passing an endless array of luxury cars: Hummers, Beamers, and a shockingly pimped-out Caddy, I sighed in relief at the sight of a Chrysler sedan. Touching the door handle with my signet ring, there came a hard click, and the door unlocked. Although long dead, Walter P. Chrysler had been a Freemason and made sure all of his vehicles were accessible to a Brother in an emergency. Henry Ford had done the same thing, and if I ever found a Model A flivver, with just a few special Words, any thirty-second-degree Mason could make it fly. Although not a Freemason, Walt Disney was a member of a friendly organization, the DeMolays, and had made a training film about how to fly a car, and then liked the footage so much he recut it into a family comedy starring Fred MacMurray. Also not one of Us, but a tremendous actor. Although, not quite of the same caliber as: Al Jolson, Harold Lloyd, Jack Benny, Laurel and Hardy, Abbot and Costello, or John Wayne, of course. But not bad for a civilian.

Slipping inside, I spoke a Word of Power at the ignition, and the engine started with a soft purr. Pulling away from the curb, I raced across town toward my one chance, the last hope of the world.

Breaking a hundred traffic laws, I made it to the lodge in record time, my brakes squealing as I parked illegally alongside a fire hydrant directly in front of the Chicago Freemason Lodge.

At this ungodly hour, the door to the building was locked. Pulling a dollar bill from my wallet, I carefully rolled my thumb across the All Seeing Eye on the back of the American currency, then slid it into a crack along the jamb. There came a low hum, a series of clicks, and then a hydraulic sigh as the armored portal swung aside.

Rushing across the foyer and dining hall, I heard the front door close and lock as I burst into the temple. Dodging around the BTK in the center of the room, I dashed up the stairs to the chair of the lodge president, plopped down, and shoved my ring into a small recess. With an electric hum, the chair rotated around, and moved through the curtained alcove, the brick wall sliding back into place behind. The chair was still moving when I hopped off and dove for the alarm button on the Master Mason communications panel. Instantly, fifteen million Freemasons across the world suddenly got an electric jolt from their signet rings and rushed to their computers. We owned the Internet, as well as most other forms of mass communications. As the good book says, Know Thy Enemy. Or was that Sun Tzu?

Slowly, lights came on in the control room and in tagged stages hundreds of small video screens lining the four walls of the room pulsed alive. A wide assortment of faces stared at me in curiosity and wary annoyance.

"The Key has been stolen," I announced bluntly.

"Which key?" an elderly man demanded sleepily. The label on his monitor read New Zealand. "The key of knowledge, or the key of power?"

"The *the* Key," I replied succinctly.

Everybody gasped, and half of them went pale.

"You mean, the Key to That Which Should Never Be Opened?" Russia gasped in horror, tightening the towel about his waist.

"Yes. And it is probably being opened right at this very moment," I added, glancing at the rooftop monitor. But there was no sign of a rain of fire, or crack of doom. Which meant that Satan didn't have the weapons yet. But when he did . . .

"Activate the homing beacon!" New York commanded. A soft knocking in the background was probably his knees banging together, or else a mariachi band warming up to perform.

"There's a tracking device?" Tokyo asked in stunned disbelief before I could.

"There has always been a tracking device on the Key," Paris declared, brushing back her wild crop of uncombed hair. "But the Guardian didn't need to know. It would have made him lazy."

"Oh, yeah, good thinking," Mecca sneered, and Brazil agreed.

"Tracking beacon is alive," London said, doing something offscreen. "All right, our satellites place the belt on a plane to Australia . . ."

"What flight?" Canberra asked, lifting a telephone into view.

"Shoot it down!" Rome demanded, shaking a fist.

Both were ignored. ". . . however, the Key is still in the United States," London continued unabated. "Central states . . . Illinois . . . Chicago . . ." His face lifted and he looked directly at me. "Brother, the Key is in the parking lot of your lodge!"

"Impossible!" the Apache Nation cried out.

"The demons have the Key, but don't know where the Lock is," India cried out, slapping a palm to his forehead. "And so they assume . . ."

". . . that the Guardian . . ."

". . . would know the location . . ."

". . . of both?"

Curses were snarled in every language on Earth.

"Run!" Beijing, Boston, and Bora Bora shouted in unison.

"Never," I growled, pulling the HK 9mm and working the slide. "I'll keep them busy here while the rest of you send troops and gunships to protect the Door-of-Doors. If my death can . . ."

"But you're at the Armory!" Paris screamed, grabbing at her hair. "That lodge holds the Weapons of Heaven!"

Everything reeled for a moment, I had to swallow twice before words came out of my mouth. "What the freaking hell is it doing in the same town as me?" I demanded furiously. "The door should be . . ."

"On the other side of the world?" Iraq scoffed. "Then, if the clarion call sounds, the Guardian would have to fight halfway across the world through the amassed armies of hell before we could get the swords."

Fury boiled within me, but then eased. The argument was sound, and there was a dull slam on the front door of the lodge. The demons were trying to get in. Well, hopefully, it was them. Satan had made his demons damn tough, but if the Dark One sent any of the Fangels, the fallen angels, that had stood by his side and declared war on God . . .

The pounding got louder. The entire building shook. A couple of the monitors wavered and went dark.

Muttering a prayer, I pressed the cold barrel of the police gun to my forehead. Maybe if the demons found me dead on the floor they might go away. Reluctantly, I eased down the weapon. No, they'd only tear the place apart in frustration, and find the Door. *Think, man, think!*

"Are there any weapons here?" I demanded hopefully, sweat trickling down the back of my neck. "Anything I can use to hold back the demons while the rest of you send troops?"

"There are already a thousand Brothers surrounding the lodge you're in," Chicago replied proudly. "Mostly police, firefighters, and doctors." Then the man frowned. "Although I am not in radio contact with anybody at the moment," he muttered unhappily.

Then if the demons had reached the front door, my

Brothers were no more. *A thousand Freemasons dead*, I realized coldly. *That was just the beginning of the slaughter to come.*

"All right, F-22 Raptor jet fighters are on route from Edwards Air Force base in California," Los Angeles replied, setting down a red telephone. "They're armed with holy Sidewinder missiles, and blessed tactical nukes. ETA, sixty minutes."

"There's nothing closer?" Poland demanded.

Hunching her shoulders, Los Angeles scowled. "Nothing that will stop a Fangel."

"Brothers, we have no choice," London stated. "The Guardian needs weapons, and the request cannot be denied. Insert your signet rings into your control panels and turn on my command. Ready . . . set . . . mark!"

A dozen of the men and woman on the screens turned their arms, and there came a deep metallic sigh from behind me.

Spinning around fast, I saw the southern wall of the lodge iris open, and there were granite racks of weapons, swords, shields, lances, halberds, bolos, katanas, and war hammers.

"Send more Masons!" I shouted over a shoulder, dashing out of the control room.

Sprinting through the temple, I raced past the pretty antiques and thankfully found some modern weapons. Stacks and crates of revolvers, automatic pistols, assault rifles, combat shotguns, machine pistols, land mines, rocket launchers, and grenades.

A shadow filled the doorway of the armory, casting me into darkness, and there came the stink of a burning sewage plant.

Grabbing a couple of revolvers off the wall pegs, I turned and pulled the triggers. Automatic weapons could not be stored away fully loaded, or else the springs inside would get weak and they'd jam. But revolvers could be loaded and safely placed aside for a hundred years, always ready for instant use. I was gambling everything that my Brothers had a couple of wheelguns ready for action, just in case of an emergency.

The twin S&W .357 Magnums roared in booming thunder, stilettos of flame extending from the big bore muzzles toward the hulking demon tromping closer. The hellspawn screamed as the silver bullets hit, but I kept firing until the hammers clicked on empty shells.

Lowering the guns, I could see that the demon was still standing. Then it sighed, dropped the bloody mace in its gnarled fist, and fell over to shatter into a million pieces on the concrete floor. *Ah ha! Silver bullets save the day again.* That Masked Ranger down in Texas and his faithful Apache companion had shown us the way to kill demons lo those many years ago. Why else would they have carried silver bullets?

Tossing away the revolvers, I grabbed a brand new US Army M60 machine gun from a rack, ripped off the plastic protective coating, and flipped open the breech to lay in a long belt of silver-tipped .308 ammunition. Each cartridge was marked with an Egyptian hieroglyph, Buddhist pictograph, Christian cross, Mogan David, Moslem Moon, pink stars, and lucky clovers. *Perfect.* That was when I noticed on the nearby wall a red box closed off with a pane on glass. Break in case of emergency? *Yeah, well, the downtown fire department wouldn't be of too much help at the present moment, let me tell you.*

"Look out, Brother!" Chicago shouted dimly from across the lodge. "I have a report of a . . ."

Just then, the entire left panel of monitors went dark, and a clawed hand punched through the glass and electronics, clawing the opening wide, and a Fangel crawled into the building, eyes glowing red from the hellfires burning inside his veins and heart. Obscenely fat, the nude Fangel stepped to the litter-covered floor and spread his wings wide. Every feather was adorned with a different sin, and the overall effect was like an LSD trip in Las Vegas.

"You there, Guardian!" the Fangel growled, reaching out a plump, pink hand the size of a Buick. "Come to me, mortal fool!"

Yeah, right. Yanking back the arming bolt, I rode the bucking machine gun and stitched the Fangel from knees to nose. Sagging into nonexistence, it puffed into vapor and disappeared.

But then another Fangel appeared at the hole in the wall. I killed it before the Fallen One could get inside the lodge. But another was right behind, and another . . . and a fifth . . . tenth . . . twentieth . . . The hammering sound of nonstop machine gun fire and unholy screaming seemed to last forever. The assorted brothers on the few remaining monitors shouted advice, but I couldn't hear a word over the deafening fusillade of the yammering machine gun.

As the last Fangel vanished in a puff of smoke, I dropped the hot M60 and flexed my aching hands. Okay, that bought me some time. Now all I had to do was . . .

Suddenly, a policeman walked out of the swirling clouds of pungent smoke. Incredibly, it was the old cop from the street!

"What in Hades is going on here?" the officer demanded, looking about in shocked confusion.

I started to reply, but that was when I saw he wasn't wearing his Masonic ring anymore. *So how did he get past the automatic defenses of the lodge?* In a surge of cold adrenaline, I pulled the HK 9 mm from inside my coat and shot him twice in the face.

Staggering backward, the cop hit the cracked wall and

his outer layer of chitin, or whatever it was, broke off
to reveal the most amazingly beautiful woman I had ever
seen. Er, no, she was a man. No, a woman . . .

"May the Great Architect of the Universe protect us!"
Luxembourg called from the smoky ruin of the control
room. "That's the Dark Lord!"

That caught me by surprise. This was The Morning
Star, Lucifer, Beelzebub, the Big "S," his-own-damn-
unholy-hairy-ass self? *Oh, crap.*

Holding a tiny golden Key in his pearlescent hands,
Satan turned toward the flickering bank of video monitors, smiling with indescribable beauty.

"Guardian!" London screamed hysterically. "Use the
Emergency—"

"Be still," Satan interrupted, rising a hand. All of the
monitors exploded, throwing the entire lodge into a Stygian gloom.

Knowing who was next on the hit parade, I turned on
a heel and pelted back into the arsenal to ram my fist
through the glass of Emergency Alarm. I sure hoped this
was what the Brother had meant, because if not I was
about to have a close encounter of the 666th kind.

I tried not to hold my breath, but did anyway. However, nothing seemed to happen for a very long second.
Then the concrete floor broke apart, and a smooth jade
obelisk lifted into view. Lying on top was a tiny crystal
dagger. That made my stomach lurch. I knew this blade.
It was shown prominently in our most secret book. This
was one of the Weapons of Heaven.

When Satan and his angels had rebelled, they used
crystalline weapons to attack the guardians of Heaven.
Special weapons designed to kill Angels. Maybe even
God. Who knows? As the thousands of Fangels and
Angels died in combat, their weapons fell gently upon
the Earth. A rain of flaming swords.

Famous for not being a moron, King Solomon quickly

figured out what was happening and sent out his army to gather the weapons, and hide them away from Satan and his minions. Then he built a temple to protect the weapons, a really mucking huge temple that took every skilled mason in the world to complete. And thus, the Freemasons were born, guardians of the Key to the Door of the Arsenal of Heaven and Hell.

Just then, a magnificent golden light flooded the armory and Satan glided into view, his/her face taking the breath away from me. I started to weep with joy at the sheer magnificence of his smile, and got an erection at the same time from the womanly curves. His beauty was indescribable! Yet there was something sinister about the Dark One that gave me the impression of absolute insanity. *Bedbugs had nothing on this guy!*

"Henry, please take me to the Door," Satan asked sweetly, the words hitting me like velvet fists.

He knew my name? I wanted to tell him to get stuffed. But incredibly, I started to obey. With a sheer effort of will, I managed to shake off the compulsion, snatch the dagger and whip it toward the Dark One with all of my strength!

The knife turned over twice and slammed into His shoulder like an avenging thunderbolt. Gushing a torrent of golden blood, Satan screamed in pain as he was driven backward to crash into the wall, the impact shattering the resilient stonework for yards in every direction.

As the Great Traitor weakly clawed at the crystal blade embedded in his perfect flesh, I stumbled closer to grab the handle, ready to pull it out and strike again.

"Wait," Satan whispered, his breath sweet as a spring breeze on my face.

As a Master Mason, I knew better than to look the Father of All Lies directly in the eyes, but still I paused, damning my own weakness. I could feel his presence, the warmth from his body, and it made me giddy, almost drunk. I wanted to obey him, to serve, to yield, to *pull out the blade and kill this asshole. Pull it! Pullitpullit!* But my hands refused to move; they were numb, locked in a tempest of conflicting urges.

"You do not dare kill me," Satan chuckled softly, a hand gently touching my arm. It was icy cold and electric pleasure at the same time. "God bade me to live after losing the war, so there must be a reason for my existence. Who are you to deny the will of Him, the Creator?"

That was a mighty good question. "You rebelled against Him once," I retorted through clenched teeth.

"Ah, but I was given free will," Satan answered, a flood of glorious promises cascading into my mind and soul.

Ignoring everything I had ever been taught, I looked the Dark One directly in the eyes. "Yeah? Guess what, asshole. Me, too!" And I yanked the blade free to plunge it directly into his hairless chest.

At the blow, Satan went stiff, and screamed for only a second before I went stone deaf. In silence, I leaned inward, putting my weight and strength against the dagger as I moved it about trying to find whatever a fallen angel had in place of a heart. Golden light erupted from the wound, and He beat against me, but the blows fell without impact, and I seemed to grow stronger as He became weaker. A hundred thousand voices cried out inside my head, promising me anything, *everything*! Grimly determined, I ignored them all, concentrating on the task. Let hellfire burn me, or demons eat my soul, I didn't care. But this pretty little sombitch was going down for the count, here and now!

Suddenly going limp, Satan whispered something too low for me to hear, and then crumbled into a silvery ash.

As I stepped away from the disintegrating form, the

entire planet seemed to shudder and the ceiling cracked apart, admitting the cold blue moonlight. Then the sun rose over the horizon, filling the world with a clean clear light that banished every shadow of Darkness. And then, the darkness of every Shadow.

Dumbstruck, I gazed in awe and wonder at the quite unexpected sight of dawn occurring in the middle of the night. Then the sun appeared to tremble, and for the first time in recorded history the burning lid raised and the Great Flaming Eye of God looked down upon the world, oddly appearing exactly as it did on the back of the American one dollar bill.

"I'll be damned," I whispered, almost dropping the dagger.

As if in reply, the Eye looked through the millions of miles of space and directly into my upturned face. *No, you will not.*

Instantly, I felt refreshed and renewed, young and healthy and full of beans. My hearing returned, as did a tooth missing from childhood. "Thank you," I shouted.

But the Eye had already moved onward, healing, fixing, finding, repairing. Now images of the world poured into my mind, and I could actually "see" a million demons vanish into smoke, and ten thousand Fangels crumble into sheer nothingness. Then the floor of the lodge cracked open and the crystal weapons faded away from sight. Gone back to wherever they originally came from.

Now, His gaze moved on, the pollution disappeared from the land, sea, and air. An endless bounty of fish returned to the barren oceans, extinct species sprang back to life, and every nuke turned to solid stone.

As the new dawn swept the globe, cripples began to dance, the blind suddenly could see, the deaf could hear, and every disease vanished: cancer, AIDS, rabies,

acne . . . along with killer bees, army ants, and almost
every other blood-sucking parasite, including TV evan-
gelists, telemarketers, and used car salesmen.

The Age of Miracles had returned, and once more
God was in our everyday lives, watching benignly down
from above. Satan and his hellish minions were gone
forever! Which would mean an end to war, and most of
the other brutalities that we did to each other on a regular basis. However, this was also the end of the Freemasons, our millennia-old trust finally fulfilled in dirty
old . . . er, in beautiful, glistening, downtown Chicago.

Unfortunately, this meant that I was out of a job, and
I had really enjoyed being the covert guardian of a divine mystery for an all-powerful, world wide secret
society.

Hmm, I wonder if the Elks have anything special that
needs protecting?

*Nick Pollotta has been a ditch digger, inorganic
chemist, martial arts instructor, stand-up comic, and
a chicken rancher, but much prefers typing pretty
songs on the alphabet piano. Regularly attempting
to break lightspeed, Nick has over fifty published
novels under a wide variety of pseudonyms. His latest novel is* Damned Nation, *a Dark Fantasy set
during the American Civil War.*

THE THINGS EVERYONE KNOWS

Tanya Huff

"BUT I'M A thief."

"Why, so you are. It's interesting that never occurred to us, what with this being the Thieves Guild and all."

Terizan's lip curled in spite of all efforts to keep her expression neutral. Tribune One's lip curled in return. Tribunes Two and Three shuffled their seats out of the direct line of fire as surreptitiously as only master thieves could shuffle. Gaze locked on One's face, Terizan's right brow flicked up.

One laughed.

When that was it for confrontation, Two and Three exchanged nearly identical expressions of chagrin.

What they'd missed, and what One hadn't, was that Terizan had no intention of becoming part of the Thieves Guild Tribunal, at least, not yet. Granted, she'd been taking reading lessons on the Street of Tales, but she wasn't ready to make an irreversible challenge to the Tribunal's authority. Besides, the thought of spending any significant amount of time in close proximity to

Tribune Three and the scent of sandalwood oil he'd recently started rubbing all over his not inconsiderable bulk, turned her stomach.

Terizan hoped he was doing the rubbing himself because the alternative just didn't bear considering.

"The job you're talking about," she continued, scratching her nose to keep from sneezing, "is a job for a spy."

"And what is a thief but one who steals in and then steals out again holding something belonging to another. In this instance, the something is information. Otherwise, there is no difference." Tribune Two sounded more emotionless than usual—probably in an effort to make up for the earlier reaction.

"It's simple," Tribune One sighed, lacing ringless fingers together. "If the rumors are true and there actually is a conspiracy to overthrow the Council, you steal into one of their meetings, then you steal out with the names of those involved."

"If," Tribune Three snorted.

"The Council is convinced . . ." Two began.

"The Council has its collective head so far up its collective ass that it's run out of air," Three interrupted.

"Tribune Three has a point," Terizan noted. "What if the Council's wrong? What if there is no conspiracy?"

"Then bring them proof of that."

"Proof of nothing?"

"That should be no problem for a thief of your skills," One said, not bothering to hide her smirk. "Unless your failure at the wizard's tower has shaken your confidence."

Oh, yeah. She was never going to live *that* down. That she'd succeeded at the wizard's tower was beside the point since no one could know of it. "I'm not questioning my skills; I'm questioning the Council's requirements."

Two's pale eyes narrowed. "Rumors of conspiracy make the Council understandably paranoid. If this matter isn't settled conclusively, they will begin making random arrests. They've already hired another two dozen constables."

"We don't need to tell you that increased security will adversely affect our membership," One added. "Of course, you may refuse the job . . ."

Terizan held up a hand and slid off the pile of stolen carpets that seemed to be a permanent fixture in the Sanctum. "If I turn down the job, you'll offer it to a thief with lesser skills who'll get caught and probably killed and I'll be responsible and blah blah blah. We've been through this all before."

"If you turn down the job," Two told her, voice cold, "we'll offer it to a thief who might be less than scrupulous about the names he or she offers the Council. Who might add names to the list for personal reasons."

The pause after this declaration was triumphant.

"Did the Council give you any idea where I should start looking for this conspiracy?" she sighed.

"They've heard rumors of meetings in the Necropolis. You have three days."

The Necropolis was haunted. Everyone knew that. From all reports, the winding paths that led from the gate to the top of the hill were as busy with the restless dead as Butcher's Row was with the living on market day. Only the lowest plateau down by the river where the very poor were buried in trenched graves remained untouched by ghostly activity.

Terizan figured the very poor were probably glad of a chance to finally rest.

She'd never seen a ghost. Mostly because she never went to the Necropolis, a decision of a very early

Council having made sure the dead had nothing worth stealing.

"When it has been decided by a physician of Oreen that in death the citizen shall pose no danger to the city, then the body shall be wrapped in an unbleached cotton shroud and laid to rest in that part of Oreen designated for the dead."

The City of the Dead; where the wealthy built mausoleums like mansions and everyone else marked their family's place with as much ornately carved stone as they could afford. The Thieves Guild, like many of the city's professional organizations, had an area in the catacombs for their members without family although, for obvious reasons, thieves' funerals were seldom well attended.

If an organization intent on overturning the Council *was* meeting unseen in the Necropolis, they were probably meeting in the catacombs. Cut into the lowest level of the hill, the narrow passageways and chambers carved out of the rock would provide a perfect hiding place for any number of secret societies—underground in more ways than one.

As the wall around the perimeter was low enough that any reasonably determined adult could easily get over it, and the Necropolis was large enough that there wasn't one place to watch all access points, Terizan decided she might as well go directly to the catacombs. Where she found the black, iron-bound doors securely locked.

They were the kind of locks a merely competent thief like Balzador could get through, but even by fitful moonlight it was obvious to Terizan no one had. Not for some time. If this rumored organization was meeting in the tunnels under the Necropolis, it was getting in another way. She peered up toward the crest of the hill, past the hundreds of tombs cut into the walls of each terrace. Any one of them could be a secret entrance to the catacombs below. She couldn't break into all of them. Well, she could, but there was no time and less need.

Moving to a less visible position while she considered her options, she crouched in the velvet shadow cast by the cracked sandstone box that held the remains of Hanra Seend, Wife, Mother, Weaver, and something else too worn to be read in the moonlight. She could climb to a better vantage point and hope she spotted one of the conspirators skulking about the graves, waiting to be followed. Or she could just pick these locks and go through the front door, then decide on her next step once she got inside.

"He'll let her use my loom!"

Terizan pivoted slowly in place to find her nose barely a finger's width away from the nose of the pale, distraught, and translucent woman crouched beside her.

"He'll let her use my loom," the woman repeated. "She won't take care of it, I know she won't. You have to tell him not to let her use my loom."

". . . and then she touched my arm and I bolted."

Poli raised a delicately arched brow higher still. "Everyone knows the Necropolis is haunted, Sweetling."

"That's not the point." Terizan paced across her best friend's bedchamber and back again to stand at the foot of the bed. "She was dead, Poli, and she was talking to me. She wasn't just moaning and wafting about, she was interacting. And when she touched me, I could feel this flash of despair."

One elegant shoulder lifted and fell. "Well, as you said, she was dead. That's a valid reason to be depressed."

"Poli!"

He sighed. "So the poor woman carried the concerns of life over into death. You just got in her way; stop taking it personally." Moving a fringed cushion aside, he patted the edge of the bed. "Come and sit and tell me why you were in the Necropolis after dark. You know you're going to anyway, so you might as well get it over with. That way we can both get some sleep."

"It was Guild business . . ."

"Anything said in my bed, stays in my bed—or *my* guild wouldn't *have* much business." He patted the blanket again. "Come on."

So she told him how the Council had heard rumors of a conspiracy and how rumor had placed the conspiracy in the Necropolis. She told him how the Council had come to the Thieves Guild and how she was to steal into a meeting and out again with the names of those involved. "Although how I'm supposed to get the names of those I don't recognize, I have no idea. I doubt they do a role call before every meeting." She deepened her voice. "Ajoe the Candle-maker?" And up again. "Aye."

"Don't tell me Ajoe the Candle-maker's involved!"

"I was just using him as an example because I was at the Necropolis and his wife's just died and that's not the point," she sighed. "The point is, I have no idea how I'm supposed to steal these names."

"You'll think of something. You always do." He spent a moment staring at his reflection in the hand mirror he'd taken from the tiny table by the bed. "What will the Council do with the names when you get them?" he asked at last, tucking a strand of hair behind his ear.

She shrugged and plucked at the blanket. "They'll arrest everyone involved, probably execute them."

"People are always complaining about the Council." He lifted a thoughtful gaze up off the mirror. "Taxes are too high, the constables are never there when you need them, there are holes in my street deep enough to swallow a donkey—but it's never come to action before.

I wonder why now. This lot's certainly no worse than any other."

"Better than some," Terizan allowed. It hadn't been that long ago that the Council had executed three of their own who'd been taking bribes from a bandit chief.

"The rumors could be wrong."

"Could be." Rumor moved through Old Oreen faster than weak beer through the Fermentation Brotherhood. "But then they want proof of that."

"Proof of nothing?"

"That's what *I* said," she snorted. "What do you think I should do, Poli?"

"I think you should have sex more often, let your hair grow out, and wear brighter colors."

Her hand went involuntarily to her cap of short dark hair. "I have to get into the catacombs," she said. "But I think I'd best check the place out in daylight first."

"Well, if you knew," Poli sighed. "Why did you ask?"

The maintenance of the Necropolis was handled by acolytes of Ayzarua, the Gateway. She wasn't exactly a death goddess—two hundred years ago, after trouble with competing death cults, the Council had made the worship of Death illegal. Ayzarua represented the passage from life to death, a definition just vague enough to get around the law. She had no temple; her followers believed that all living creatures carried her temple within them.

Terizan thought the whole thing was kind of creepy but she had to admit the Ayzaruites took good care of the Necropolis. The paths were raked, the cracks in the rock were weed-free, and the small amount of vandalism she could see appeared to be in the process of being either repaired or removed. The Ayzaruites were a definite presence in the Necropolis. Something to remember.

In daylight, the locks on the catacombs looked no more difficult than they had by moonlight and just as infrequently used. Shooting a nervous glance toward Hanra Seend's resting place as she passed, Terizan started along the first terrace trying to look fascinated. Apparently, the City of the Dead was a popular destination for visitors to Oreen. Took all kinds, she supposed.

The basic design of the wall tombs included four shelves on each of three walls with a stone crypt in the center for when bare bones were ready to be removed and the shelf refilled. Tombs in the Necropolis were used for generations, and they were all variations on the theme. Individuality showed up in the ornately carved facades and in the narrow gates that led through them. Steel gates, stone gates, wooden gates; bolted, mortared, chained in place; every one of them, even the most solid, with a small horizontal window just at eye level.

The reason for the window had long been forgotten, but as newer tombs copied the oldest tombs, everyone knew it was supposed to be there, so the window remained. It reminded Terizan of jail cells.

Approaching the first tomb, she hesitated, afraid that when she looked in, something would look out. Bodies were no problem; she'd seen plenty and robbed a couple, but Hanra Seend's ghost had prodded her imagination.

Terizan rubbed at her arm. It was just turned noon. Ghosts, like thieves and traitors worked under cover of darkness. Of course, *she* was here now, so . . .

Just look!

It took a moment for her eyes to adjust to the faint spill of sunlight past her head, but eventually she managed to make out the vague outlines of cloth-wrapped bodies. There was a faint smell of rot, a stronger smell of incense, and nothing at all to suggest either a secret entrance into the catacombs or a restless spirit. Relieved, she kept moving.

By midafternoon, her legs ached from the constant climb. With about a third of the Necropolis examined, she'd seen nothing out of the ordinary. Trying to ignore how hungry she was, she crossed to a particularly ornate tomb and peered through the opening in the big double gates.

Years of practice kept her from shrieking. She leaped back, the heel of her sandal came down hard on something soft and yielding, and she leaped forward again as it moaned.

Too close to the tomb for comfort, she whirled to see one of Ayzarua's acolytes hopping in place, rake forgotten, both hands wrapped around one bare foot. Well, she knew what she'd stepped on. That was a start.

Heart pounding, she managed a fairly coherent, "Sorry, I didn't see you."

"I know!"

"Are you hurt?"

"Pain is transcendental," he gasped.

Terizan figured that was a yes. She watched as he put the injured foot down and shifted his weight.

"But I'll live," he concluded after a moment. He studied her in turn. "What frightened you?"

"I wasn't," she began, saw his eyebrows rise, and surrendered bravado. "There's something in there," she told him, nodding toward the tomb. "It grabbed for me."

"Did it now?" He limped past her and peered through the gate. "Ah, I thought so. Pardon her ignorance, Gracious Lady. It is my Lady," he explained turning toward Terizan with a smile. "Her likeness at least. She reaches out to help the recently dead through the gate."

Dared by his smile, Terizan leaned forward, eyes narrowed. Even knowing it was a statue, her heart still jumped at the sudden sight of a hand nearly at her nose. The Goddess herself, back in the dim depths of the tomb was barely visible. Terizan thought she could see friendly eyes and a gentle, welcoming smile within the depths of a stone hood, then suddenly . . .

"Okay." She jumped back again. "Skull."

"The best images of my Lady recognize she stands between life and death," the acolyte explained. "This particular image, commissioned by the Harl family and sculpted by Navareen Clos, has a spell attached. If you look long enough into the darkness beyond the Goddess, you'll see the Gateway open. There are only two other tombs like it in the entire Necropolis, up on the crown of the hill in crypts of the two of the oldest families in Oreen—the Aldaniz and the Pertayn. Unfortunately, the Aldaniz didn't specify . . ."

Terizan let his voice wash over her, paying only enough attention to nod where it seemed appropriate. The sort of person who'd spend the day methodically climbing the Necropolis peering into tombs was the sort of person who'd actually listen to this kind of lecture. It had obviously been a long time since this particular acolyte had found an audience, and he seemed determined to make the most of it. Fortunately, he wasn't trying to convert her, he was just talking.

And talking.

Terizan kept nodding and amused herself by watching the shadows move across a particularly ornate carving on the next tomb over. She frowned slightly as the shadows caressed the edge of the highest bolt holding the gate to the tomb. That bolt had been removed and, from the raw look of the surrounding stone, both recently and frequently. Why bother to unlock the gate when it could be lifted, locked, away from the stone? Not the oldest trick on the scroll—she seemed to remember it was actually number eleven or twelve—but useful.

"And what brings you to my Lady's city?"

"Me?" Jerked from her reverie, Terizan searched for an answer that didn't involve conspiracy or the Thieves Guild. "It's uh, peaceful." Disturbingly peaceful. Uncomfortably peaceful.

The acolyte nodded. "There are few places more peaceful than the grave."

Hard to argue with that, Terizan acknowledged. She needed to find out if he'd seen anything. But just in case he was in on it, she needed to do it subtly. "So, do many people come here at night?"

His brows rose. Poli was right. She really sucked at subtle.

"The gates are locked at sunset."

Everyone knew that. "And your lot makes sure other people stay out?"

"There's no need. The Necropolis is haunted."

Conscious of the Ayzaruite's attention, she went out the gate just before sunset and back over the wall shortly after. Moving quickly from shadow to shadow on a path that took her well around the weaver's crypt, she finally climbed into a hiding place on top of the tomb with the loosened bolts. Everyone knew that conspirators met in the dark of night when cloaked figures scuttling about empty streets were likely to be noticed, and they'd have no plausible excuse if they got caught. If she was running a conspiracy, she'd have them meet in the late evening and have them head home with the crowds when the cantinas closed, hiding them in plain sight. Of course, she *wasn't* running this conspiracy and that became obvious as time passed and she saw no one but a few translucent figures wafting by, moaning.

She determinedly ignored them and they ignored her.

Finally, after the bells of Old Oreen rang midnight, the sound strangely muffled in the City of the Dead, Terizan saw two cloaked figures approaching. They opened the tomb, exactly the way she'd known they would—the bolts whispering out of the stone—and slipped inside, replacing the gate behind them. She would never have noticed the faint spill of lantern light a moment later if she hadn't been waiting for it.

Hanging upside down over the gate, she could just make them out as they crouched by the rear wall and together slid the shrouded body from the lowest shelf. Setting it carefully to one side, Conspirator Number One lay down in its place and crawled into darkness. Conspirator Number Two passed the lantern through and followed.

Terizan waited a moment for her eyes to readjust to full dark, checked that there were no more cloaked conspirators approaching, and flipped down to the ground. The gate was heavy for one person, but she didn't need to open it very far. She slipped through, closed it, and, keeping her fingertips on the center crypt, made her way to the back wall. By the time she reached it, she was in total darkness. She knew she was holding her hand in front of her face but she couldn't see it.

Fortunately, it was impossible to get lost.

There was room to stand on the other side of the corpse shelf but just barely. Her fingertips danced over rough stone; a crack in the rock, a natural fissure. She counted twelve paces, felt the air currents change, and stopped. Barely an arm's length from her face, the fissure opened up into a much wider passageway.

When she held her breath, she could hear a quiet hum of sound. When she crept silently forward and peered out of the crack, she could see a faint graying of the dark off to her right.

The conspirators were meeting in one of the catacombs' square tomb-within-a-tomb areas and enough light spilled out the entrance that Terizan could just make out the carters' crest carved over the arch. As she came closer, the sound fractured into a number of voices all making the kind of anticipatory small talk that suggested the meeting had yet to start. Since there were more people present than the two she'd followed, there were clearly other routes in.

She could lie down and peer around the corner into the tomb well below where most people would even think of looking for intruders, but there was no way of telling how many more conspirators were still to arrive and that would leave her exposed—provided this was the meeting of conspirators the Council had hired the Thieves Guild to find. For all Terizan knew, she'd stumbled on a social club for necrophiliacs.

Pressed up against the stone niches that lined the passageway, she glimpsed a line of gray at the edge of her vision. Peering over the shrouded body on the shoulder-level niche, she could see a crack in the rock as wide as her thumb. Moving quickly, she scooped up the corpse—breathing through her teeth at the intensified smell of rot—and stuffed it in with the body occupying the niche below. Any small sounds she made were covered by the sudden rhythmic rise and fall of a single voice inside the tomb. It sounded like . . .

Poetry?

Not surprising, given the venue, images of death were prevalent.

The niches were narrow and not easy to get into, but Terizan had been in more difficult places and, with a minimum of bruising, she managed to get her right eye lined up with the crack. There were seven cloaked figures in the tomb. Not a large conspiracy, but she supposed seven motivated people could do some damage. After all, she'd managed to destabilize the throne of Kalazamir all by herself.

As she watched, the poet finished, slid the scroll into a pocket, and blew his nose, clearly overcome. She could see three faces clearly and didn't recognize any of them. Then a fourth raised both arms, the cloak sliding back as he gestured for silence and with some surprise Terizan recognized the heavy gold links he wore around one wrist. She'd had her eye on that bracelet for a while. It seemed as though Ajoe the Candle-maker *was* involved and not only involved, but in a position of some authority. Maybe grief at the death of his wife and infant son had addled his brains and turned him from law-abiding artisan to . . .

Poet?

"We ask justice for the dead," Ajoe declared, his voice rough with grief.

Terizan hoped the next couple of lines would rhyme. She liked Ajoe and didn't want him involved in anything that would result in his head on a spike in the Crescent.

"Overcrowded streets slow the arrival of what few healers there are. The high taxes paid by the apothecaries keep medicines too expensive. The rulings of the Council kill those we love. Those who lead have failed us and must be removed."

Not poet.

"Who will lead us to justice?"

The other six mirrored his position, arms up. "Who will lead us?" they repeated.

Terizan had assumed the question was rhetorical, the sort of thing secret organizations chanted to get in the mood for conspiracy, but as she watched a translucent figure floated down from the ceiling in the far corner of the room. Pride kept her from bolting this time. Pride and—well—it seemed there was some truth in familiarity breeding contempt.

It took her a while to recognize the ghost but, in her

own defense, the last time she'd seen Councillor Saladaz, his head had been on a spike in the Crescent after he'd been executed for betraying caravans to the bandit chief Hyrantaz for a percentage of the stolen goods.

He seemed to have gotten his head back.

His voice a distant whisper, he began to speak of how the Council had been responsible for countless deaths in Oreen. Men, women, and children all lost to life and love because of the actions or inactions of the Council. "We all know the Council is corrupt. We all know the Council must be stopped before more loved lives are lost." Thought about rationally, nothing Saladaz said made much sense, but it was obvious to Terizan watching the seven people listening that they weren't thinking rationally. Like Ajoe, these men and women were lost in grief, and that grief was being expertly manipulated by the dead councillor. He'd always been able to work a crowd into near hysteria; while death had lowered his volume, it had focused his skill.

In a weird way, she admired Saladaz' ability to hold a grudge beyond the grave. The Council had him executed, and now he was using what he had—grief-stricken visitors to the Necropolis—to exact his revenge. It was probably a good thing he didn't know she'd been the one who'd exposed his dealings with Hyrantaz.

"The Council must be removed," Saladaz whispered, moving about the tomb and touching each of the conspirators in turn.

They shuddered and chanted, "The Council must be removed."

Terizan shuddered with them, remembering the weaver's touch. It was a small step from grief to despair.

"The dead must have justice."

"The dead must have justice!"

Terizan would have bet serious coin that when Saladaz spoke of the dead, he meant only himself.

"We must take action to avenge our dead."

"We must take action to avenge our dead!"

"When the time of mourning is done, we will take action," Ajoe the Candle-maker added in a tone as definite as the dead councillor's had been suggestive.

Saladaz' face twisted as the other six repeated, "When the time of mourning is done." Throwing off their cloaks, they began to wail and beat at their chests. His mouth moved, but it was impossible to hear his rough whisper over the grieving, and finally he surrendered to the inevitable and wafted back up through the tomb's ceiling.

Leaving seemed like a good idea to Terizan. Besides Ajoe, she'd recognized another of the seven by the silver-and-lapis clasp that bound her thick gray hair. She didn't yet know the woman's name, but she knew she worked on Draper's Row—and that was enough. Sliding silently out of the niche, she waited a moment for her eyes to adjust and then, fingertips stroking the stone, moved into the dark of the catacombs, counting her footsteps back to the crack in the tomb wall.

The name of the woman who'd owned the silver hair clasp was Seriell Vanyaz; her eldest son had recently died in a construction accident in the new city, crushed under a load of stone. Terizan settled the clasp in her pocket and crossed the bridge into the Necropolis. It would be easy enough now to find the other names. All she had to do was ask an acolyte for the names of those who'd been interred over the last few months and match the faces of the mourners to the faces of the conspirators.

She could hand the names to the Tribunal a day early. The Tribunal would hand them to the Council and then, probably before Terizan had even counted her share of the payment, the Council would add another seven bodies to the City of the Dead.

She'd thought about telling the Tribunal that Councillor Saladaz was the only actual conspirator.

"A dead Councillor? Not only dead but beheaded? You saw him then? Conspiring? Alone?"

Council might believe that Saladaz wanted revenge; they'd known him in life after all, but they'd never believe a dead man was working alone. Ajoe and the others might be grief-addled puppets, but they *were* conspiring.

Of course, now she wanted an acolyte there were none around.

She stood for a long moment outside the tomb that held the entrance to the catacombs and, frowning slightly, traced on the surface the path of the underground passage, climbing up and over terraces and tombs. When she was fairly certain she was as close to the meeting room as she could get, she began to read the names carved into the stone.

Councillor Saladaz's family name was Tyree. Terizan knew it because she'd robbed his town house once. Well, twice actually, but it hadn't been his town house the second time because he was already dead.

The rear wall of the Tyree family tomb was directly over the part of the catacombs where the meeting had been held.

"The carving of the colonnade is thought to be exceptionally fine."

Terizan had often been accused of walking silently, but the Ayzaruites could give her lessons. Heart pounding, she turned to find the same older man who'd spoken to her the day before. At least she assumed it was the same man; one acolyte looked pretty much like another and, besides, she was better with jewelry. "The what?"

"The decorative columns." He gestured helpfully.

"I was wondering . . ."

"About the mason?"

"No!" She didn't think she could cope with another lecture on stone carving. "I was wondering about the recently . . ." She paused and stared into the Tyree crypt. Saladaz had been dead for nearly a year. "I was wondering why the ghosts of the Necropolis don't move out into the city."

"They are tethered to their bodies by my Lady's will. They are not alive, and she will not give them the freedom of life."

"She won't?" That was interesting. "She seems a little annoyed about it."

The acolyte shrugged. "My Lady is the Gateway and she would prefer the dead accept her assistance."

"But if the body was moved out of the Necropolis . . ."

"If a body with an active spirit was removed from her influence, then it could go where it would." His tolerant smile suggested he didn't know why he was bothering to explain what everyone knew. "Except back into the Necropolis, of course."

That answered the one question that had really been bothering her. None of the seven conspirators were violent people. Violent in their grief, maybe, but not the sort to start whacking councillors even with the encouragement of a dead politician. She couldn't believe it of Ajoe the Candle-maker, and she doubted the others were much different. So what was Saladaz actually working them up to?

He wanted them to remove his body from the Necropolis.

Once he got them to commit, they probably wouldn't bother being subtle; they'd crowbar the gate off the tomb, bundle him up, and bury him secretly in the city somewhere. After that, he could haunt anyone he wanted to.

Terizan rubbed her arm. If forced to choose, she'd

take Ajoe and company over the Council in a heartbeat. Unfortunately, unless they were going to move Saladaz tonight, she didn't have that option. The Council would have either the names of the conspirators or proof there was no conspiracy by tomorrow or they'd begin to implement their extreme new security measures. As a thief, Terizan wasn't fond of the idea of extreme new security measures.

Nor, as it happened, did she particularly care for the idea of someone like Saladaz wafting about Oreen.

If she gave the names to the Council, they'd deal with both the living and the dead, and things in Oreen would continue on the way they had been. No extreme security. No dead Councillors being a bad influence on the grieving. No Ajoe the Candle-maker. No Seriell Vanyaz. She reached into her pocket and stroked the silver-and-lapis hair clasp.

Good thing the Council had given her another option.

The acolyte cleared his throat, breaking into her reverie. "It is, of course, a crime to steal a body from the Necropolis," he declared.

"How do you prevent it?"

He stared at her as though she was out of her mind. "We are a presence in the day and no one comes into the Necropolis at night. The Necropolis is haunted."

Terizan sighed. "Trust me, that's not the deterrent you think it is."

"He'll let her use my loom!"

Terizan backed away from the crypt. Hanra Seend followed.

"He'll let her use my loom!"

And a little farther away.

"She won't take care of it. I know she won't."

And farther still.

"You have to tell him not to let her use my loom!" Between *my* and *loom*, Hanra stopped following.

And that gave Terizan the rough length of Ayzarua's tether.

Terizan moved quickly between crypts and tombs, touching nothing. Unfortunately, there was one ghost she couldn't avoid, but she did her best to delay the inevitable by waiting until she saw a pair of cloaked figures slip into the catacombs and then humming all twelve verses of *Long-Legged Hazra*. If tonight's meeting followed the same pattern as last night's, that would give Saladaz time to appear and begin talking.

Motivated, Terizan got through the three locks on the Tyree tomb in record time. Once inside, she carefully lit her tiny lantern and swept the narrow beam around the shelves. It wasn't hard to find the Councillor's corpse; he was the only member of the family to have been beheaded.

Breathing through her mouth, she wrapped the shrouded body in waxed canvas and tied off the ends, leaving a length of rope just a little longer than Ayzarua's tether. Then holding the end of the rope, she dragged the body out of the tomb.

"The dead must have justice!"

Apparently, she'd pulled him away from his rant. She kept moving and didn't look back.

"Thief! Stop, thief!"

He could yell all he wanted. Unless there was a horde of dead constables around, there was no one to stop her. A quick, nervous glance from side to side determined that there were *no* hordes of dead constables.

"Do you know who I am, little thief? I am Councillor Saladaz Tyree!"

"You were," Terizan muttered, picking up speed on the raked gravel off the path. The ranting turned to threats behind her until she stopped by the tomb with the loosened bolts and the entrance to the catacombs.

"Fool! I learned the secrets of the City of the Dead. I gathered those who would hear my voice. Everyone knows you cannot stop the dead! I will have my revenge."

Terizan ignored him and moved one tomb further.Her arm barely fit between the bars, but she managed to put the end of the rope in Ayzarua's outstretched hand. The moonlight extended just far enough for her to see the Goddess' welcoming expression turn to grinning bone.

A little unnerved by the sudden quiet behind her, she turned to come face-to-face with Saladaz. He roared and reached for her. With the rope in the Goddess' hand, his body was now close enough that she was just within the limit of his tether.

Oh, that was clever!

She spun around, pressed hard against the bars, and stared into the darkness behind the Goddess. The acolyte had said that if she stared long enough, the gateway would open.

She needed that gateway open.

Goddess. Skull.

Skull. Goddess.

Five lines of icy cold down her back. Again. And again. Overcome by a despair so deep she wanted to die, Terizan sagged against the bars and reached to take the Goddess' hand.

When flesh touched stone, the darkness behind the statue lightened. A tiny circle of gray growing larger and larger until the Goddess was silhouetted against it. Only the cold wind roaring past her into the gray kept Terizan on her feet.

One last glimpse of Saladaz' face. Not a cold wind roaring past her then but his spirit being assisted through the gate. His translucent form stretched into caricature, he howled, "The dead must have justice!" as he disappeared.

Terizan lifted her other hand just far enough to flash a rude gesture.

She dropped to her knees as the gateway closed. Dragged her tongue over dry lips. Realized with the clarity that came from nearly dying, that it was the despair brought on by Saladaz' touch that had opened the Gateway. Without it, she could have stared into the darkness until she starved and nothing would have happened.

Well, if she'd starved to death, the Gateway would have opened, but she didn't have that kind of time.

She took a moment to convince herself that she'd meant to do it that way.

As soon as she could stand, she'd put the body back in the tomb. Without Saladaz, there was no conspiracy, just seven grieving men and women.

Unfortunately, the Council had asked for proof of nothing, but even she wasn't that good. She'd have to bring them proof of something else.

In the morning, she needed to have a word with an acolyte and get those names.

"There is no secret organization meeting in the Necropolis and conspiring against the Council."

One steepled her fingers and smiled over them. "Prove it."

Terizan threw a small crumpled scroll on the table. She'd picked the poet's pocket when he left his shop to get some lunch.

Two snatched the scroll from Three's fingers before it could get covered in scented oil. Unrolled it. Frowned. "This is a ballad mourning a dead love."

"And not a good one either," Three muttered reading over Two's shoulder.

"Poets?" One asked, lip curled. "There are poets in the Necropolis?"

"Dressing in black. Wearing silver jewelry. Rhyming *into the darkness* with *broken hearted*. And I'm not going back in there for another poem, I barely escaped as it was." Lines of cold across her back. Her shudder was unfeigned. "You can send someone else if you need more proof."

"We will."

"Go ahead."

She meant it and that convinced them. After all, if there was a conspiracy, and she turned down the job, it would go to a thief who might be less than scrupulous about the names he or she offered the Council. Terizan would never be responsible for something like that.

And everyone knew it.

Tanya Huff lives and works in rural Ontario with her partner Fiona Patton, six and a half cats, and an unintentional chihuahua. Her twenty-third book, The Heart of Valor, *is due out in hardcover from DAW Books Inc., in June 2007. When she isn't writing, she gardens and complains about the weather.*

THE INVISIBLE ORDER

*(Being a most small and concise part of the
Hidden Histories of Mankind)*

Paul Crilley

O N THE DAY she found out about the hidden war
being fought in the streets of London, Emily Doyle
woke up praying for snow.

It was four o'clock in the morning, and Emily pushed
aside the ragged sheet that covered the lead-paned window. She wiped the mist of her breath away and stared
out into the near-darkness. Frost winked and glittered
in the moonlight, a thin layer of gleaming white that
reminded her of the powdered icing on Mr. Warren's
cakes.

It always looked pretty at this time of the morning.
Then it melted away to reveal the dirt and grime that
was the norm in St. Giles.

Her prayers went unanswered. There was no snow.

She knew it was selfish, but if it snowed she wouldn't
have to work. She could crawl back into bed with her
two younger brothers and sleep till sunup. No such luck,
though. Now she had to trek to Farringdon and buy her

penny's worth of watercress to sell in the freezing weather.

She pulled her oft-patched shawl tight around her shoulders and stepped over the prone bodies of the new tenants. Emily didn't know who they were. Just that they paid their money to Mrs. Hobbs yesterday, and she told them to sleep on the floor in their room. That was the way of it in Cheapside. Her mother said they were actually the lucky ones. Some landladies put fifteen people into a room at the same time. Emily'd heard tell that when they did this, they sometimes died in their sleep. They sealed the windows in an effort to keep warm and breathed each other's air until there was nothing left to go around. When she'd heard about this it terrified her, and for days afterward she would wake up and listen to make sure her brothers were still breathing.

Emily pulled open the front door and felt the sharp bite of the air against her cheeks. She breathed in deeply and felt the last remnants of sleep leave with her explosive exhalation of white breath.

She stepped onto the deserted street and couldn't help but wonder if this was what all ten-year-old girls had to go through every day of their lives.

Emily had to get to the market early that morning as Mrs. Eldridge promised to give her an extra bunch of watercress if she got there first. She turned into Church Lane; she knew a shortcut from this road that would get her there in half the time. She hurried down the street. Washing lines crisscrossed the road high above. Someone had left a sheet out overnight. It was now a solid square of material that hung heavily on the line, weighing it down so that it looked like the rope would soon snap.

A broken railing between two of the tenements gave

her access to the labyrinth of courts and yards that wove around and behind the main thoroughfares of London. The maze of back streets and dingy pathways was like a vast shadow cast by the city streets. The alleys were thin and claustrophobic, the buildings leaning in on her like Uncle Thomas when he'd had too much gin. She gritted her teeth and broke into a jog.

She was halfway to the market when she heard the noise up ahead. She stopped short, skidding and almost falling in a puddle of something slimy. She held her breath and listened. There it was again. A scuffling sound from around the corner, and a strange clacking noise.

Emily looked around. A lot of people used these alleyways as shortcuts, although that didn't mean they were safe. But the alley ahead was the only way if she wanted to get to the market in time.

She crept forward until she was leaning against the exposed red brick of a lodging house. She listened for a moment but still could not place the sounds. She laid her hand on the corner of the wall and started to edge her head around.

Something stung her. She jerked her hand back with a stifled yelp and stared down at it. There, stuck in the soft skin between her thumb and forefinger, was a splinter of wood. Where had that come from? She grabbed hold of it and pulled.

It wouldn't budge. She frowned and pulled harder. The skin puckered and stretched but the splinter stayed firm in her skin. Not only that, but she imagined she felt it pulling back, as if it were actively resisting her efforts. Emily let go of the stick, intending to pull out her knife blade and dig the stupid thing out, but as soon as she did so, the splinter jerked and sank deeper into her flesh.

Emily's breath caught in her throat. She grabbed hold

of it again. It was definitely resisting her. She set her mouth. Nothing else for it. She tightened her fingers and with one sharp tug, she yanked the splinter from her flesh.

She could not keep a small cry from escaping. The splinter tore her skin as it came free, bringing with it a dark bubble of blood.

She ignored that, however. Her attention was focused on the piece of wood.

It wasn't a splinter. It was an arrow. A tiny arrow with a piece of flint as an arrowhead. She stared at it in bemusement for a moment, then turned and looked around the corner into the alley beyond.

A scene of carnage greeted her.

An almost silent battle was being fought, the only sound the frantic scraping and scuffling of feet on the wet cobblestones and the fierce clattering of wooden swords and daggers. Emily stared in amazement. The participants in the battle were tiny, no more than the size of her forearm. One side wore black skins and old leather, and had painted their faces so that only their eyes and teeth shone in the shadows. The others wore more natural clothing—brown leathers and earthy-colored clothes. Dark blood covered the fighters as they skirmished in the tight confines of the passage.

As Emily watched, one of the creatures broke away and limped in her direction. An arrow caught him in the back and he collapsed, twitching, not five feet from her. He lay there for a second, then he melted into the cobbles, his skin liquefying into a bloody puddle that gave off the stench of bad meat.

Emily realized that she was watching a battle between the fey. *The stories were real.* They existed, just like her little brother believed.

She stood transfixed, wondering what she should do.

She wanted to take it all in, but the ferocity of the fighting frightened her.

A moment later the decision was made for her. A piercing whistle echoed through the morning air, sounding like it came from a few streets over. It was answered a moment later by others, although they were fainter and farther away.

As if they were some kind of prearranged signals, the whistles brought the fighting to a stop. The fey froze in place and cocked their heads, listening as they drew in ragged breaths. Emily could hear voices now, still far away but shouting to each other as they drew closer.

They sheathed their weapons and stepped away from each other. The black-painted faeries closed their eyes and faded into the shadows. The others slipped between gaps in the walls or into drainage holes in the gutters. Emily saw a few climbing the dirty facade of the building that faced onto the alley, pulling themselves onto the roof and vanishing from view.

In five seconds they had completely disappeared. Emily stepped into the lane. She looked at the spot where the faerie had died, but there was nothing there; even the puddle had dried up.

The voices were coming closer. She should leave now. She didn't want to be caught here.

"You, girl," said a voice.

Emily whirled around, heart racing.

"Over here," said the voice, irritation clear in both words.

Emily took a hesitant step forward.

"If you move any slower they'll have us both."

She quickened her pace and found the voice's owner leaning against an old orange crate. It was one of the faeries, the ones that didn't paint themselves black. His long face was twisted in a grimace as he stared down at his leg. Emily could see an arrow sticking into his thigh, identical to the one she had pulled from her hand.

The creature turned his attention to Emily. She could see him trying to figure out what to say, how to work the situation to his best advantage. She'd seen that look before, when her brothers tried to make her do something she didn't want to do. She had no patience for it.

"You're injured," she said.

"How observant you are. And all this time I thought humans were stupid."

"And you need my help, so if I were you, I'd think about being a bit more polite. Are you a faerie?"

"Bones, girl, do I *look* like a faerie?"

"I don't know, I've never seen one before."

The creature thought about this for a moment. "Fair point. No, I am not a faerie. Faeries are stupid creatures with wings. Faeries are a waste of space. I am a Piskie—from Cornwall."

"Fine. Are those men I can hear coming for you?"

"Yes."

"Why?"

"Look, can we talk about this while we move? Only, those footsteps sound like they are getting awfully close."

"Fine," said Emily again, and picked the piskie up. He weighed next to nothing, his bones sharp against her flesh. "What's your name?" she asked.

"Corrigan," said the piskie.

"Mine's Emily Doyle. Pleased to meet you," she said. She tucked the piskie beneath her shawl and stood up. She turned to the entrance of the alley.

The was a man standing there. He was so tall and thin, his clothes so tightly fitting, that Emily's first impression was that of a skeleton in a velvet suit. But then the man doffed his top hat and stepped forward.

"Good morning to you, Miss Doyle. My name is Mr. Creely, and I see you are in possession of something that belongs to me."

Emily backed up a step.

"Come now, Miss Doyle. I am afraid my patience is thin so early in the morning. Just hand over the piskie."

"Why do you want him?"

"Why? Because they are vermin, Miss Doyle, and my group eradicates vermin before they can overrun the city."

"You kill them?"

"We have no choice. London holds some sort of symbolic meaning for them and they want it for themselves. That's why they fight each other."

Emily took another step back. "I don't believe you."

"That is beside the point." Mr. Creely's eyes flicked over Emily's shoulder. She turned swiftly, and saw a fat man sneaking up on her. She didn't hesitate. She ran toward him, dodging at the last moment and sprinting for the alley's entrance. She heard Mr. Creely cursing behind her, but she didn't look back. She burst out of the lane and took the first turning she came to. She knew these backstreets well. They'd never catch her.

Some time later, she stopped in the recessed back doorway of a shop and uncovered the piskie. He didn't look good. His limbs hung limp over her forearm and for a horrible second she thought she had suffocated him. But then he groaned and swung his long face around.

"What is it?"

"The arrow. It must have been poisoned. You must take me—"

Emily's heart leaped in her chest. "But I was hit as well! One of the arrows got me!"

"All the more reason to take me to Merrian. I'll give

you directions." He winced, and gently repositioned his leg. "He's a bit on the gruff side, but if you remember to give him his due respect, everything will be fine."

"I'll not give him respect if he doesn't earn it," said Emily firmly.

"You will."

"Why?"

"Because," said the piskie, "he used to be a god."

He may have once been a god, thought Emily, looking around the cramped shop, but he certainly didn't know how to keep things tidy. Dust covered every available surface. The front window was so dirty you could barely see in or out. Emily wasn't even sure what type of shop it was meant to be. There was no clear indication of what he sold.

"Just . . . ring that bell."

Emily looked and saw a bell on the counter. She was surprised she hadn't seen it before, as it was the one thing in the shop that looked as though it was routinely polished. The handle of the bell was carved from a pale wood and featured a delicate scrollwork carved carefully into the grain. The bell itself was white, and it shimmered with blue highlights as she looked at it. Emily gently placed Corrigan on the counter and picked it up. The slight movement this caused drew from the bell a clear, high ring. Emily quickly replaced it.

"Now what?" she whispered.

"Just . . . wait."

No sooner had Corrigan uttered those words than the curtains at the back of the shop were torn aside and a giant lumbered through, ducking his head to avoid banging it on the doorframe. The man was bald with a long braided mustache that trailed down to his chest. He stopped short when he saw Emily and glared at her.

"Who in the name of all the Gods are you?" he shouted in a deep voice.

Emily stared in awe. Then she cleared her throat to make sure there wouldn't be a squeak to it. "Emily," she said. "Emily Doyle."

"Well, Emily Emily Doyle. What are you doing in my shop?"

"I told her to come here, Merrian," said Corrigan.

Merrian looked down at the counter. His brows knitted in surprise. "Corrigan? What are you doing here?" He stepped forward. "You're hurt! Was it her?" He glared at Emily. "I'll kill her—"

"Relax, Merrian. It wasn't her. She saved me. It was the Unseelie."

"What? Gods, have they broken their word already? Who were they?"

"A tribe of Tylwyth Teg out of Wales. We followed them in from Bath."

"Ah. That explains it."

"What?"

"There's a truce on. The Dagda Himself has asked to meet the Queen tonight at Hyde Park. Said he wants to end all the fighting."

Corrigan looked surprised. "Just like that? And what of London?"

Merrian shrugged, and cast a sidelong look at Emily. "Greater minds than ours will decide her fate. Here, let me look at your wound." He bent over and examined the piskie. "Nasty," he said. He sniffed. "Unicorn shit and . . ." he sniffed again. "Unicorn shit mixed with the dead flesh of a Slaugh."

"Can you heal him?"

"Aye, I think so."

"Can you heal me as well?" asked Emily. She held out her hand. "One of the arrows got me."

Merrian took hold of her hand. It looked like a doll's limb resting in his huge palm. He bent over again and sniffed. "Not too bad. You got it out quick enough. I'll give you a poultice, though."

Merrian opened a drawer and took out a tiny glass vial. He handed it to Corrigan. "Drink this while I look for the ingredients. It will take away the pain." He moved off to the shelves and started taking down dusty jars, muttering to himself as he examined them.

Emily watched him for a moment. "Who are the Unseelie?" she asked, turning her attention back to Corrigan.

"They're the Black Sidhe," he said. "Our enemies. We've been fighting them for thousands of years."

"And who are you?"

"We are the Seelie."

"But why are you fighting?"

Merrian laughed. "Why does it rain? They fight because they always *have*. All through the centuries there have been hidden wars between the fey."

"Rubbish," scoffed Emily. "Why don't we know about it, then?"

"Some do," said Corrigan. He looked over his shoulder. "This is good stuff, Merrian. Does the job." He turned back to Emily. "There are groups of humans—secret societies—who know about us, who try to stop us. That Mr. Creely you met? He's in one. The Invisible Order they call themselves. Founded by Christopher Wren. You know who he is?"

Emily shook her head.

"He started the Royal Society a couple of hundred years ago, a society for men who worship on the altar of science and logic. But the Society itself was just a cover to hide his real purpose. The eradication of the fey, the destruction of Faerie itself."

"Why would he want to do such a thing?"

Merrian lined up five jars on the counter. He opened them and took out bits of bark and leaves. "Your kind have always hovered on the outskirts of our wars, like hungry dogs eager for scraps of meat, but Mr. Wren—the reason he got involved was more personal."

Corrigan sat up. "You mean that was true?"

Merrian grinned and stuffed the contents of the jars into his mouth. He chewed on them and nodded.

"Bones, I thought that was just gossip."

"What are you talking about?" snapped Emily. "I'm not magic, you know."

"Mr. Wren had a thing for our lady the Queen, but she in her infinite wisdom saw fit to spurn his advances."

"I see. So you're telling me that faeries and goblins and spriggans and all kinds of strange creatures live in London?"

"All over," said Corrigan. "We're just good at hiding."

"Not that good. I found you."

Merrian spat the brown mess he had chewed into his hand and laid it on the worktop. He scooped some out with his finger and held it out to Emily. "Here. Put this on the wound. It'll draw out the remaining poison."

Emily grimaced and took the warm sludge from the giant. She pasted it over her wound.

"What were you doing in the alley anyway?" asked Corrigan.

"Taking a shortcut." Emily suddenly remembered where she was supposed to be. "The cresses!" She looked to the window, where she could just see the building across the street through the grime. "I'll never get any good bunches now." She unconsciously patted her threadbare dress, where a pocket sewn on the inside held her penny.

She couldn't feel it.

She turned her pocket inside out, but the money was gone. She must have dropped it in the alley when she escaped from Mr. Creely.

"I have to go," she said urgently. If she didn't get that penny back her family wouldn't eat tonight. She took one last look before she opened the door, trying to freeze in her mind the image of a giant God bending over a trembling piskie, then she hurried out into the watery gray dawn of a winter's morning.

The alley looked deserted. Emily hugged the wall and watched for what seemed like an hour, but there was no movement. But then, why would there be? The piskies were all gone, what need for Mr. Creely and his men to linger?

When she was satisfied she was alone, she moved to the spot where she had found Corrigan. The sky had lightened enough for her to see and she scanned the wet cobbles for her money.

"Looking for something, Miss Doyle?"

Emily felt as if her heart simply stopped in her chest. She turned quickly and saw the skeletal figure of Mr. Creely blocking the alley mouth. Her heart made up for lost time and thudded painfully in her chest. She turned, intending to run to the other end of the passage again, but a hand grabbed her painfully about the arm and a sack smelling strongly of onions was thrown over her head.

Emily felt suffocated by the darkness. She wasn't sure how much time had passed, but she still had the sack over her head and her eyes were streaming because of the stench of onions. She was angry—not because she was crying, she wasn't—but because Creely would *think* she was crying.

She tried to move, but her hands were tied behind her

back. She shifted, and something sharp dug into her spine. She realized she had been propped up against some crates. She fell forward onto her knees, then stood up, feeling with her hands until she touched the sharp corner at the top of the crate. Then she tried to wedge it into the knot, pushing down with her wrists to get it as deep as possible into the loop and then pulling forward, slowly loosening the binding.

It took over ten minutes, and each second she expected Mr. Creely to walk through the door and discover her attempt to escape. She dropped the rope to the floor and yanked the sack from her head. Light exploded across her vision. She squinted to block out the brightness and looked around. She was in some kind of storeroom. Crates were piled against three of the walls and a single window let in the rich light of afternoon. She must have fainted in the hansom cab Mr. Creely bundled her into.

She hurried over to the door and pressed her ear against the rough wood. She could hear voices on the other side. Mr. Creely talking to someone.

"I ain't gonna to do it. I'll go to hell for that, Mr. Creely.

"My dear man, the last thing someone such as yourself should be worried about is going to hell."

"Oh. Thank you very much, Mr. Creely."

"You misunderstand, Mr. Vance. I think it *inevitable* you will end up in hell. But at least the monetary recompense will allow you to damn your soul with some style."

"But—"

"Mr. Vance! Please! If we are to play our part in the Dagda's betrayal, we must be at the Serpentine Bridge before midnight. And you still have to pick up the weapons. Just go in there and find out where she took the piskie. Use whatever means necessary."

Emily stepped away from the door. The Dagda's betrayal? Wasn't the Dagda the person meeting with the Faerie Queen tonight? To discuss a truce? Were the Seelie headed into a trap? She turned and studied the window. She had to warn Corrigan.

She climbed onto the crates and pushed open the window, pausing only to stuff some potatoes and oranges into her shawl for her family's supper. Then she clambered out into a yard piled high with mounds of moldy sacking and disappeared through the open gate.

Two hours before midnight, Emily slipped through the massive arches at Hyde Park Corner and hid at the bottom of a huge statue of a naked man. She waited for a few minutes to make sure there were no police around, then she jogged across the grass, following the road that ran along the Serpentine River.

The full moon hung crisp and bright, and finally revealed the stone parapets of the bridge arching across the river. She climbed up into a tree that gave her a good vantage point of the surrounding area. It was bare of leaves, but the thick branches twisted so much that they hid her from view.

The run had warmed Emily somewhat, but now the chill set in. Her old dress and threadbare shawl did nothing to keep out the cold. Her teeth started chattering. They sounded so loud that Emily thought anyone passing below would be able to hear her.

She finally decided to distract herself by eating the orange she had kept aside when a voice spoke to her.

"Would you like a drink?" it said.

Emily almost fell from the tree. She craned her neck up and around and saw Corrigan sitting astride a tree branch, his feet dangling over the side while he drank from a tiny horn.

"What are you doing here?" she gasped.

"Actually, I could ask you the same thing."

"I came to warn you! The meeting is a trap. The Unseelie are in league with Mr. Creely."

Corrigan swung his legs and took another sip of his drink.

"Didn't you hear me? I came all this way to warn you."

"I heard you."

"But if they kill the Queen, who will stop them taking over London?"

"That's not a problem."

"What do you mean?"

Corrigan sighed. "We know it's a trap. The Dagda told us."

Emily shook her head. "What?"

"The truce is real. Tonight we wipe out the Invisible Order and then the Queen and the Dagda will divide up London between them."

"They can't do that!" said Emily, horrified.

"Yes, they can. The weapons the Invisible Order were given are fake. Not iron like they thought. Now hush. The meeting is about to start."

"But . . . but what will happen to us?"

Corrigan frowned down at her. "Is that important?"

"It is to us!"

"I don't know. All I know is that London stands on a piece of land sacred to the fey. We will burn the city down. Properly, this time."

"But, my family—"

"Hush. The Queen comes."

Emily turned. A small hill lay in the center of a sward of grass. As she watched, a white light blossomed at the base of the hill and slowly grew until it was the size of a door.

Then a tall silhouette appeared and moved forward.

Emily was vaguely aware of dancing and capering shapes spilling out around the tall figure, but her attention was riveted on the face of the Faerie Queen as she stepped from the hill and surveyed the landscape around her. Her features were perfect, a cold white face framed by copper hair that fell in loose waves past her slender shoulders. She had lips so red they could have recently tasted blood. A long, wispy cloak, looking like it was made of spiderwebs, floated behind her as she walked. Its edges were held above the grass by a troop of dirty and unkempt children. Their clothes were torn and muddied, their eyes vacant of expression. Beside the Queen walked a blackcloaked man with a hood pulled over this face.

"That's the Dark Man," whispered Corrigan. "If he comes for you, there is no escape. He'll follow you into the Depths and more if the Queen wishes it."

He stood up on his branch. "I have to go. The river will soon run red with the blood of the Invisible Order." He hopped down and joined the rapidly growing group emerging from the hill. There were so many different kinds now. Hairy gnomes with spears. Goblins with sickly yellow skin. Taller creatures, more elegant, and closer in size to the Queen. Emily wasn't sure who they were. All she knew was that right now she was the only one who knew the fey meant to betray Mr. Creely and his men. She might loathe the man, but it looked as if the Invisible Order was the only thing standing in the way of London being burned to the ground.

She clambered from the tree and retraced her steps until she was out of sight of the faeries. Then she headed down to the river and hurried along the bank until she saw the bridge. She could hear the fey off to her left, giggling and squealing like demented children. Then there was a commanding voice, high and perfect like a clear note of music, but with undercurrents of ice and danger. The creatures fell silent.

Emily scrambled up the bank and slipped onto the bridge. She bent low and ran across. She could see the trees on the other side, and if Corrigan was right, Mr. Creely and his men should be hiding somewhere nearby.

She ran into the trees. She couldn't see anyone. "Hello?" she called softly. "Mr. Creely?"

Movement to her right. She turned and saw the tall man emerge from the shadows. His face was drawn and pale, filled with tension. "What in God's name are you doing here?"

"Saving your life," said Emily. "If you cross that bridge, you will die. The fey have double-crossed you. They've called a truce so they can get rid of your order. Then they plan to burn London to the ground and divide up the land."

"Nonsense. How could you possibly know this?"

"The faerie I carried this morning. I saved his life and he told me." She gestured at a rude looking spear he carried. "And that's not iron. You were told it would be fatal to them. It won't be."

Mr. Creely cursed under his breath. He turned. "Mr. Vance," he hissed. "Get over here!"

The fat man who threw the bag over her head shuffled forward. By this time, others were emerging from their hiding places. Emily looked around at the wall of faces, all armed with the useless spears.

"Mr. Vance, you picked up the weapons today, did you not?"

"Yes, sur. Just like you tol' me to. One of those ugly gnome things helped me load them into the cart seein' as I was runnin' late."

Silence greeted this. Mr. Creely turned fully around to tower over the cringing man. "The gnome *helped* you load these?"

"Yessir."

"He touched them?"

The man nodded mutely.

"These are supposed to be iron, you buffoon. Iron is fatal to the fey."

"Ah."

Mr. Creely turned to the others. "Spread the word. This night's work will have to be completed some other time. Go now."

The cloaked figures ran into the forest. Mr. Creely turned back to Emily and stared at her. "I think you can see for yourself that the fey are not about light and dancing. They are cruel, sadistic hunters who think humans should be their playthings. They are closer in nature to cats than they are to us."

Emily heard a loud crashing behind her. Voices raised in shouts. Creely looked up.

"That was to be the signal for us to join in the attack against the Seelie." He sighed. "And so the battle continues." He bowed low in front of Emily. "Good night to you, Miss Doyle."

Before Emily could utter another word, he turned and walked quickly into the darkness. She should leave as well. Before the faeries came to find out what happened to their plan. She set out into the trees, intending to leave by one of the other gates.

She was close to the edge of the woods when she heard the giggling. She stopped. The sound seemed to come from up ahead so she turned to the right.

Corrigan dropped from the tree and leveled a bow at her. "Stupid, stupid," he said.

"Corrigan." She looked around frantically, searching for a way out. "Won't you let me go? I . . . I saved your life, after all."

"And that is why we will spare yours. Deed for a deed. Life for a life."

Emily turned. The Faerie Queen stood before her, tall

and terrible. The giggling sound she had heard came from the children holding her cloak. They stared at Emily with hungry eyes.

"You . . . you won't kill me?"

"No."

"Then I can go?"

"I did not say that."

Emily felt anger rise up despite her fear. "Then what?"

"You have a choice. You will live—if you accompany us to Faerie."

"For how long?"

"Why, forever. You will never see your home again."

"And if I refuse?"

"Then I'm afraid you will have to be punished."

Emily looked around. More of the fey had gathered, forming a tight circle around them. There was nowhere to run. She looked back at the Queen. "It might be better to be dead than a prisoner for the rest of my life."

The Queen raised an eyebrow. "Do you think so? Then let me add a bit of incentive." She raised her hand in the air. The fey behind her silently moved aside, clearing a pathway into the trees. A dark shadow detached itself from the darkness and glided forward until it stood by the Queen. Emily swallowed nervously. It was the Dark Man. The Queen leaned toward him and whispered something in his ear. He turned to Emily and stepped toward her. She tried to move, but someone grabbed her from behind and held her in place.

The Dark Man lowered his head to her hair. He made a noise like the snuffling of a horse as he moved his head over her clothes and skin. Emily realized he was smelling her.

When he was satisfied, he stepped back to the Queen's side.

"Now," she said. "The Dark Man has your scent. If you do not accompany me, I will send him to hunt down your family. Their deaths will not be quick."

Emily looked despairingly for Corrigan, but there was no sign of the piskie. There was nothing she could do. She felt tears well up in her eyes. She could not condemn her family to death simply to save her own life. She had to go.

She hastily wiped the tears away. She would not let them see her cry. And besides, she told herself. At least if she were alive, there was always a chance of escape. She looked up at the Queen.

"I don't have much choice, do I?"

"There is always a choice. Just not always good ones. What is your decision?"

"I'll come."

The fey erupted into excited chattering. The children behind the Queen grinned feral grins. She pointed at them. "But I won't do that."

"Oh, my dear, you're much too intelligent for that. No, you will be a storyteller. You will regale our feasts with tales of heroism and danger." She leaned forward. "But be warned. If you ever run out of stories, I'll cut out your tongue and make you eat it. Now come."

Emily hesitated, then stepped forward. The Queen put her arm around her shoulders and guided her across the grass. They took three steps and left the trees behind. The small hill stood before them. The doorway was still open, the fey disappearing back through in carousing groups.

Emily let the Queen guide her. Just before they stepped inside, she took one last look over her shoulder.

Snow was starting to fall. It drifted like silent feathers through the winter air.

"It's snowing," she said, and smiled.

Then the light enveloped her and she stepped into the lands of summer.

Paul Crilley is a Scot currently living in South Africa with his partner, his daughter, seven cats, and two dogs. He recently turned thirty, and much to his surprise the world did not, in fact, come to an end.

He is a writer on a prime time sitcom due for broadcast on South African television early next year, and is hoping to finish the first novel in his fantasy series, "The Sundered Land Cycle" in the next few months. He is also working on numerous screenplays, some of which may actually have a chance of getting made.

BORROWED TIME

Stephen Kotowych

THE LOOK ON Vincent's face confirmed for Kayla that she was the last person he expected to see when he answered the door. She pushed past him into the apartment.

"Hey!" Vincent said sharply.

The apartment was much the way she remembered it: looking (and smelling) of bachelor. In the half-light through the closed drapes—the ones she had made him the year before—she saw magazines and newspapers scattered on the couch, a pizza box under the coffee table, and dirty plates full of desiccated pizza crusts and worse sitting on top. She was sure the kitchen sink would be full of unwashed dishes.

"Still don't clean?" she said, stepping over a fallen T-shirt. Reaching into her shoulder bag, Kayla pulled out a gold pocket watch, and popped open the cover. She studied the four small dials of its chronograph face by the dim light. Each of the tiny hands turned at a different speed, some forward and some back.

Vincent gave a frustrated sigh. "I haven't spent a lot of time here lately."

"So I hear."

He straightened. "What does that mean?"

Kayla's brow furrowed. The readings from the chronograph dials synced with the time reading from the large hands. She held the watch out for Vincent to see. "There's no variation from baseline here."

"Why would there be? I'm hardly having a good time." Almost at once Vincent's eyebrows arched. "Oh, *that's* what this is about. You're checking up on me. You just can't get over—"

"What the hell is the matter with you?" she interrupted. "I thought you were going to stop stealing time."

"You wanted me to stop. There's a difference."

"Because I knew you'd get caught!"

"No, Kay, you were worried *you'd* get caught. That's different, too."

"So who is she?" Kayla demanded, crossing her arms. "Another new recruit?"

"I'm through dating younger women," Vincent said, wandering into the kitchen.

Kayla's eyes narrowed. Though he'd meant to hurt her, she was angry with herself for taking the bait. The Chronographer's Guild had recruited her right after grad school and assigned Vincent—only *four* years older—to train her. He'd hardly robbed the cradle. Besides, she'd been just as interested in him and had sent all the right signals. She'd been surprised it took him so long to clue in.

Light spilled into the dim apartment from the refrigerator. *Pop-snap.* Vincent stood in the open door of the fridge, bathed in light, drinking a soda. His wasting energy still bothered her.

"Did I ever get my key back from you?" he asked casually, in between gulps.

Kayla gave no answer.

"Kay?" he said. "Where's my key?"

She made no motion, no response.

Vincent's eyes went wide. "Oh, God," he said. "You turned me in." He tossed the empty can to the counter. Stepping past her, he turned the dead bolt and slid the door chain across.

"I didn't turn you in," she said, defensive. "They came to me. You stopped meeting your quota, and then you stopped checking in altogether. They notice that kind of thing. They want me to bring you in."

"You? Why you?"

Kayla hesitated. "Because of our . . . history."

Vincent scoffed. "Is that what they told you? Doesn't matter. I don't work for them anymore." He looked out the door's peephole.

"They don't see it that way." Kayla didn't believe him, either. Vincent still wore the bracelet that, along with the chronograph, was the mark of their secret profession. A braid of rope in gold—a reminder of their first lesson, to think of time as a piece of rope, and of each moment a fiber twisting together to make up the whole. The bracelet was a constant reminder to all chronographers of their mission and oath to gather lost time, moments people skipped over, which would otherwise slip away into nothingness.

Kayla, like most chronographers, came up with her own simile for time after considering the lesson of the rope. She preferred to think of time like oil; as nonrenewable a resource, and just as slippery to deal with.

"Things are so black and white for you, Kay. I wish it were that simple."

"You steal lost time and use it for yourself. Seems black and white to me. Chronographers are supposed to collect lost time and use it for the future! Without the Guild and the chronographers, who knows how much time we'd have left?"

He laughed. "Still such idealism? I always loved that about you. But it drove me crazy, too."

"I am idealistic," Kayla said. "And I'm not ashamed. The work we do," she caught herself, "the work *I* do is important, noble."

"Noble? You're the one who's stealing time, not me— you and the other chronographers."

"That's ridiculous. What we do, we do for the good of everyone, the whole human race. You know our days are numbered if we do nothing about it."

"How many tomorrows do we have, hmm?" He crossed the apartment. "Have we ever been able to tell how much time remains unused, in reserve? The Guild would have you believe that all we have left is what the chronographers have saved and put back into use. What's that make our lead time? A year? A bit more? Are we that close to oblivion?"

Vincent pulled one edge of the drapes back a bit, letting in a sliver of the day, and looked out across the skyscraper skyline. "All those people out there using up time, skipping over baseline like rocks over a pond, unaware of the moments they have. Humanity entered the twentieth century with one billion people; it exited with more than six. That number will only rise. There aren't enough of us," he waved his hand back and forth between them, "to keep up the quantities of time people are using. There never could be. It's diminishing returns. We're fighting a war of attrition, one that entropy is destined to win."

"We delay the end of time as long as we can. That's all the Guild could ever do," Kayla said.

He rounded on her. "What if the Guild is wrong? We could have a hundred years left, or a thousand, or maybe aeons more. Then what would that make the chronographers, if not thieves?" He crossed back to the door and looked out the peephole again. "It's one thing to *lose* time, and another to have it *taken* from you. How many hours have you stolen, Kay? How many days or years of someone's life have you taken?"

Kayla's mouth worked, but no words came out. She'd never heard anyone speak about the Guild or the chronographers that way. She was not like Vincent! She gathered time the way all good chronographers did—when it wouldn't be missed. And she returned it to the Guild, for the benefit of all to use, not for herself.

She would gather moments from the sleeping, from the excited, from the distracted. So someone would wake up feeling like they'd only just closed their eyes, or someone would see that time flies when you're having fun. Their sacrifice meant those moments would be recycled, available for someone else to use, cheating entropy of its victory for another few seconds. Vincent made it sound like she killed people.

"We all steal time," Vincent said. "I just use it differently than you."

He pulled a jacket and small duffel bag from the hall closet. He'd been preparing for an escape. He slammed the closet door.

"Where are you going?" Kayla asked. She turned as if to block his way as he headed for the window. Vincent bumped her out of his way with a shoulder.

"Vincent, where are you going?"

He pulled the drapes open, violently, ripping one from the curtain rod. It peeled away like a skin, and fading daylight streamed in. Vincent pushed the window open and threw one leg out onto the fire escape.

The sound of the bullet entering the pistol's chamber stopped him. He stood frozen for a moment, straddling the window frame, before Kayla finally spoke.

"You can't leave, Vincent. Unless it's with me and back to the Council."

Vincent looked at her, studied the automatic she pointed at him, and turned back to the window. "If you want to stop me, you'll have to fire . . . and shoot me in the back."

"They're in the alley, waiting for you!"

Vincent hesitated. "Nice try. But I always knew when you were lying. The Guild knows as much about bringing in a fugitive as a bunch of librarians. Don't take this the wrong way, hon, but if you're who they sent after me I don't think they bothered putting anyone in the alley."

He waited for a moment before pulling his other leg through the window. There was the sound of footfalls on the fire escape, and he was gone.

Kayla rushed to the window and leaned out. She could hear him getting farther away, rattling down the escape toward the ground, but couldn't catch sight of him.

Dammit!

Strangway, the Guild agent who had assigned Kayla this task, had given her the gun, but she'd never intended to use it. The threat would be enough. But no, not for Vincent. Idiot.

There was a knock at the door. Kayla checked her watch. Twenty minutes and they'd follow her up, they said. Right on time.

Muffled voices outside the door, and then the key she had given them turned in the lock. The door opened as far as the chain would allow. A body slammed against the door. The chain held, but Kayla knew it wouldn't for much longer.

What would they do, she wondered, when they found out Vincent escaped? It would be the end of her career, at best. They might let her stay on as one of the rank-and-file, patrolling every day, gathering stray bits of time day after day for years, until retirement. She didn't relish the idea of such mediocrity.

"Stop! Freeze!" she yelled. That sounded like the

right kind of thing. The crashing at the door stopped momentarily. She scrambled on to the fire escape and held the gun high above her head, pressing a finger in one ear and the other ear into her arm. "Freeze!" she yelled once more for good measure, and squeezed the trigger.

She jumped at the sound, but the kick was what really surprised her. There wasn't normally any call for a chronographer to use a firearm.

There were shouts in the hall, and as Kayla flew down the first set of metal stairs she heard the splintering wood of the doorframe giving way.

When her feet finally hit the ground, she ran hard down the alley. Would they know that she'd hesitated, or that Vincent had a three- or four-minute head start?

As she cleared the alley, which opened on to a busy city street, Kayla looked to the darkening sky. She couldn't take the chance that he was right about how much time was left. She had to find him. Otherwise, her charade wouldn't make much difference—she'd be finished in the Guild, and time itself would be in danger.

Though she had her chronograph out, Kayla relied more on feel to guide her through the city streets, in what she hoped was Vincent's direction. She found the usual fluctuations from baseline, but nothing out of the ordinary.

Sitting on a park bench, Kayla clicked shut her chronograph. She needed to gather her thoughts, focus her attention. She drew deep, slow breaths, emptying her awareness, focusing on becoming a vessel for time to pass into. Kayla waited for . . . *something*, some clue to where Vincent might have fled.

The glow from a hundred office towers, each a shimmering finger of glass, steel, and light, illuminated the downtown core. People in suits emptied from them, filling the streets to teeming. Each of them rushed somewhere, distracted, minds racing ahead of them. The city intruded on her awareness.

She'd never considered how many moments she could gather from these rat-race types. There was no need to check the chronograph for confirmation. She could tell there was time here, ripe for the taking; she could see it in their eyes, feel it in her bones. It would be hard to find Vincent through such a jumble.

Learning the true nature of time—that it was a real and tangible thing, as elemental as fire, as invisible as the wind—was one thing. Look at how time ravaged and wrinkled the faces of the elderly, or how the monuments man built wore and decayed as the ages passed, and it made sense. Learning the ebb and flow of moments people use but don't observe, how to take those seconds or minutes without being noticed, was something else entirely.

She had skill for it, more than some Guild recruits, and she found her own instinct often as good as data gleaned from a chronograph. So she closed her eyes, and imagined herself reaching out to them, scooping up their unwanted time like sand on a beach. Instants, seconds, moments slipped through, each one distinct to her, like sand against her skin. She could not save them all. Entropy would have its due. But she could save some.

Something indistinct pulled at her, there, over her right shoulder. Her attention shifted. There was a definite pressure, familiar . . .

Vincent!

Into the park she ran, deep into its darkness, with no thought of what might lurk there. He was close, she was sure, and that was what mattered.

She slowed her pace as the pressure built, like pinpricks all over her skin, like the tingle of a sleeping limb. It was right in front of her, and it was . . . nothing. Kayla paced near a stand of trees, feeling the pressure stronger here, weaker there, the boundaries of a bubble.

Kayla knew something of such spaces from her time with Vincent. She closed her eyes, preparing. She moved through the barrier. How seductive it was. How easy it would be to give in as she had so many times, unaware, with Vincent.

Opening her eyes, she saw the world overlaid upon itself. Night and day flexed and jostled, each trying to impose itself over the other.

Kayla was still within the same stand of trees, but there were children suddenly, half a dozen, all nine or ten years old, playing in the dying sunlight of a late August day.

Each part of Kayla's awareness fought for dominance, just as the flickering night and day did. Two moments: one theirs, one hers. Their moment was an echo for her, she realized, a flash into how they were experiencing time. Children wove around her, running after one another. Did they see her? Was she really there?

Kayla's brow tightened. Guild agents used time differently from others, were more "in-moment," in Guild parlance. They observed baseline more closely, used time at a fairly constant rate regardless of circumstances. But even they sped through moments sometimes. Everyone, even chronographers, lost stray seconds without noticing, like losing eyelashes, or shedding skin cells.

Those children, though, did not. They had every second at their disposal. There was no room for Kayla to reach in and take moments. She could feel them using and attending to every moment individually, perfectly, like no one she'd ever encountered . . . But how? They couldn't all be so naturally in-moment.

Until she had appeared at his door that afternoon, Kayla hadn't seen Vincent in almost a year; he'd made no effort to contact her. But now he wanted her to find him. It was the only thing that made sense.

Vincent had somehow given these children time. He knew that she would recognize the strange sensation and track it. The children were a marker, part of a trail. Vincent led her to them, and was leading her to himself. But why?

Time began to move faster around her. Kayla turned to see the sun falling behind the skyline, felt coolness against her skin as buildings' long shadows raced over her, filling the park. In the same moment, she saw the moon, the starless urban sky, the glistening office towers.

The flickering between moments intensified as they moved to merge at baseline. It was her presence, she realized, her observation of this strange sliptime, that was bringing things back into synch so rapidly.

And it was night again suddenly, Kayla's moment. The children called good-bye to one another, promised to play again the next day, as they scattered in all directions.

A young boy collided with Kayla. Perhaps he hadn't seen her, she thought, for there was surprise on his face at running into a strange woman who, for him, had not been there a moment earlier. He ran off without an apology.

Kayla began running, too, in the other direction. Vincent was close now, she was sure. And he wanted to be found.

She rounded a corner. Another *something* was nearby. Time rushed away from her like water through a burst dam, pulling her along in its current. He was here, on one of the restaurant patios that lined the sidewalk.

Kayla felt an unmistakable tingle and turned. Instead of Vincent, she stood in front of another trail marker: a blissful young couple. They were having coffee and dessert, holding hands, lost in each other's gaze.

"I've spent my whole life in this city," said Vincent, suddenly beside Kayla. "Maybe people are different somewhere else, I don't know. But here, watching people always in a hurry, always thinking about what's next, I realized that we need to do more than just make sure there's a tomorrow. We need to make sure that, once they have them, people use their *todays*. Or what point is there in keeping the wheel turning?"

"How are you doing this?" Kayla asked, awed. "*What* are you doing?"

"You're seeing what I do with the time I take. I've applied the same principles I used when we—when *I*— took time for us."

"You steal time for them?" she asked, confused. "Do they pay you for it?"

"They don't pay me." His voice had an edge at the accusation. "They don't even know what I've given them. You know they rarely see us."

Moving in moments where others were not meant rarely being seen by those people, like the children in the park, or the couple at the restaurant. Even standing so close you could reach out and touch . . . It was one aspect of the job Kayla knew she'd never get used to.

"I *borrow* time for them, Kay. The Guild will take other moments from them, I just borrow against that. I took a cue from something you said when we, well . . ."

A lot had been said the night she walked out, a great deal of it hurtful, and designed to be. She didn't look at him.

"You said I was selfish," Vincent continued. "In fact, you said stealing time, even to spend whole, perfect days

with you, was the most selfish thing you'd ever heard of,
as I recall your exact words.

"You know," he said in hushed tones, "some women
would find that terribly romantic."

She could tell without looking that he was smiling.
She smiled, too.

"That really stuck with me," he said. "It hurt. Mostly,
I guess, because it was true. I was selfish. And one day
it occurred to me: What if I gave time back? We know
what happens when we take time, but what happens if
we give time back to people? If we let them use the
seconds or minutes we would otherwise snatch up and
store away, what then?"

"You can do that?" Kayla asked.

"I have been, for months now. The results, Kay! This
is what life was meant to be like! This is how it was in
the beginning, how all our hominid ancestors experienced existence before we became self-aware. A perfect
now. We lead such short, fragile lives . . ."

Was that a tear Kayla saw in his eye?

"Don't we deserve a chance to slow things down, to
expand our finite lives sometimes? And when they have
those moments, people just let time wash over them,
know how to handle it, the same way newborns will hold
their breath underwater—instinctive!"

"You knew I'd find you. You left a trail. Why?"

"Because I wanted you to see this. You are the only
one who could find me. You don't really think they sent
you after me because we used to date, do you?"

A denial died in Kayla's mouth.

Vincent shook his head. "Oh, Kay. So naive. They
sent you because you were there when I started stealing
time. You know it's possible. You know what it feels
like, how to sense it. The Council knows I can borrow
time, but could any of them track it like you could?

"It's a test of allegiance," Vincent said, turning to face her. "The Council wants to know whose side you're on. They're wondering—will you turn me in, or are we in league?"

Kayla considered the idea. Did the Council question her loyalty? Perhaps they were right to. Turning Vincent in had been clear-cut when she thought he was robbing time for his own use, but now she wasn't sure. What would they do to him if she handed him over? What would they do to her if she did not?

"How are you doing this, Vince?"

"I'll tell you, but there's something I need to show you. Then see if you still want to bring me in."

He took her hand and they ran into the night. And as they ran, he explained.

The last time Kayla had been in a hospital was also at Vincent's side, during her training.

A tour of the coma patients was a required part of training. Whole days, months, even years could be taken from them. There were chronographers who specialized in coma patients, slipping unseen into the rooms of patients over and over . . . It was an easy way to make quota, but it struck Kayla as ghoulish, like preying on the helpless.

The cold and the antiseptic smell brought it back to her as she and Vincent again walked hospital halls.

Vincent found the room he wanted and they stood in the doorway, watching. An old man lay in bed connected to a web of wires, tubes, monitors, and machines. Racking coughs shook his withered frame; his voice was thin and raspy. A middle-aged man sat at his side, holding his hand. They talked in hushed tones, and sometimes the old man would smile meekly, or weep gently.

"James is dying," Vincent said quietly. "He won't last

the night, the doctor says. That's his son, Derrick. He's come to say good-bye."

Kayla said nothing. She could feel the tingle of moments all around her, like an itch she wanted to scratch. She wouldn't let herself.

"The world won't let children stay children for long these days," Vincent said. "The kids in the park deserve one golden summer to always remember, so I've been giving them time for weeks now.

"That couple on the patio? Today was the day they fell in love. And, well, you know how relationships go."

Only hours ago, Kayla realized, she would have taken that as a veiled accusation. Now, she nodded her head and understood.

No matter what happened later in their relationship, the couple would always have that magical, intensely lived day they fell in love. That's what Vincent had given them. Just as, Kayla realized, he had tried to give her.

She didn't want him stealing time for her, but had she misjudged him? She considered him for a long moment, seeing perhaps for the first time what she loved in him.

"And them?" Kayla asked, turning her attention back to the old man and his son. "This is an awful time to be in-moment."

"But it's not, Kay! That's what you made me realize. With us, I tried to prolong all the happiness, all the easy moments. I didn't want the difficult ones. No one does."

He became very still. "My father died last year."

"Vincent . . ." Kayla took his hand. Vincent's father had been ill for several years, the whole time Kayla and Vincent were together. Vincent hadn't wanted them to meet until he recovered, saying his father didn't want people seeing him as an invalid. Now it was too late.

"It was a lot like this," he said, looking over the hospital room. "I sat with him, held his hand. We were close,

I thought. We talked a few times a week; I'd go visit him. But then he was gone, and I realized there was so much unsaid. I could have taken time, spent weeks and weeks with him in-moment . . . but I didn't. It was too hard, too scary. And now . . . Now it's too late." He wiped away tears.

Kayla's throat burned. She squeezed his hand, and felt him squeeze back.

"That's when everything you'd said about my selfishness made sense. Even if we don't want those moments, even if they scare us, we need them. They make us see what we don't like about ourselves; they shake us up and change us.

"Look at this man, dying in his bed, and tell me that he hasn't been robbed of his most precious possession— *time*. For him, it's lung cancer, but it could as easily have been some Guild agent who took just enough moments . . . I can't make him say the words, but I can give him time, and give him the chance. Time to say all the things he never said. Time to bring some peace to his life, and his son's, before the end." He turned to look at her. "If you want to put me away for that, well, you're welcome to it."

Kayla leaned up and kissed him, standing on tiptoes as she'd always had to. As their lips met she felt her resistance melt away, and she gave in. Every second— every one!—washed over her like a warm rain. She was there with Vincent, and with the old man and his son, in the moment, fully living each instant. It was all she remembered it being, and more. This was how life should be lived!

She broke the kiss when she realized the hushed conversation by the bedside had stopped. Kayla could feel eyes on her. The old man could see her, was looking at her! She was so used to not being seen she could find no words to answer the questioning look on the old man's face.

"Sorry," said Vincent. "We must have the wrong room." He took Kayla by the elbow. They stepped into the hall and back into baseline time.

Waiting there for them by the nurse's desk was Strangway, the tall, grandfatherly Guild agent who'd set Kayla after Vincent.

"Don't move," Strangway said. Men appeared at Strangway's side, and others blocked possible avenues of escape. They were the kind of men librarians wouldn't know to hire.

Cold slipped down Kayla's spine as Strangway settled his gaze on her. He knew, didn't he? He knew that she had let Vincent escape his apartment, that she now did not intend to turn him over to the Guild. They'd just been using time—had he been able to sense it? Is that what drew him here?

A pair of the men with Strangway moved to either side of Vincent, each roughly taking an arm.

"Hey! Easy!" Vincent said.

The gun. It was still in her bag, Kayla realized. Could she get it before they stopped her? She slumped her shoulder, trying to slide the strap down her arm.

"You're a little late to the arrest," Vincent said, as the men pushed him toward Strangway. "Kayla was about to bring me in. She's convinced me to turn myself over."

Kayla wanted to scream that was a lie, but his look as she caught Vincent's eyes held her back. I know what I'm doing, they said. Don't stop me.

"Well done, Kayla," Strangway said. "I knew I was right about you."

Kayla didn't like the implication.

"You know," Strangway said, stepping to within

inches of Vincent, "what we do is like building a bridge of stone. All of humanity walks as one across the endless span of this bridge, except for us. We walk a few steps ahead on the leading edge, laying down the next course of brick, the next row of stones, so everyone else will find safe footing for their next step. What you do, though, is monstrous—stealing bricks from under the very feet of your fellow man!"

He nodded his head and the men ushered Vincent down the hall, through a set of swinging doors, and out of sight.

As she motioned to follow, Kayla felt an arm slip around her shoulder. She fought the urge to shrug it away.

"It's gratifying to know that you are on our side, Kayla," Strangway said. "This wasn't easy for you, I'm sure. You realize by now that this wasn't a simple assignment from the Guild."

Kayla considered the slipperiness of his statement, the layers of meaning: a veiled reminder of his secret knowledge of her crime; a kind of congratulations on passing the test and expiating her sin. It was how Vincent would have picked apart the statement, she realized. He was right—she had been naive.

Not anymore.

"I think any lingering doubts have been put to rest," he said, slowly guiding her down the hallway. "You made the right choice in the end, and that's what counts. There's no need to discuss your, hmm—youthful indiscretion?—ever again, as far as I'm concerned."

Kayla mumbled false words of thanks and forced her attention to stay in the moment. Trauma was one instance where it was easy to skim the seconds, awareness shutting down as you went into shock. She was determined to have every instant of the pain, to feel it all, remember it. Like Vincent said, the hard moments helped you change. . . .

"It's clear you're a person of special talents," Strangway continued, "one who won't be content in the trenches, gathering time forever, yes? I have something of an eye for talent, and you have greatness in store for you, I'm sure of it. I don't doubt eventually you'll be sitting on the Council with me. It might do you good to have a friend in high places as you make your way."

She allowed herself a moment of dark pride at the confirmation. Pieces had fallen into place after Vincent said her mission was a test. Of course Strangway was on the Guild Council: who else would be trusted with the knowledge that you could turn time to your own purpose?

Something about keeping enemies closer crossed Kayla's mind as she forced the effusive thanks for Strangway's patronage that he would expect.

He smiled softly and disappeared through the swinging doors at the end of the hall.

Kayla headed for the elevator, tears in her eyes at last.

Strangway wasn't the last person Kayla expected to see when she peered through the peephole, but she thought he would wait longer before coming to see his new protégé. It had been less than a week.

He knocked again.

She watched him, strange and distorted through the peephole, grow increasingly impatient with waiting. He checked his watch—not his chronograph, Kayla noted; that was a good sign—knocked once more, then turned and walked down the hall.

Kayla waited, ear pressed to the door, until she heard the elevator open and close again. She exhaled a deep and ragged breath. Had she been holding it the whole time? She slid the door chain across and decided to have more dead bolts installed; she'd seen how little help chains could be.

She closed the blinds on her living room windows—the ones she'd made herself when she made Vincent's—and returned to work on her chronograph.

Did Strangway suspect? Had he taken apart Vincent's chronograph, seen how its gears and counterweights, its crystals and wires had been modified?

Vincent had explained the basics of his borrowed time during their hurried trip to the hospital. The chronograph was the key. Simple modifications turned it from a meter for time into a *conduit* to dispense it.

How many others, in the long history of the Guild, had happened upon this secret? How many of those had the Council also "disappeared?"

She'd heard the rumors, of course, the urban legends chronographer trainees told each other. Cross the Guild, they said, and you'll end up in the coma wards, your body kept alive as Guild agents steal away every moment of the rest of your life. . . . She'd never had reason to believe that, until now.

Was that where she'd find Vincent—a John Doe in some faraway coma ward? And would she find other chronographers who'd made the same modifications Vincent had? Did they share his vision? As she soldered wires and reweighted the mechanisms in her chronograph, Kayla vowed to find out.

Stephen Kotowych has is a member of the Fledglings, a Toronto-area writer's group brought together by Robert J. Sawyer in 2003. He has his Masters in the history of science and technology from the University of Toronto, which serves the dual function of looking pretty hanging on his wall and being good fodder for his fiction. He is currently an acquisitions editor at the University of Toronto Press. This is his first published work of fiction.

SHADOW OF THE SCIMITAR

Janet Deaver-Pack

SWEAT STREAMED THROUGH his short mud-brown hair and down the back of Percival St. Croix's neck. Unrelenting sun hammered on his head, shoulders, and back. Climbing a pitted rock spire in the Arabian desert in the middle of the day wasn't his idea of intelligent action, but he needed to speak to the rebel leader on the summit.

I bounce around on a camel across half the desert to get here. Then circumstances dictate that I climb this rusty spine for a meeting with an old friend. Well, he's not exactly a friend—I never got to know him that well at Oxford.

Percival grinned, an expression bringing boyish enthusiasm to his oval sunburned face. "The things I do for my Order and people who need my help," he grumbled aloud, enjoying himself despite the heat.

A twenty-nine-year-old man of forgettable features, mild mien, and average height, Percival's blandness hid remarkable talents. He was the only Advocate of the Rosicrucians, appointed by the eminent Council of

Twelve and the Order's leader, a seldom-seen figure known as the Liberator. Percival's lifelong assignment was to seek out and annihilate Chaos.

And now, during the first third of 1917, one of the greatest threats to mankind's peace and security is gaining power in the Middle East, Percival thought. *The war has little to do with the real menace: conflict between nations makes a convenient curtain for the growing power of Devlin Quint.*

He stopped climbing, right hand digging into a crevice while his toes balanced on a protruding bulb of ancient lava. Percival wore smoke-colored lenses rimmed by silver wire to protect his eyes. Lifting them, he swiped a blurring tear from his left eyelid with a brown sleeve. That eye felt tired and grainy, the white likely still deep red from the ritual dust he'd employed yesterday to ferret out his path through the desert.

Settling the lenses back on his nose, he reached upward for the next handhold. Sudden peculiar fluttering, like cotton robes whipped by a dust devil, made him stop. A dark form crossed the sun. Percival looked up, seeing nothing.

"Things are not right here," he whispered. "I must hurry."

It took him a good fifteen minutes more to grasp the sand-scoured ledge of the volcanic plug. As Percival's eyes lifted above the shelf, he discovered a dozen rifles pointing at his face.

"The peace and blessings of Allah to you," he said in calm Arabic to the Bedouin holding the rifles, knowing use of their language would confuse them. *I can tally on one hand all the British in this country who speak Arabic. Two of them are on this blasted rock.* "Please, may I see your leader Aurens?"

They shifted their feet and argued about what to do.

Finally one lowered his gun, looked at the top of the ridge, and called, "Aurens. Aurens! Someone asks for you."

A conspicuous figure in white and gold glanced at Percival, then back out into the desert. "Very well, but not for long." He turned, skidding down from the summit, spitting Arabic. "You'd better have an extraordinary reason for interrupting us. Who the hell are you, and what are you doing here?"

"Spy, he's a Turkish spy!" suggested several nomads.

Careful of the rifles, Percival levered himself up enough to sit on the ledge. "I wondered where you were, Thomas." His English wheezed and cracked from dust. "I came partially in response to your letter."

Captain T. E. Lawrence slid to a stop near him. "Ahmad, get some rope. We'll have to tie him up until we're finished with the train . . . wait." Lawrence squinted blue eyes beneath sun-bleached brows, barely shaded by his head cloth. "Is it—no, it can't be." He switched to English. "Percival St. Croix from Jesus College at Oxford, is that you?"

"In the flesh." He nodded, and couldn't keep mischief out of his tone. "Only you would endeavor to confuse the enemy by wearing Arabic wedding robes, Thomas."

Malice faded from the nomads as Lawrence held out a hand. Percival stood and took it: dry and gritty, it felt like leather-wrapped bones with a minimum of wiry muscle, very much a part of this desiccating desert.

"What's this?" Lawrence fingered the six-inch Latin cross Percival had pressed to his palm while shaking hands.

"My calling card, the Rosae Crucis."

Leaning to shade it from the sun, Lawrence studied the cypress cross with its delicate carved rose. He turned it over to scrutinize the mystical symbols on its back. A long moment passed as he considered what it meant. "The Rose Cross." Turning to the tribesman beside him, he ordered, "Give him water."

Percival felt as if he'd passed a test as a goatskin bag was thrust into his hands. He upended it, drinking the warm stream of mineral-tasting liquid. He returned it with thanks in Arabic.

Lawrence handed back the cross. "I've heard about the Rosae Crucis, of course, but I've never seen one." He squinted as Percival's fingers made the cypress disappear, apparently behind a fold of his cloth belt. Indicating his own costume, Lawrence shrugged. "This is a necessary ploy. These were a gift from Prince Feisal, meant to bring me more credibility among the tribesmen I live among these days. And they're much more comfortable than British military kit while riding camels."

Percival looked deep into the shrewd eyes that had a startling ability to assess both minutiae and men. Suddenly he remembered Lawrence's sensitivity about his short stature. There were four inches of difference between the two. Percival discovered a wide hole in the rock with his toe and eased his sandals into it, putting his and Lawrence's faces on the same level.

"You look well despite this heat," Percival grated in English, his throat somewhat relieved by the water.

"As well as can be expected." One side of Lawrence's mouth quirked upward in a wry smile, and he shook his head. "None of us are getting much rest charging around the desert at all hours, chasing trains and befuddling the Turks."

"By the way, I bring greetings from Prince Feisal. He hopes your mission is going well."

Lawrence waved a hand at the desert beyond the top of the rock. "So you stopped at the prince's camp. I'm sure he told you that we're awaiting a train along the

Hejaz Railway. We're going to blow it off the tracks and pillage what's left. Damned Turks aren't always punctual, but they often send wagons fat with horses, mules, and staples for stations up the line. The only ones we let pass have cars of women and children whom the Turks have decided to uproot and send away."

He squinted suddenly at Percival. Tension gathered about him like electricity, carrying an unmistakable question.

"Yes," Percival replied. "I'm here to investigate the odd deaths of Turkish soldiers you mentioned in your letter. And hopefully glean more from the train."

"I really didn't expect your appearance in the middle of a war zone in Arabia, or your ability to climb rocks," Lawrence stated in a soft voice. "I thought perhaps you'd reply by letter. Figured that was more your style: you were always quiet at school, chasing from one place to another with an intent look on your face."

"I had other duties. They more than filled any spare time."

"I must say, your arrival is a pleasant surprise. Frankly, I'm impressed that you'd come all the way from Feisal's camp to find me." His expression hardened, looking much like the rock he stood on. "Few of the military higher-ups bother to respond to anything I tell them. I've been talking myself silly to no effect in almost every meeting I've had. Most think this is a mere sideshow to the important side of the war." His voice gained passion. "If they only realized how pivotal this area is!"

"Indeed. I agree with you completely, old chum." *It's even more important than you think, Thomas.* "What goes on here will set up much of what happens in politics and policy for generations to come. And it will generate problems, too. That's another part of the reason I'm here."

Lawrence leaned forward. "I had to take a chance and write you. You have some experience with . . . odd goings on, I think. Heaven knows, some strange events happened during our years at school. Excuse me, I need to keep watch on that train." He turned, climbing crabwise to the top of the rock to check the still-distant Turkish transport. Percival waited as Lawrence gauged the time of the train's arrival, conferred with the lookout, and slithered back down.

Lawrence's intent eyes bored into Percival's ice-blues behind the gray lenses. "You *must* have received my letter."

"No. Serious consequences necessitated my hasty departure from England. I gained your information through other channels."

Lawrence's eyebrow lifted. Percival kept his silence.

"I wasn't sure the information would get all the way home, least of all to you." Lawrence scratched a stubbled cheek. He hadn't taken time to shave. "It had to go from me, to Feisal, to his father Grand Sharif Hussein by special courier, then into a diplomatic pouch for the trip overseas, then through God knows how many hands in the army. I wouldn't be surprised if it had disappeared. Let's face it, the details within are peculiar."

Percival nodded. *It almost didn't get to me,* he thought. *Extraordinary means were employed by a Rosicrucian who appropriated the letter as soon as the messenger set foot on English soil. He sent the information on to me by metaphysical means. Otherwise, it would have been buried as nonsense in someone's trash bin at the Home Office, or sent for decryption.*

Aloud, he replied, "I found your descriptions quite disturbing, Thomas."

The rebel leader sighed. "You are the only one I know who might understand what's going on. I hope you can explain it to me." He peered at Percival, his expression pleading. "You do really have some connection with occult forces, don't you?"

Percival allowed the corners of his mouth to turn slightly upward. "You remember that day at Oxford when you fought invisible flies for twenty-four hours?"

"Yes." Lawrence's long nose wrinkled. "Nasty, that. Most of the house thought I'd gone barmy, slapping and scratching at nothing."

"You sprang a trap meant for me. I assure you, the creatures involved were much worse than invisible flies. Thank God they couldn't do much to you except irritate. For me, they would have been poisonous."

"Knowing I was beset, you could have at least conjured something to help alleviate my misery," Lawrence said with a touch of sarcasm. "I scratched till I bled."

Percival lifted his left lens and wiped away moisture from his irritated eye. He kept his voice level. "I helped you as much as I could. I was, however, preoccupied with some nasty things myself for a few days."

"Is that why you disappeared for a while? The rest of us wondered. Just who are you, really?"

"I'm a dealer in antiquities and a scholar in ancient texts, Thomas. This allows me to roam the world buying artifacts for clients, authenticating antiques, and lecturing. I also sometimes apply expertise in occult subjects to . . . shall we say, certain situations."

Lawrence's voice gained an eager edge. "Do you have any clue what made those odd marks on the Turks?"

"I won't know for certain until I've had a close look at them. I need to get on that train to find out. Time is of the essence. There's something very wrong here."

Lawrence looked far into the brassy desert at a dust devil, then turned back to Percival. "I've been pressed into service again on this front," he said in a quiet, frustrated voice. "I tried to get out, but my superiors sent me back. They said Prince Feisal and the Arab Revolt needed me. That the war needed me." He shook his head. "This killing and killing; it's too much. I can't bear it."

"It's what you get for being competent, old chum," Percival said, trying to soothe his friend. "And having a willingness to charge into the fray when no one else will. Admit it, you've always enjoyed a challenge."

Lawrence frowned. "Not one of this type. I'd almost rather return to Cairo and spend the rest of the war bored to death in the map department. I wanted action, but not like this."

"Drawing maps of terrain in Cairo would be a waste of your extraordinary talents."

Lawrence looked hard at his schoolmate, his own analytical ability making an odd connection. "Percy," he said slowly, pointing a long index finger, "did you plan my posting to Cairo, then set up my appointment as adviser to Feisal?"

"Not entirely."

"What do you mean?"

"The British war effort would have been mad not to post a man like you in Cairo, or ignore you for the Arab Bureau. I merely suggested your name at a likely moment in a certain military someone's ear during a dinner soirée. I also gave my highest recommendation when another general questioned me about you some time later."

"So, you were in the right place at the right time to determine my destiny." Shaking his head, Lawrence looked distressed. Tension built again as he stared at Percival. He opened his mouth to retort, then laughed as a mercurial thought changed his mood. "I should have bloody well known you stirred that pot. It all happened too fast and too thoroughly to believe that someone's hand wasn't pushing somewhere." He glanced upward at the lookout again, answered a question in Arabic from one of the tribesmen, then switched back to English. "Your timing is excellent, by the way. The train will get here within the half hour."

"Hopefully, it will offer important information for both of us." Percival kept tiptoeing between the mundane world and the mystical, searching for a plausible explanation to give Lawrence an inkling without revealing too much. "You know, you're assisting the fight on two fronts."

"What?" Lawrence's penetrating eyes probed Percival's face.

"Trust me," he said, the seriousness evident in his voice. "There's much more going on than you think."

"So, the odd marks on the dead Turks are part of this second front?"

"I'm not certain yet," Percival repeated. "But I suspect that's true."

"I'm quite worried." Lawrence's tone warned Percival to listen. "If the same strange thing starts happening to the Arabs, Grand Sharif Hussein's revolt could be in complete disorder in a matter of days. I doubt even Feisal could hold them together if word got out. The tribesmen are bad enough as it is. When they get what they think is enough booty, or we haven't won decisive victories in three or four fights, they disappear like summer clouds and go home." He shook his head. "It's a completely different mind here, one most Europeans don't understand. There are no contracts for two-year involvements, or dedication to a national cause. These people are loyal only to their tribes and the sharifs who lead them. Feisal lost more than half of his army earlier this year just because many nomads decided their raids weren't successful."

Percival appreciated his passionate tone. It was no surprise that Lawrence had moved at least one or two of his superior officers and Prince Feisal to listen to his assessments. It was also no surprise that Lawrence had been assigned to ascertain which of Grand Sharif Hussein's four sons was ready to shoulder the responsibility of leading the Arab Revolt. After meeting them all, Lawrence had endorsed Feisal.

"We have to keep the Arabian front active, attacking with these people's strengths and minimizing their shortcomings," Lawrence continued. "If the defense here collapses, we not only lose the Levant, but this entire side of the world."

Percival smiled at his fervor. "You're more a part of this fight than most Arabs."

"Someone has to be. I seem the only consistent advocate they have outside of Prince Feisal and Grand Sharif Hussein."

I understand exactly how you feel, old chum, Percival thought. *It's not easy being a force of one.*

From the top of the ridge, a Bedouin called out to Lawrence. He replied in Arabic, then faced Percival again, continuing in the same language.

"Want to have some fun?" he asked. "We can always use a hand with the explosives. If you've had experience, of course."

"I have," Percival smiled. "Thought you'd never ask. What have we in resources?"

"Several mule packs of dynamite, plus blasting caps. A few mines and remote triggers. Camel and mule teams to pull down the telegraph poles and wires, after we've appointed someone to ascend and yank apart the important bits. I've taught several of these men to do just that recently." Lawrence waved his hand at the surrounding tribesmen. "And some of the finest marksmen in Arabia, handpicked from Feisal's top rifles. These Juheina are particularly good."

The adulation raised a cheer from half the tribesmen. Others glowered. "And the Beni Salem are superior shots." A roar came from those who'd been frowning a moment before, making the first group subside into grumbles.

"I take it the trains come armed?"

"Always," Lawrence nodded. "Two or three small guns, and usually dozens of soldiers with rifles and extra ammunition. How dull things would be if they weren't."

"Right." Percival stepped back while Lawrence gave orders.

"Ahmad, Gasim, choose your crack shots. I want them up here to pick off as many soldiers on the train as they can. Hold your fire until the mines go off, then choose targets with care, shooting as soon as the locomotive derails and the dust cloud allows sight. Aim for the artillery gunners first. Shoot at the same time, so several enemies fall together. That always makes a better impression.

"We'll lay a couple of mines under the front and back wheels of the locomotive, ensuring that the entire motivating force, as well as a majority of the train behind it, derails. Turkish soldiers still alive will be in confusion then. We can take cover behind that dune," he pointed to a mound below, halfway between the tracks and the rock where they stood, "and deal with the rest at our leisure."

The excited nomads followed his orders. In minutes a line of riflemen, divided into Beni Salem and Juheina, lay prone in firing positions across the top of the rock, padded against heat by rugs. They tested their sights on the railroad, challenging each other's prowess. The rest of the Arabs, led by Lawrence and Percival, made their careful way down the crag to the sand.

Lawrence directed the unpacking and division of explosives. He cradled one mine as Percival picked up and inspected another. "I thought I'd grow up enough by now to stop playing with fire crackers," he teased in English.

"Haunted by our evil pasts," replied Percival in the same language. "Where were you thinking of setting these? And approximately how long are these Turkish locomotives, from camel-catcher to the back wheels?"

Lawrence grinned at his joke. "Come on, I'll show you."

Lawrence led the way around the foot of the recumbent stone, Percival at his elbow. The tribesmen followed, their callused bare feet whispering through hot sand. Their dark eyes glinted with the promise of adventure and riches.

"Does your cadre always trail you with such devotion?" Percival asked.

Lawrence tossed a twisted smile over one shoulder. "For the promise of treasure, they'd follow me to the gates of hell."

"Not farther?"

"I haven't tested them beyond that yet."

The sun cooked the sand without mercy. Heat waves shuddered on either side of the shining rails, and the omnipresent dust overrode all scents except sweat. The Turkish train puffed toward them, its engine appearing to swim along the desert. Percival listened as Lawrence described the locomotive's length, then arbitrarily picked a mile-marker, its total measured from Damascus, at which to bury the first mine. Percival paced off the distance estimated by his friend, knowing Lawrence had a keen eye for size and length, honed by years of map making and gauging the sizes of walls and floors while working at the Hittite archaeological dig at Carchemish, in northern Syria. His reckoning would be almost as accurate as measuring the locomotive with a yard stick.

Percival dug into the coarse sand between the timbers, appreciating the unyielding surface. The hard grains abraded his fingers. With a fundament such as this supporting it, his explosive would not shift as the approaching train vibrated the rail bed.

Lawrence rose from his task before Percival did, and walked over to observe his friend's work. He squatted to double-check the second mine.

"Does it pass?" asked Percival.

Lawrence studied the explosive connected to wires with a critical eye. "A small adjustment here, and it should. Now we hide it." They scooped coarse sand over the mine until it looked like part of the rail bed, then covered the wires leading back to the plungers behind the dune. When they stood, dust wafted from their robes.

"We've tracked through that area enough that the Turks will notice," Lawrence said, pointing to the sand between the railroad and the mound. "I think we should do more."

"Walk the men and camels through it," nodded Percival. "Good thought."

Lawrence called to his tribesmen. While he and Percival planted the explosives, they had pulled down the telegraph wires and poles with the help of camels, dragging the debris out of sight around the hip of the rock. The nomads fetched their mounts and turned the trampling into a game, shuffling across their own footprints followed by their camels. When they finished, the sand between the railway and the dune revealed only that it had been churned by many feet going multiple directions.

Lawrence nodded in satisfaction. "Let's get behind

our dune, Percy. That train's getting close." His voice softened. "I hope it has some odd victims you can look at somewhere within."

"Ah. Thanks for reminding me." Percival doffed his head cloth and fished for something beneath his clothing. The sun beat on his unprotected head and neck. "One of the reasons I came here was to give you this. Wear it at all times next to your skin. Never take it off for any reason. Don't let anyone touch it. Above all, don't lose it."

He held out his hand. On it sparkled a silver chain. A fat oval of lapis lazuli hung from it, gleaming in the sunlight. The stone was carved into a rough heart shape, and showed an engraving of a vulture-headed figure holding a spear in one hand and a serpent in the other, flanked by Egyptian hieroglyphs.

"Lovely gift," Lawrence said as he took the charm and fingered it, studying the jewel. "It's cool—unusual in this climate. I read 'truth' and 'strength' here. Who's the figure? I don't recognize it." Looking up after draping the chain around his neck, he saw something in Percival's expression. "It has occult properties, I assume."

"It's powerful protection," Percival replied. "That's the old Egyptian heart symbol. Found it in my collection. It's now ritually tied to your spirit. I thought the strength of Abrasax, also known as Abraxas, might help protect you. I repeat: do not ever take off that talisman, nor allow anyone else to touch it."

"Right. Thank you." Lawrence buried the stone in his robes. "You'll have to tell me more about it later. Ah, our target's almost within range." He replaced his head cloth and its golden rope, then motioned with an imperative hand for the tribesmen to crouch behind the dune.

The locomotive rolled toward them, dragging nine cars along a curve taking it around the volcanic pinnacle. The middle one carried two small field artillery guns pointed in opposite directions, with piles of ammunition, and crews of four men each. Two flat beds carried nervous horses and mules meant as replacement mounts for Turkish soldiers at depots up the line. Others were open, mounded with canvas-wrapped bundles. One car was full of soldiers, elbows and heads hanging out glassless windows to catch the breeze. The other enclosed wagon promised staples such as coffee, sugar, and flour.

"A fat haul, if we can stop it," murmured Lawrence.

"We'll stop it," returned Percival.

Lawrence teased, "You're truly a scimitar of the desert."

"No, just its shadow. Old chum, what I'm about to do must remain between us. This, and my presence here, must never surface in the book you intend to write."

His friend looked surprised. "How do you know about . . . ?" Then he stopped, obviously recalling Percival's extraordinary talents. "Of course not, old boy. Any knowledge you offer becomes my own. And whatever you do stays in here." He tapped his temple.

"Your tribesmen shouldn't see this." Lawrence moved his men away from the Englishmen in the center, then gave orders for the Juheina and the Beni Salem to keep eyes on the train.

Turning his back to the dune, Percival detached a leather pouch from his belt and opened its brass catch.

Lawrence inhaled sharply, peering inside. "Is that what I think it is?"

"Yes." Percival gently lifted out a small alabaster canopic jar surmounted by a beautifully carved and painted head of Anubis. Muttering an incantation, he opened it, took his spectacles off, folded them and put them in the pouch, then pinched a bit of pale powder from the jar. Turning his face upward, he opened his left eye wide, dropped in the dust, and closed both eyes.

"That always hurts," he sighed. By feel, he hooked out his lenses with a finger, put the jar away with great care, and reattached the pouch to his belt.

"What in heaven's name did you do?" Lawrence whispered.

Percival smiled, faced his friend, and opened both eyes. Lawrence stared, amazed.

"I've just performed the 'Eye of Anubis' spell with ritual dust made from the mummy of a golden jackal. I now see the mundane world through my right eye, and the metaphysical world through my left." That eye appeared obsidian black against an angry red background. Lawrence's energetic, restless aura glowed like fire in Percival's enhanced sight. "It's what will show me the creatures that left those strange marks on the dead Turkish soldiers you found. And perhaps other things." He fitted the lenses over his eyes again. They disguised, but not quite hid, the change.

The train chuffed closer. The nomads crouched to both sides of the Englishmen. Percival faced the tracks, inching upward until he could see over the dune's crest, shoulder to shoulder with Lawrence. He fumbled for the detonator attached to his mine. Lawrence grabbed his own plunger.

"I'll make the Turks' eyes slide away from us," Percival muttered in English. "I must also pray to my patron, the Archangel Michael, and to Sekhmet." He grinned. "They make a fine team when they decide to work together."

"I think," Lawrence said, "that I contacted the right man for this job."

Turkish soldiers pointed out the trampled sand from the train's forward vantage points. The engineer slowed the train. Five men armed with rifles jumped from a wagon, approaching the area and avidly discussing reasons for its disturbance. Two, more curious than the rest, neared the dune.

"We're discovered," whispered Lawrence.

"Not yet. Wait."

The Englishmen remained motionless, their noses just above the dune's edge. Percival's normal eye focused on the pair of Turks as they closed the distance. The soldiers stopped, craning their necks and lifting their rifles as if hoping to provoke anyone in hiding to break cover. The train crawled forward at walking speed. The Arabs and their leader held their breaths.

One of the Turks shrugged and returned to his compatriots. The other seemed to sense something odd and stepped toward the dune, rifle ready.

He took another step, and another. He was so near that the hidden men heard the rasping of breath in his dust-sore nose and throat.

"Now," whispered Lawrence.

He and Percival pushed their plungers. Seven, eight, nine heartbeats and more passed—nothing happened.

"Damn!" Lawrence abandoned his plunger and thrust to his hands and knees, reaching for his pistol, preparing to lead a charge.

Percival grabbed his friend's forearm and yanked. Lawrence tumbled against sand, his features contorted with anger until odd accents reached his ear. Percival's lips already moved in patterns of archaic language. The eyes of the hidden tribesmen flicked between the curious Turk and Lawrence. Their faces showed alarm; in moments, they'd be discovered.

"Change in plan," Percival muttered in English, centering his internal force as he turned to Lawrence. "Shoot the guards. I'll stop the train."

With a bloodcurdling yell, Lawrence leaped up, followed by trigger-happy nomads. Turkish soldiers fell, riddled with bullets. Seconds after, the tribesmen atop the rock opened fire. The soldiers manning the gun car all dropped, dead within moments. At the second volley, the engineer opened up the train's throttle, obviously hoping to get away.

Percival scrambled to the top of the mound, his body quivering with power. Sekhmet and the Archangel Michael had both answered his request. Reaching out his right index finger, he pointed toward the locomotive, and to the rails. Forming both hands into a triangle and lifting them to center on the engine, Percival sent a metaphysical command.

The locomotive groaned, cracking in several places with sharp reports. A blinding blue flash came from the rails beneath. Belching smoke, the engine skidded sideways and toppled. The tender and the car behind it skewed off the tracks and plowed into the sand on their sides. Turkish soldiers in the passenger car yelled and swore as it leaned, uncoupled from the wagon ahead of it, and crashed in a dusty cloud.

It took long moments for the battered Turks inside to recover. Some began shoving heads and shoulders through the train windows. Lawrence's rebels stormed forward, yelling dedications to Allah and insults at their enemies. They shot each soldier climbing out.

An imposing figure in his white robes, Lawrence strode among the tribesmen, pistol in hand but firing at no one. Percival stood alone atop the dune, aiming his enhanced eye at each car of the train. He slid the holster of a pistol hanging at his back along his belt to his right side.

"I know you're here, Devlin Quint," he murmured to his real enemy. "Or your minions are. Your evil makes the hairs on my neck quiver. Come out, come out, wherever you are. There's little cover left."

His left eye halted on the caboose. "Ah. Found you." Skidding down the dune, he strode toward the last car of the train as if no bullets sang around him. A few Turks from the passenger car had mustered, and now fired back at the Arabs.

The caboose still stood upright, bullet holes in its thin wooden walls. Climbing its metal rungs, Percival pushed open the door in the back and looked in.

An empty chair meant the trainman of the caboose had fled into the questionable security of the desert. In the other two seats, flies already buzzed over bodies slumped there. Above-standard Mauser rifles with state-of-the-art telescopic sights were still clutched in their hands, revealing that the deceased were marksmen sent with a specific purpose.

Expressions of surprise and horror froze the Turks' bruised, distorted faces. Making a quick job of it, Percival unbuttoned their uniform shirts one after the other, finding the same hideous black-purple-red marks over each heart.

He sighed. "Good thing I expanded Lawrence's protection to include the ugly things that made these wounds, as well as bullets, swords, knives, and poisons. Quint, I'm sure the Arabs appreciate your consumption of their enemies. The vessels holding the spirits of these two have probably already started their flight back to your stronghold."

Rebuttoning their shirts, he left the soldiers as he'd found them, and turned to leave. Percival hesitated, hearing an odd noise. Something of power still inhabited the caboose. Taking care to make it look like his interest was the Mausers, he searched the compartment with both eyes.

Got you! There was a panel in the front wall. *Let surprise be my advantage.* Percival called a neutralizing spell to mind, and whispered it just before he lunged forward and split the partition open with a double-fisted blow.

A mage stood in a niche barely wide enough to hold him, intoning a spell in ancient Egyptian.

"Robbie Chickering!" Percival controlled his emotions and damped his surprise as his old friend from the Servants of the House of Light refused to recognize him. "Sekhmet, be my strength," he said quickly. "Archangel Michael, protect me." Wards around him became as thick steel. Wrapping his arms around his head, he crouched.

The mage's spell slammed against Percival's metaphysical shield and rebounded, blowing the walls and roof of the caboose to flinders. The metal bed of the car rocked violently.

Momentarily deafened by the concussion, Percival straightened as the mage's body, impaled by hundreds of splinters, sagged to the floor. His eyes were still open, registering shock. His spell had returned to him threefold.

"Robbie, my good friend. I'm sorry. And I'm sorry that Devlin coerced you to his side." Percival's head ached from the explosion, and his heart with loss. Working quickly, he tried to tie the spirit of Devlin Quint's mage to the section of desert where he stood. He was too late: the body had already lost too much essence in the explosion. The rest of Robbie Chickering's spirit fled as Percival touched the cooling flesh. He recoiled.

"He's linked to Quint. That scoundrel will feel Robbie's death, and know there's someone with power in this area," Percival muttered. "Ah well, I'll just have to figure out how to deal with that little problem later."

Slipping on his protective lenses, Percival leaped from the caboose into the sand. An odd pulse in his left eye made him hesitate. He looked upward to see two narrow inky wisps, foreign to this land of bright contrasts, hovering above what was left of the car. They snaked off against the wind.

"You hid them well, Quint," Percival said, trotting away from the ruined caboose. "I thought those vessels of yours would already have fled back to you. Heaven help the rebellion if Prince Feisal ever stays in one place long enough to attract your ravenous attention." Satisfied that nothing else at the end of the train merited his attention, he jogged back toward the dune.

The Arabs were busy pillaging Turkish bodies for gold, jewelry, coins, and intriguing objects. Lawrence stood supervising, elevated on a rim of the tender fallen on its side behind the locomotive.

Percival's trained senses saw a tragedy in the making. "Get down, you fool!" he shouted, leaping into a run.

A shot sounded. Lawrence jerked, spun, folded, and dropped to the sand. Percival's trained eyes picked out motion in a shadow between prone rail cars. Drawing his pistol without aiming, he shot the wounded Turk through the eye.

"Aurens! Aurens is hurt!" Ahmad cried, shocked. The rebels abandoned their work as the stunning news traveled from mouth to ear in moments. Gathering around their English leader and good luck symbol, they stared downward in consternation, too amazed to do more.

"Let me through," Percival demanded in Arabic, pushing tribesmen out of the way to get to Lawrence. Kneeling, he checked for a pulse.

"He's alive. Get water. Hurry." A skin sloshed into his hands. Percival squeezed it, splashing liquid on Lawrence's face.

"Ah, uh," the reluctant rebel leader sputtered, looking

upward. Incomprehension changed to surprise. "How did I get here?"

"You were shot, old boy," Percival replied. "Lie still."

Lawrence struggled against friendly hands to attain a sitting position. "Shot!" The nomads forced him to remain down. He raised his head, looking at his chest from beneath furrowed brows. "There's not enough blood."

"Shot slightly, I should have said, by a Turk when you were standing on that tender. You're bruised where the bullet glanced off, but no worse. It'll hurt like the very devil for some days, especially when you ride camel-back." Percival sat back, grinning, swiping away moisture streaming from his left eye. "You're a lucky fellow."

"Fine, I'm fine," Lawrence assured the worried rebels. "Look." He surged to his feet. Breath hissed between his teeth and he staggered as bruised muscles in his chest protested. Worried tribesmen supported him as his knees buckled.

"Thomas." Percival's sudden voice of command shocked the tribesmen to stillness. Lawrence's eyes jerked to gaze at his friend. "You can do no more good here. Rest for a few hours. I know that's difficult for you, but these men can offload goods and herd horses and mules without your help." He gestured to Lawrence's Juheina assistant. "Ahmad, help Aurens to a place in the shade behind the rock. Have someone make coffee. Give him several cups with plenty of sugar. And dates, if you have any. Make him stay still until everyone's ready to head back to Prince Feisal's camp. When you leave here, travel slowly."

Ahmad nodded, and gave orders to the tribesmen. A few strode toward the saddlebags on their camels for coffee-making utensils, while the others assisted Lawrence to a comfortable resting place.

Percival recovered the mines and the wires, digging

them from the sand along the rail bed. There was nothing wrong with the connections. *Robbie's magic stopped them. Poor Robbie.* He repacked the explosives, then sought his own camel.

"Percival." Lawrence's voice shot through the air like a bullet. "You're not leaving until you've answered my questions."

He walked back to where Lawrence now sat on a rug, sheltered by a tattered canvas anchored to the rock. He knelt. "Very well."

"Your gift deflected that bullet, didn't it?" Lawrence asked in English, touching the talisman beneath his robes.

"Likely. You're going to have to be more careful."

"I know," Lawrence sighed. "There's quite a bit of Turkish gold offered for my head."

"Exactly. And I found two sharpshooters with excellent long-distance rifles in the caboose."

"Sent for me, you think?"

"None other."

"Were they . . . were they dead?"

"Yes."

"Did they carry the marks I described in the letter?"

"Yes."

Lawrence squinted at him in frustration. "Did you learn anything at all from looking at them?"

"Yes."

"Well?"

"I suggest that you keep up your work here, Thomas. If you and I both fail, it will brew a whirlwind that will make this war appear as a tempest in a teacup. Time is of the essence. My Order has pledged to fight a man corrupted by power named Devlin Quint. He's gathering as many ancient artifacts as he can find, such as the Spear of Destiny, the Ark of the Covenant, the Song of Mary Magdalene, and Buddha's Jewel, to further that power. He won the race for the 'Papyrus of Nesser-Khamit,' and used the rite on himself." *He's now a living mummy, sustained by the spirits of those dead Turkish soldiers you discovered,* Percival thought, unwilling to share too much.

His voice gained an edge sharp as a scimitar. "I will not allow him to succeed again. I must save the Tablets of Takhisis."

"The first codified law that the goddess of the Sumerians wore on her breastplate, the ancestor to the Code of Hammurabi?"

Percival nodded.

"So you're mounting a one-man assault." Lawrence's eyes glowed. "If I could win free of my responsibilities to Feisal, I'd join you in a snap."

"Sorry." Percival shook his head. "I couldn't allow it. I'm afraid you'd be a liability when I meet Quint and his minions. Their vanquishing requires . . . uhmmm . . . specialized knowledge."

"Ah." Lawrence's ebullience deflated.

"Take comfort in the fact that Grand Sharif Hussein is already quite safe. And I've set my best protections around the prince: Feisal wears a brother to your stone. It's time I continue my quest."

His voice softened. "My calling is sometimes a lonely business, Thomas. It was good seeing you again. I'd like to stay longer, but I cannot."

"One more question." Lawrence shifted position, and winced. "Why under Heaven do the Rosicrucians send only one man to accomplish such a huge task? I'd think there should be an army."

Percival smiled. "Because my Order is eternally optimistic, Thomas. And we don't normally need an army. Too, it would be an admission that there's more evil in the world than an individual can conquer."

Lawrence had to think about that. Percival stood.

"You brought us luck today, you know." Lawrence said. "If there's ever anything I can do to repay you . . ."

"Keep up the good work with Prince Feisal. There's likely to be more for you to do on behalf of the Arabs after the war. And think positive thoughts in my direction."

"Too bad I can't send anything with you except water." Lawrence called to a nomad, who handed Percival a full skin.

"That's enough. Farewell. Your friendship rides with me, Thomas."

Percival turned, ordered his camel to kneel, looped the waterskin around the peaks of the saddle, and hopped onto the padding. He prodded her to rise. Turning her with the halter and tapping her neck with his stick, he rode through the tribesmen and swirling dust. As his camel settled into her best walking pace, he intoned a spell.

"Be careful, Percival!" Lawrence's shout tickled in his ears.

He smiled and raised a hand in acknowledgment, aware that it was the only part of his body still visible as the swirl of metaphysics and desert consumed him.

Janet Deaver-Pack and Janet Pack are the same writer. She lives in an antique farmhouse-turned-duplex on the eastern border of Williams Bay, Wisconsin with cats Tabirika Onyx, Syranis Moonstone, and Baron Figaro de Shannivere. She has over thirty-five fantasy, science fiction, mystery, and horror stories on the market, also many nonfiction pieces for local newspapers and magazines. Her furry trio helps her edit them. This is Janet's first extensive excursion into fact-based fantasy; she did comprehensive research, urged on by her "silent partner" Bruce Heard. This tale, and the book trilogy based on it soon to come, is partially his fault. Janet has her work cut out for her, but is looking forward to more research, especially if it requires travel to Europe. Her website is www.janetpack.com.

THE GOOD SAMARITAN

Amanda Bloss Maloney

I AM SEVEN years old again. The earth spins beneath me as I lie on the grass and watch dark clouds race through the sky, like an armada struggling to reach a critical battle. It's hot, but some of the humidity has lifted as if a valve has been opened to ease the pressure.

It is twilight, and dinner is late because we lost power in the afternoon. Between the storm and the rolling blackouts, electricity is erratic throughout the city. Some lights still shine at the core to the east, a beacon of civilization. It almost hurts to look at them, like staring at the sun. They cast an eerie glow on the clouds skimming just above the tallest buildings. Everywhere else is gray; the sunset is a distant haze, not really trying to pierce the clouds. It's too much effort and the day is coming to a close, so why not rest?

Mrs. Hudson is with me. Her flashlight is off now, but I think she still sees me by the final burn of the day. She climbed the small hill where the hydro towers march in the field behind our neighborhood, said she'd seen me leave through the gate and didn't want me to get lost. We sit for a while, watching the storm clouds and pointing out interesting shapes that remind us of familiar things. She braids my hair, her warm, wrinkled face smiling down at me.

She lives alone on our street and sometimes has dinner with us. She tells wonderful stories with so much detail they almost seem real to me; of beings who share our world but cannot be seen. There are tales of the Seelie Court—the benevolent Faeries—who sometimes entertain mortals. I listen to her stories about the Faerie folk and dream of visiting the Court. I would wear a dress woven from moss and drink dew from the heads of flowers. Mrs. Hudson says I'd have other human children to play with: there are no Faerie children at Court. She always says a blessing for them at every meal. "Must make the *Daine Side* feel welcome," she says. Mum has explained in hushed tones that Mrs. Hudson is talking about beings that don't exist. *She* thinks they are real and Mum doesn't want to upset her with the truth.

I am alone now. Mrs. Hudson has gone just down the hill to pick some flowers to decorate my braids. We'll have to go home soon as dinner will be ready. I close my eyes so I can't see the hydro tower looming above me and picture myself in a forest instead, full of colorful flowers and sweet-faced faeries dancing in a glade.

The crickets are suddenly silent and the wind has stilled. Something is very wrong. I open my eyes and stare up at four figures. They are pale phantoms of men in long, black coats. Their skin has a luminous quality and their hair is long and silver. The faces are poor imitations of being human. Their features are oddly spaced; the noses too narrow and the eyes and mouths are too large. I recognize these creatures; Mrs. Hudson has an attentive seven-year-old sponge absorbing everything she says. They are the Slaugh, or The Host, unsanctified dead who fly above the earth, steal mortals, and take great pleasure in harming them. They are part of the Unseelie Court, the unblessed faeries, the damned. I don't know how they can be here. They are creatures of myth: Mum said so. Having them real is too much. I blink but they don't go away.

"Lookie-look," a strangled male voice says. It sounds like he's choking. Something wet lands on my cheek; it isn't rain. *Drool* . . .

I try to roll away, but sharp hands grab my arms and lift me from the ground as if I were a doll. Their bones tighten against my flesh. Something tugs on one of my braids.

"Pretty," another voice says. I kick and squirm but to no avail. "Can we have it?"

"It's only a snack."

"Maybe we should take it to the King."

"You have to go home now, young Nattie," Mrs. Hudson says from behind me, her voice strong and clear. I don't know when she arrived, but my tears of relief are making it hard for me to see.

"Ooooo," the choking one says. "Main course."

I am dropped like a broken toy. I cry out, but my voice is too small to be heard.

The Slaugh ignore me and direct their attention to my neighbor, circling her, hissing. Their limbs are restless and their long, long fingers click together like branches in the wind. They are fast, too, and I don't know how Mrs. Hudson is going to survive if they attack her. She seems small and frail by comparison.

Mrs. Hudson is motionless, as if waiting to take a breath. She makes an abrupt gesture with her hand and one of the attackers keens loudly before dropping to the grass. He doesn't move again. I suddenly realize she's fought them before.

She is going to lose this fight.

I have to help. I get to my knees, scared but determined. A strange feeling sweeps over me, as if I'm being covered by a heavy blanket, and I collapse. I cannot move.

Mrs. Hudson is protecting me.

My eyes remain open, and I am only a spectator as the hydro tower fifty feet away groans under the strain of a force that pulls steel free of welds and concrete. It crashes toward the hill, dragging wires, ripping bolts, and crushing one of the creatures that doesn't move fast enough. The remaining two scatter, silver hair and black coats floating behind them, and then return angrier than before.

The wind has come to play. It rushes over my head and howls like the dog next door when it's left alone. I try to scream, but the invisible blanket muffles my voice. I think I'm going to die. I want to close my eyes, but I can't. Helpless, I witness the end as Mrs. Hudson staggers under the assault of their slashing claws and cries out. Her head is severed from her body and she falls from my range of vision. There are sounds I can't identify. I lie there in shock, heart racing, waiting for them to find me.

I wake with a scream crawling up my throat, scrabbling to get free. It takes me a moment to relax my rigid limbs. Tears burn my face as they track, unchecked, down my temples to dampen my ears and run into my hair. The Slaugh fled when family and friends, having witnessed the collapse of the hydro tower, rushed to the field. I was carried away without seeing the remains of Mrs. Hudson.

Fourteen years ago. The creatures of silver and black linger in my memory and haunt me when my headaches are at their worst. I have never encountered them again.

*   *   *

"Irish, Spanish, Chinese."

I glanced up from the newspaper I'd borrowed from Mrs. Wu in 1B. The guy in 2A had his radio blaring again; some kind of modern jazz/funk mix, and the base-line was thumping through the brick building with all the subtlety of a gang war. I didn't know him very well. His mailbox in the lobby read "Jack;" I was tempted to add "ass." It irritated me that we seemed to work within blocks of one another and I often encountered him during the day.

I peered down toward his small balcony, my expression of annoyance clear. He straddled an old wooden chair and fiddled with the radio, his short hair standing on end as fashion dictated. The frat boy look was complete with a taupe cotton T-shirt, coordinating khaki pants, and old cowboy boots. He grinned up at me and demonstrated that he knew how to lift his middle finger; I returned the gesture in kind. At least we were keeping it friendly today.

"What?" I asked, trying to tune out the noise.

My roommate, Ali Jones, squinted her pale blue eyes against the sun, too lazy to find her sunglasses. Her short, blonde hair held the shape it had assumed when she rose that morning. She was curled in the old vinyl office chair like a cat, sipping from a small glass that contained some of the orange juice we'd bought the day before.

"Your family. Irish, Spanish, Chinese."

"Um, yeah," I managed, feeling like I should say something just to fill the space. She was looping back to a conversation I thought we'd finished about five minutes before. I'd just revealed my immediate ancestry after almost three months of watching her not ask me about it.

My glass of juice was already half empty—or half full, depending on your perspective—and we only had enough left for another two servings each. Anything imported always came at a price, especially with the U.S. being so picky about shipping their produce lately. The reserve list at the market was long, and affordable orange juice with pulp was rare.

"Doesn't sound like a family tree," she stated after a lengthy pause.

I shifted in my lawn chair, avoiding the strap that was broken, and took another sip of juice, savoring it. "What does it sound like, then?"

Ali snorted and smiled impishly. "Fusion cuisine."

Well, I guess the "fusion" part works.

When I looked in the mirror, I either saw a young woman still getting her bearings in the world or a puzzled girl who was trying to hide. It depended on the day. Genetics had given me the dark hair and pale coffee complexion that was my mother's Spanish heritage. Mixed in was an Asian influence contributed by my grandmother on my mother's side, especially noticeable in the shape of my eyes and the roundness of my face. I wasn't sure if the Irish part was responsible for my height—five feet, eleven inches—or for my obsession with potatoes. Physically, I didn't hit my stride until I was fifteen. According to a guy I played basketball with at school, that summer I went "from gangly to gourmet." Whatever. I didn't mind discussing my background with Ali. It just wasn't a subject I wanted to share with the whole building.

"Fusion cuisine?" I wrinkled my nose and tried to redirect her. "You've been listening to that guy at the sushi place too much."

"Hey, he listens to me, I return the favor."

I nodded, put my glass on the crate beside me and

skimmed the pages for anything interesting. I handled the paper very carefully in order to prevent unnecessary wear as several people were still waiting to read it. There weren't a lot of presses left that could afford to produce a paper daily and they didn't print as many copies as they used to: took too much power, too many resources. Mrs. Wu fit a paper into her budget every other day and had it reserved at the convenience store two blocks away. As well as the newspaper, she shared her plot of vegetables with most of the building's inhabitants. She had been in that ground floor apartment more than half her life and had taken over a fair portion of the court-yard for her garden. In exchange for fresh produce and time with the paper, I gave her a manicure and pedicure every two weeks and styled her hair when her family came to visit.

Three brothers from a small village on the Baltic Sea near Kaliningrad lived in 1C, and they helped her maintain the garden. Ali told me they also shoveled snow for our building in the winter. I thought of them as "The Brothers Karamazov," though they weren't mired in angst like Dostoevsky's characters. They were always energetic and in high spirits despite having the thankless job of city sanitation engineers. Most of the tenants contributed to some aspect of the building's care. Mrs. Thomas in 3C, generally known as "That Bitch," and the guy in 2A were the exceptions.

I pursed my lips and turned the page. Everyone bartered for something. I could give manicures in my sleep now. When I'd studied the art of nails at the age of twelve so I could freak out my friends, I had no idea how valuable a skill it would be. It was the most popular form of barter I had.

There were a few merchants over the years that had expressed interest in another option, but I was determined never to go down that road.

I turned the page and folded it neatly. The article at the top proclaimed: "Hydro Issues Continue." Like that was news. My parents had lived through the economic changes, and I grew up hearing all about it. For twenty-five years Ontario had dealt with brownouts and black-outs and "no lights between 8:00 AM and sunset." The struggle for electricity along the eastern seaboard had played havoc with essential services until the Special Permit Program had given them the unconditional right to run required equipment by restricting other usage. The average citizen could apply for more time so they could use their computers, lights, and so on into the night, but they had to pay extra, by the hour. The population of the GTA had initially panicked and Internet addicts had to make life choices. They adapted quickly, though, as Canadians were stereotypically known to do, a "fact" right up there with everyone north of the forty-ninth parallel owning a team of sled dogs.

"Well, I gotta go." Ali drained the rest of her juice and stood.

"What's up?"

"Mrs. Petrovich needs her massage."

We grinned at one another. Mrs. Petrovich was very good to us. A massage meant we were having chicken for dinner.

"It isn't as exciting as it might seem, you know."

"What isn't?"

"My family tree. I'm Canadian, right? This kinda thing is normal." I released one side of the paper long enough to make quotation marks with my fingers. "We're a 'Mosaic.' "

Ali shrugged and grabbed her knapsack. "Hey, I'm Canadian, too, but I'm just a boring white chick. Whatta I know? Later."

"Later," I echoed and returned to the paper.

There was a short blurb on the back page regarding

the latest homicide. It was the third bizarre death in the last two months. The police were frustrated and the answers seemed to elude them like the threads of a spiderweb. You'd think it would be front page material, but no, that was reserved for some fluff actor who was in town to cut a ribbon on a new theater.

Thirty-three years into the "clean slate" of the twenty-first century and we still had our priorities screwed up.

I reread one of the sentences. *Third* bizarre murder? Surely they meant the sixth? I sighed. Journalism was going down the tubes. I could keep better track of what was going on than the pros.

The sun was getting hot, and it was still fairly early. Such was the nature of the weather my generation had inherited from our great-grandparents. No doubt there was an article about that on page nine. I sighed again and turned my baseball cap around so the brim shaded my face. My sunglasses had shattered the previous week during a short struggle with a thief on the TTC. The driver and I had the kid pinned on the floor of the bus in fairly short order but not before my knapsack was crushed in the struggle. They'd been nice glasses, too, found them at the Salvation Army soon after I'd arrived in Toronto. I hadn't made the time to replace them. They didn't help my headaches, either way, so what did it matter?

At least the lady was happy to get her purse back. Mission accomplished. I thought of the sunglasses as a small price to pay for being a Good Samaritan compared to other ways that situation could have ended. It turned out the kid had a knife in his boot.

I glanced at my watch: almost nine. The paper was due at Mr. Bernard's in 2C in seven minutes. He was a spry man in his sixties who had a huge laugh and didn't leer at me. Ali thought she knew what he shared with

Mrs. Wu in exchange for his turn with the paper and fresh vegetables. None of my business: they were both widowed, consenting adults, after all.

I didn't want to think about it.

Mrs. Wu was scheduled for a wash and set at ten. Her son and daughter-in-law were visiting around noon and bringing grandchildren and lunch. I eased from the chair.

Carrying the paper and the rest of my juice, I spared one more glance at the radio below me, rather pleased when it lost the signal, giving the guy nothing but static. Maybe there was a God. Listening to his curses, I sought refuge from the sun—burn in five minutes, the paper reported about yesterday's weather—and focused on planning my day.

The TTC at street level was running slowly so lots of people were walking. There was a joke about that, referencing a time when it wasn't really "slow," just not always as frequent as the commuters would have liked. That was before I was born. The fact that remnants of the Toronto Transit Commission still functioned at all said something about the persistence of humanity in the face of adversity. The surface vehicles were usually on schedule—when they worked.

The subway was another matter, only running during the day and sometimes not at all. There were designated hours when pedestrians used the tunnels as sheltered routes around the city: no sun and low pollution. Steps and ramps were placed into position and then folded away when the subway was operational. The tunnels provided refuge from the winter storms, too, and some people lived down there, staking claim in the disused areas. The city evicted them periodically, but that didn't seem to deter them from returning. An exception was Union Station, which was still a very busy spot for commerce but could definitely be considered an official community. The merchants and restaurant owners lived at their stores, raised their children, and held worship there.

A modern Depression with its own evils and ingenuity. What was it some wit at the sushi bar had said? "Economic collapse is a bitch, but sometimes the puppies are cute."

In the summer, it was still hot under the city, as vents were free but air-conditioning was prohibitive. I walked there now, pushing my precious bike and moving east from Bathurst Station with a throng of others. I was wearing my standard uniform of sneakers, jeans, and a T-shirt, so I was fairly comfortable. Above us, Bloor Street was probably equally busy—but down here, I didn't need to use my sunblock.

I emerged at Yonge Street, deciding the crowd going south on the subway was a little too much. Catching the sun in my eyes, I silently cursed the thief who had destroyed my sunglasses and made another mental note to replace them. After liberally applying sunblock from a bottle I kept in my knapsack, and pulling on my nylon jacket so my arms were covered, I mounted my bike, pulled my cap as low over my face as I could, and entered the rhythm of riding south with the traffic. My shift at Levar's started at one; I had half an hour to make it to Front Street.

No matter what, folks needed to eat and "Levar's Kitchen" was there to ensure groceries and home-cooked meals could still reach the customer, even those without gas for their cars. At the current price of fuel, many couldn't afford any drive that didn't involve an emergency or abandoning the city for a better place.

Marie and Extreme Phil had loaded their bikes and were leaving as I arrived.

"Lots today, Natalie," Marie commented, sounding tired already.

"Busy, busy," Extreme Phil added, chipper despite the shiner he sported on his left eye. I raised an eyebrow in question, but he just said his usual response: "You should see the other guy."

I laughed and went to check my route.

By nine that night I had one delivery left.

The Taylors were nice folks and bought from Levar's regularly. They always placed their orders early, so I'd known since six o'clock that I'd see them that evening. We'd chat a bit and they'd offer me a slice of the pizza I was bringing, then I'd be off home to eat my share of Mrs. Petrovich's chicken.

I parked my bike in the lobby of their Bloor Street apartment. It was more a narrow hall than a lobby as the access door was squished to the right on the ground floor next to a used bookstore. *Living above books wouldn't be too bad*, I thought, having been an enthusiastic reader as long as I could remember.

I could feel the heat from the bottom pizza even through the insulated bag. Both of them smelled delicious. One had mushrooms and pepperoni, and I couldn't wait to sit at the kitchen table and catch up on all their news while I savored the gooey cheese. The wooden stairs creaked as I climbed to the dimly-lit landing and looked up at the apartment door, expecting Mrs. Taylor to be waiting for me with a big smile.

My own smile was stillborn as I froze in place, like a butterfly pinned in a display case. A crease of light crept from the lower hall to meet the faint light leaking down the steps to my feet. Shadows flexed around me and I held my breath. Something was very wrong.

The door to the apartment wasn't quite closed. This alone wouldn't have caused any alarm—it helped to have the door open on the really hot nights. It was the silence. There was no sound, no footstep or snatch of

conversation or laughter. For a moment I couldn't move
or think through a sudden rush of panic. A part of me
wanted to run, but the Taylors were good people. I
couldn't abandon them.

My headache was off the scale. It had been irritating
me with bursts of static during the day, but now it surged
to the fore with a vengeance. I took a deep breath and
let it out slowly. Transferring the insulated bag to one
hand, I climbed the final flight of stairs, mentally noting
the ten steps like they were part of the countdown to a
launch. I avoided all the spots I thought might creak and
made it to the top silently.

It turned out I needn't have bothered.

As I reached for the door it swung open suddenly. A
strong hand grabbed my wrist and yanked me inside.
Amazingly, I kept my hold on the pizzas.

"Look what I found," a woman said, her voice like
frost on winter glass. I was pushed toward the sofa and
landed awkwardly.

"It smells like cheese." A man's voice spoke from the
window on the other side of the room. He sounded barely
interested in my arrival, and I had the impression he only
spoke because the aroma of the pizza confused him.

"Maybe it tastes like cheese," a deeper male voice
suggested, sounding hopeful, and I lifted my head to
look at them.

Slaugh. They were all Slaugh, in long black coats. Immediately I looked away. The female had stayed near
the door. The deep voice came from the kitchen table.
The one at the window had seen me arrive and they had
waited, perhaps curious as to why I was here. It was
disorienting to focus on them and my headache . . .

"It doesn't look well," the female stated, sounding
amused. I christened her "Ice," though I doubted the
damned would appreciate the concept of being
christened.

"It can see us." The one at the window moved so quickly that he was suddenly there, in front of me, a shadow blocking some of the light from a table lamp behind him. I tried not to look at any of them and remained silent. "It can hear us." I named him "Leader," though I got the impression each of them considered themselves the one in charge.

"Can we eat it, too?"

Too? The excited tone of his voice and the implication made me nauseous. I chose the name "Hunger" for him. I glanced around the apartment, careful not to make eye contact as it made me dizzy as well.

"If you're looking for your friends," Ice said, sounding bored and waving her hand toward the kitchen. "They're in the refrigeration unit."

"Well, what's left of them, anyway," stated Leader. I fought the sudden urge to vomit. This couldn't be real, couldn't be happening. My phantoms were just figments of my imagination pulled from stories I'd read as a kid, desperate for an explanation for Mrs. Hudson's death. That's what I'd been told, over and over again. They were representations of a distant event that gave me shudders just to recall. Perhaps my headache was causing hallucinations. There was a perfectly logical reason why the Taylors weren't here—and it wasn't because they were in the crisper.

"No," I said through clenched teeth and stood. Leader pushed me back down firmly.

"Hmmm," he mused. "What are we going to do with it?"

"I'm still hungry," Hunger announced and I shivered. *I'm going into some kind of shock*, I decided, the buzzing in my ears increasing with the distant promise of passing out.

"Maybe *this* one knows where she is."

"She isn't here, I tell you." Ice seemed to glide over

to the refrigerator without moving her legs. "The ones who lived here were favored by the Queen. If anyone could provide information about her location, you would think *they* would have known."

"My lead was solid."

"Your lead was useless and is now feeding the earth." I found myself recalling the details of the last murder. A troop of camping Girl Guides had found the body parts of a man while digging their fire pit at the Scarborough Bluffs. Could this be whom they were talking about? Ice opened the door to the freezer and pulled something out. My mind couldn't wrap around the nature of the item. She tossed it to Hunger, saying, "And no more until after the job is done."

He caught it and started to move his shadowed head over it, eating noisily.

From what I could tell, it was a man's hand.

I was working on controlling my breathing and my gag reflex as the other two argued over something that was obviously a sore topic. *The Taylors. Oh, God . . .*

They would be bizarre murders number seven and eight. And by next week, the world would have forgotten a few of the earlier ones. It would be like they'd never existed.

I heard a bone crunch and realized he had bitten into a finger. I watched as Hunger chewed, my stomach roiling, still not entirely accepting what my senses presented. He sucked the marrow out and sighed.

"The hands are the best parts. So many tasty bits."

I slid to my knees then and threw up everything I had eaten in the last day. The Slaugh stepped back, apparently fastidious.

On my hands and knees, I heaved until there was nothing but bile. They were real, they were here, and they were going to eat me, too.

Oh, God . . .

"Is it finished?"

"I'm not sure," Ice replied. She sighed. "It's so hard to tell with these things."

I dragged my right arm over my mouth just so I could get the smell away from my nose. At least throwing up had cleared my head. I had to escape. I was outnumbered and I didn't need my self-defense instructor at the Y to know that if I started a fight, I would be seriously outclassed.

"Why do we even bother dealing with the herd?" Hunger asked, sucking noisily on his long fingers. "Eventually they all end up the same."

"Humans can be useful." Leader poked at the insulated pizza bag. "They usually make good spies. The Queen is so friendly with these things, after all. She trusts them and nurtures them, as if they were children and not food."

"None of us can have children." Ice sounded subdued where she had been hostile moments before.

There are no Faerie children at Court.

"She did give them fire," Hunger said, sliding from the table and stretching until his feet reached the floor. He yawned and I had a quick glimpse of sharp teeth, two layers deep. I almost wished I hadn't seen it, but it was another clue as to what they were.

"Tools were another mistake," Ice said, shaking off her momentary mood and striding to grab a pizza box from the bag, eliciting a growl from Leader. "Look where it led. Now we have to recruit and play their silly game, pitting them against those who are swayed by the Queen." She pulled out a slice and sniffed it. I nearly threw up again, though I didn't think there was anything left in my stomach. "The King should just take some of their pretty explosives and wipe them out."

"What would we eat?" Hunger reached down suddenly and grabbed me by the front of my jacket. I was lifted effortlessly to dangle with my feet off the ground. He stared directly at me and I saw his eyes for the first time. Narrow, hard, like gems that had been cut poorly, no spark, no warmth. I wasn't expecting the tongue that licked the side of my face. He smiled, all teeth. "This one does taste good, but it doesn't taste like cheese." He moved until my back was up against the wall and leaned in closer. His breath smelled like raw meat. "I can see why the Queen started breeding her Court with them, though."

Leader tsked. "You don't bed your food."

The grin before me grew increasingly terrifying. "This one might be entertaining, though." He dragged the fingers of his free hand through my long hair. "It's pretty, for a human." The face came so close that his nose pressed against mine. His voice was barely a whisper as he said, "I bet it screams."

Shit.

A part of my brain was deciphering the hints about the involvement of the Faerie Realm with human history. How long had this been going on? Another part contemplated the wisdom of kicking my captor as hard as I could in an attempt to get away. Did I have any hope of succeeding? I opted for trying to make sense of it all.

The herd. *Food.* Was humanity just one, huge free-range restaurant for the Faerie folk? Was the Seelie Court really any better than the Unseelie Court? Interfering with the course of human history was never considered acceptable in those old science fiction videos my dad collected. Was my world controlled by a race of beings that just wanted to ensure they had enough fresh meat on hand?

If so, how ironic I should work for a grocer.

Hunger grabbed my left thigh and squeezed.

"We don't play with our food either," Leader stated firmly.

Those cold eyes shifted to regard the other Slaugh. "Maybe *you* don't, but I think it might be fun."

It was becoming harder to focus or think. My head was a pounding rhythm section. Their voices continued, but I couldn't hear what they were saying, never mind work on a plan for escape. I tried closing my eyes.

The body in front of me pulled back slightly. My eyes snapped open to see Hunger raise one long finger and look at the sharp claw at the end of it, as if he was weighing an option he hadn't previously considered. He chuckled and plunged it into my left shoulder with one swift stroke. The pain was excruciating. I screamed. My headache amplified tenfold and my scream became a shriek as the claw was twisted in my flesh.

Seconds later, the claw was abruptly removed and I found myself on the floor. I stopped screaming and took a deep breath, confused by the keening sound that continued around me. I pushed myself up on my elbows and was stunned to see all three creatures curled on the floor, clutching their heads and writhing in agony. I had no idea what had happened and didn't care. Too slowly for my liking, I crawled over to the sofa, used it as a brace to stand and straightened. Though my left shoulder throbbed with pain and blood stained my hand when I touched the hole in my jacket, I stumbled to the door and fled.

I had no idea where I was going. All I knew was I had to put as much distance between them and me as possible. I made it down the stairs and was backing my bike out the door before I realized I should see a doctor or call the police or something. Did I go directly to the clinic near Spadina and risk the lives of so many people? Would the Slaugh choose not to attack if I was in a crowd?

Their collapse was probably a temporary reprieve and soon they'd start hunting me. After all, I'd seen them and knew they'd killed the Taylors, so I was likely to be their next target. They would also probably be enraged about my escape and want their revenge.

Heading west on Bloor Street, I wondered how far I'd get before they caught up with me. There were quite a few people out; it was a beautiful summer night, and curfew for the lights was still at least an hour away. I passed several busy patios and the Royal Ontario Bata Museum was having some kind of function that had spilled onto the street. Although I must have looked white as a sheet, with blood on my jacket, and I wasn't pedaling steadily, no one gave me a second glance. It was probably just as well. Somehow, I doubted the Slaugh would hesitate to kill anyone who tried to help me, so any thought of going to the police or the staff at the clinic was dismissed.

Mrs. Hudson had died protecting me. It was my fault. I didn't want to be the cause of any more deaths. I had to hide and find another solution.

At least I could think now that my headache was gone.

I crossed Spadina, diligently ignoring the officers on bike patrol. Too late, I realized I was riding on automatic and heading home. That wouldn't work at all. I turned north at Brunswick, two blocks away from my apartment building, and headed for the housing development off Lowther Avenue. The project had been abandoned about five years before when the money ran out, or so the papers said. Passing the first few hiding places that seemed too obvious, I finally chose a partially-built row of town houses with a narrow gap in the chain-link fence.

My bike wouldn't fit. *Luck of the Irish, my ass*, I thought sourly. I sighed and quickly decided to leave it behind an old garage across the road. It was away from the street lamp and wouldn't be obvious. If I survived, it would probably still be there. Resigned to hiding and hoping, I carefully slipped through the fence.

There was debris I had to avoid, which made for slow going in the pale light provided by one dim streetlamp. It felt like forever before I reached the end house. I was reluctant to get trapped inside, so settled for lying down under the porch and making myself as small and still as possible. It was hard to decide whether or not I should scour the site for a piece of rebar and face my fate.

"Natalie?"

I actually yelped. It would have been embarrassing any other time but I was too scared to care right then.

"Over here," came the voice again, a loud whisper from the gap outside the porch. I tried to see who it was but stared at the crouched shadow without recognition. My brain scrambled to figure out how anyone I knew would have been able to find me in an old construction site on a Saturday night—or any night, for that matter. The voice added, "It's me."

I couldn't help it. I snorted. "That's useful."

He chuckled. "You're holding up pretty well, considering."

I gaped and was glad he couldn't see me. I knew *that* voice—

"Jack?"

"Yep."

"The jackass from 2A?"

He laughed. "Not the first time I've heard that one."

"I'll try to think of something more original later," I snapped. "What are you doing here?"

"I could ask you the same thing."

"Go away."

"What?"

"I don't have time to explain. It isn't safe here. And they'll see you and know where I am. Go away!"

"That's very thoughtful of you," he said calmly, "wanting to protect me from harm. I'm sorry, though. They already know where you are."

I felt a cold, sharp finger of despair drag down my spine as he pulled a curved blade from somewhere. It glinted in what little light the streetlamp behind him provided. I was trapped under the porch and had no way to defend myself.

He's with them? Oh, God . . .

"You couldn't have gone far," he continued. "Not injured. It was easy for *me* to find you, so *they'll* be here soon."

I swallowed, hard. "Why are you doing this? Why me?"

There was a pause before he replied, "Because I made a pledge."

The chain-link fence started to rattle, too much to hope for rescue. My headache began a slow pulse across the back of my skull. Would that damn thing never leave me alone?

"That didn't take long." Jack stood. All I could see were his cowboy boots. "Time's up, Natalie." I braced myself.

"Stay here. Get away if you can." The boots started walking toward the Slaugh.

What the— I wriggled toward the gap and rose to a crouch as the second creature cleared the fence.

"I thought I told you to stay put," Jack hissed, not looking at me as I moved to stand beside him.

"What do you think you're doing?"

He grinned. "Saving your ass."

"Are you crazy? They're Slaugh, evil." Jack turned to

look at me then. "Friends of mine are dead, killed by these things." As I spoke, the third one landed on the gravel surface and joined the others. They walked toward us leisurely, silver hair shining like cloaks, long fingers clacking together. "I interrupted them looking for someone."

Jack's smile faded. "They've been looking for you."

I stared at him. "What?"

"*You.* They're looking for you, Natalie."

"Me?"

We were out of time. One of the Slaugh—Hunger—chose this moment to launch himself toward us with a horrific cry.

I lifted my arms in desperation as if I could stop his progress, wishing I had a blade like Jack's. I yelled something that wasn't a word so much as an expression of my anger.

The result was extraordinary. Hunger slammed into solid air and landed poorly on some broken concrete. I blinked and found four pairs of eyes watching me. *Did I do that?* My mind tried to recall exactly what I'd done in hopes I'd be able to duplicate it.

Jack's grin resurfaced. "This is gonna be fun."

Ice and Leader moved as one. I quickly raised my hands and pointed at them. Nothing happened. Jack was forced to engage Ice in a fight. She didn't have any weapon but her claws and strength and that would be more than a match for a human with a long dagger. Distracted, I didn't notice Leader until he'd grabbed my arm and slammed me against the unfinished house.

Shit.

"So," he said, faceted eyes glinting in the faint light, his anger barely controlled. "You have some Seelie in you. That will make another abomination dead this night."

I was having too much trouble thinking with a rabid badger rampaging in my skull to comprehend what he was saying. All I knew was his long, multijointed thumb was pressing into my shoulder wound, and I was going to pass out from the pain. I panicked.

"Get away!" With my remaining strength I lifted my arms as my instructor had taught me, trying to break his hold.

His expression changed to one of surprise as an invisible force yanked him backward to slam into the fence.

I regarded my hands as if someone had placed guns in them. How could this be happening? There wasn't time to wonder, though. Hunger was standing and Leader wasn't far behind him. I glanced at Jack.

And noticed for the first time that he'd been joined by three familiar faces: The Brothers Karamazov from 1C, armed with bladed weapons I didn't recognize. Ice was outnumbered now, though she had speed and agility that they didn't possess. A young man brandishing nunchucks leaped into the fray, his attentions on Leader: Extreme Phil, my coworker at Levar's.

What the hell was going on?

Jack raised his arm and muttered something, and Ice fell as if a bus had struck her. The brothers closed in. It happened so quickly that I witnessed the final seconds of her life. At the same time, Leader and Extreme Phil circled one another. The Slaugh was apparently wary of the nunchucks and he weaved when my coworker pressed him. It was like watching a bizarre dance. The whole evening was taking on a dreamlike quality where I was the dreamer.

Another figure emerged from the shadows and leaped at Hunger with a hearty battle cry and sufficient force to knock him to the ground. There was a long sword, and I thought I recognized the robe and fuzzy slippers.

Mrs. Wu? What the—?

Hunger recovered and swatted the elderly lady aside. I was startled into action. He'd hurt Mrs. Wu, a woman who tried to make her tiny piece of the city a better place. I was determined that nothing would happen to her. Undaunted by his claws this time, I charged, fists ready, screaming as loud and as long as I could manage.

The creature shuddered and wailed. He dropped to his knees, hugging himself as if to contain something, and then promptly exploded. I was too close. I stopped abruptly and had the sense to turn and duck so the back of my jacket took the brunt of whatever hit me. Too stunned to wonder if I could throw up again, I stood facing the partially insulated town house, not wanting to look. The jacket wasn't getting washed; burning was in order.

"Gross," Extreme Phil stated eloquently from somewhere behind me.

Leader stepped into my line of sight.

"*You*," he said softly. It sounded like such a cliché that I could feel my lips twitch into a smile at the absurdity of it all. "All along, it was *you*."

I had no idea what he was talking about. "Whatever," I muttered.

With a scream, he lunged. I couldn't move. I was seven years old again and the living nightmare loomed before me. Then Jack was there and the curved blade took Leader's head from his shoulders. The body slumped and landed at my feet. I stumbled away from the corpse. The back of my knees hit a stack of pavers and I sat abruptly.

I hated crying. It wasn't a bad thing, just I felt like a little girl when I did. I had taught myself not to cry in front of strangers at a very early age.

Don't cry like a girl. Don't throw like a girl.

I put my hands over my face and cried.

I became aware of someone beside me and didn't bother trying to wipe my eyes before looking at them. The night had been long and hard and terrifying—and I was capable of killing with astonishing effect. *Does this mean . . . I'm not human?* The thought left me dreading an answer. I sniffed. *Well, I am what I am, and if someone doesn't like it, that's too damn bad.*

Mrs. Wu regarded me cautiously. "Nat? You okay?"

She waited calmly in her pink bathrobe, a bruise already forming on the left side of her face. I was surprised to see one of her grandchildren standing beside her. Neither of them seemed to be afraid of me. Relieved, I grabbed Mrs. Wu, hugged her tightly, and cried even harder. She wrapped an arm around me and stroked my hair. It was almost as if my grandmother was there.

Behind her, Jack and the brothers were placing the corpses in a pile. I finally pulled away and wiped my eyes with the edge of my T-shirt. When I stood, my knees felt like jelly—but I was alive. That was something to celebrate. I clasped Mrs. Wu's hand, and together we joined the others. I started with Jack as he seemed to be the one in charge.

"First off, I want to thank you for coming to my rescue."

He blinked. "Anytime."

"Now, who are you?"

"I'm your guardian angel," he stated somberly.

Extreme Phil made a choking sound that resembled poorly contained laughter.

I rolled my eyes. "Oh, come on."

"No, really." He stepped closer to me. He was taller than I was but only by a few inches. "Well, I'm your guardian." A smile twisted the corners of his mouth. "I'm not an angel, though."

"I knew that already." I nodded to the brothers and Extreme Phil, who were gathering branches and lumber and covering the bodies, and glanced at Mrs. Wu before returning my gaze to Jack. "And they are?"

"Part of the guard," he said, as if it were obvious.

"The guard," I repeated.

"Um, yeah." He exchanged a look with Mrs. Wu and took a deep breath, as if he wanted to get this part over with as quickly as possible. "The Queen figured they might come looking for you eventually, what with you being old enough now to start exhibiting your powers, so she arranged a guard detail to join you when you moved to Toronto—"

I held up my free hand. "Whoa, whoa, whoa. Queen *who*? Powers *what*? And what do I need a guard for?"

He sighed and looked like he was developing a headache. Maybe I'd given him mine, as it seemed to have vanished. "You don't know who you are, do you?"

"Of course I do." Maybe he thought I'd hit my head on something. "I'm Natalie O'Neill."

"*You* are one of the heirs to the Seelie Court."

I blinked. "Excuse me?"

"I said—"

"I heard what you said, but you don't expect me to believe I'm some sort of supernatural creature!" I looked pointedly at the bodies, then decided it was better not to keep my focus there. I glared at Jack, demanding an explanation. It was the first time I noticed his eyes were blue.

He raised his hands in a sign of placation. "No one is saying you're like them. Those weren't Seelie."

"I know that! One of them said I had Seelie in me, and they said Seelie eat humans!" I turned to Mrs. Wu for confirmation. "Do they?"

"Maybe," she conceded, "but that was long, long time

ago. Not eat anymore." And she patted my arm reassuringly. "Friends."

I frowned. "But the Seelie are at war with the King, right? So . . . those three were from the Unseelie Court?"

At the request of Extreme Phil, Jack tossed him a lighter. "Uh, basically, yes."

I had to sit down, but there was nowhere to sit. "This is too weird."

Jack nodded. "Yeah."

I looked at him. "And you—"

"Are an 'abomination,' " he finished. He smiled, almost shyly. "I have Seelie blood, too."

"Pointy ears are myth," Mrs. Wu said when she caught me scrutinizing Jack very closely. Her grandson nodded wisely.

The flames took me by surprise. We turned and watched as the fire blazed madly, consuming the bodies of my nightmare creatures. I quickly checked my pockets and removed their contents. Slipping off my ruined jacket, I stepped forward and tossed it onto the pyre. The flames melted the nylon fabric within seconds.

I sighed. "This is real?"

"Yeah," Jack said.

"Straight up?"

He nodded. "Yep."

"And someone was going to tell me about all this *when*, exactly?"

"Oh, soon," he said evasively. "The less you knew, the less chance you had of accidentally exposing yourself." I noted Mrs. Wu sending him a stern look that suggested they had disagreed on that point. I'd have to ask her about that during her next manicure.

"Do my parents have any clue?"

"Your father knows all about it," Mrs. Wu admitted.
I gaped. "Dad knows *all* about it?"

"Who found you this apartment?" Jack pointed out.

"I'm gonna kill him," I muttered.

"Not his fault," Mrs. Wu stated firmly. "The Queen wouldn't let him tell."

"What about Mum?"

Mrs. Wu shook her head. "She is safer not to know. The Queen—"

"Yeah. The Queen. Right." God, I was tired. "Well, I don't know about anyone else, but I could use a stiff—" I caught myself, remembering there was a minor present. "A glass of orange juice. How about you?"

Mrs. Wu smiled. "Good idea," she said and her grandson started to hop and tug on her robe, speaking in Mandarin about wanting a drink *now*. It was the most normal activity I'd seen in hours.

"You should have that shoulder looked at," Jack suggested quietly. He looked genuinely concerned. I hadn't forgotten about my injury as much as it had been pushed to the back of the line by revelations.

"Yeah, I guess so." I sighed. My "guard" watched and waited. The bodies of our attackers crackled in the fire behind them. I was glad to be upwind. "You have a lot of explaining to do," I told all of them sternly, ticking off the points with my fingers as I made them. "Heir to a Court I only know from faerie tales, special powers, all this cloak and dagger stuff."

"Don't worry," Jack said, smiling reassuringly. I wasn't used to him being so nice. "We have plenty of time to get into that—thanks to you."

Maybe I should cut him some slack. He did just save my life, after all. I smiled. "No, thanks to *you*." I paused. "At least my headache's gone."

"No, it hasn't," Jack assured me, pointing to his chest.

"*I'm* gonna be your headache now. Learning to control your abilities starts on Monday, Ms. O'Neill."

"Really?" I said sweetly. "I'll remember that the next time you wanna play your music, Jack . . . ?"

"Hudson." His grin broadened at my startled look, and he nodded. "You know, Nattie, my grandmother *really* liked you."

Amanda Bloss Maloney has been writing stories for as long as she can remember, and as a chronic pack rat she still has every single one of them. She has an Honors B.A. in Drama and English Literature which, after moving to Mississauga in November of 2003, she finally put on the wall in October of 2005. She lives with her beloved husband Peter, her wonderful mother Audrey, and an endearing geriatric greyhound, Harry. "The Good Samaritan" is her first professionally published work. She dedicates this story to her father, W. John Bloss, and hopes that somewhere he knows she finally made it.

SEEKING THE MASTER

Esther M. Friesner

THE HOOD THAT the brothers jammed over my head stank of sweat and something more, a scent at once familiar and alien, sweet, yet with a faint hint of bitterness. I trembled in their iron grip, marveling that men whom I and any other sighted person would have taken for weaklings could possess such unanticipated strength. As they hustled me along, I was further astonished by the speed at which they moved. Their plump bodies and the languid, slothful way in which they conducted themselves in public had fooled me into believing that they were as sluggish as they were weak.

Wrong on both counts, I thought sourly. *I underestimated them, believed just what they wanted me to believe. Do they realize that? Will my inexcusable naïveté count against me when I stand before . . . him? Oh, God, please no! I've given so much, dared so much for this chance! Please don't let them suspect that my intelligence isn't worthy, that I'm not worthy to become one of them!*

I struggled for air inside the hood. My own breath

was hot, bathing my face in a stifling, muggy mist. I felt my heart beat faster and faster as eagerness turned to fear, fear to the blindest panic.

God, what if they do *know how badly I've misjudged them?*

Heartsick, I recalled the way in which they'd first approached me with the invitation I had yearned to receive for so very long.

"We've been empowered to tell you that *he* wants to see you," they'd said. "He believes that you show . . . promise."

It was only by the mightiest effort on my part that I did not fall to my knees at once and kiss their feet in slavish gratitude. There was no need for them to say more than that, nor would they have done so. We all knew what, if not whom they meant by *he*, even if I remained ignorant of any further means of identifying him more specifically. *He* was the Master, and he held my future in the palm of his hand.

Ah, the joy of that blessed summons! It was an invitation made all the more affecting by the fact that up until that moment, I still half-believed that it would never come because there *was* no secret league, no hidden path, that my suspicions as to its existence were nothing more than the product of a fevered brain driven to the brink of insanity by bitter frustration.

And now, had I thrown away the prize so arduously won by a simple, thoughtless act of misapprehension?

Like bats awakening from their daylight sleep, my doubts flew forth in ones and twos, then in vast swarms to darken my soul: *This chance—this one golden chance they've offered me to become one of them—what if it's only a cruel, sick joke? And who knows how a joke like this will end, given who—what—these people are? I know how their minds work, even if I underrated their bodies.*

Is there anything too devious, too twisted for them to imagine? What a short, cold-blooded step it is, from imagining a horror to making it so!

The thought froze my blood and turned my bones to jelly. I stumbled badly, and would have fallen if not for my guides, my captors.

"Careful there, little lady." Even though I knew both of my escorts, the heavy hood muffled sound just enough for me to be unable to determine which of the two members of the elite brethren spoke. "What were you thinking, wearing shoes like *that* for something like this?"

"Eh, she just wants to make a good first impression." The second man snickered. He patted me on the back. "I think it's *sweet*, you dressing up like that, honey: high heels, tight sweater, and is that a slit in your skirt? Oooh, slutty. Me like."

"Like all you want, but keep your distance," the first one commanded. "She's here for *him*, remember. You know the rules."

The other turned sulky and resentful. "It's always all about *him*, isn't it? And you know damn well that as far as he's concerned, all this is going to be wasted. He doesn't care what they look like as long as they're willing to give him what he wants."

"Act your age, you oaf. God knows you ought to be grateful that looks don't matter to him, or you'd still be on the outside looking in, slaving away, believing all the lies."

The lies . . .

I took a deep, shuddering breath. Not so long ago, that had been me, all my dreams and aspirations so deeply entrenched in the layers upon layers of wide-spread, purposely generated falsehoods that these men and others of their arcane brotherhood—men and women both—consistently maintained to keep the unworthy at bay. And I had believed those lies, every last, miserable one of them. Had I truly been that innocent?

Yes. Yes, I had.

"You know what we *should've* done?" the second man said. "We should've given her . . . *the routine*. Sure, she was sharp enough to snag the Master's attention, but she never would've seen through . . . *the routine*. Trust me, it would've been the best deal all 'round. At least with *the routine*, she'd be able to keep on hoping forever. Honestly, is that so bad? Once she meets the Master, it's win or lose, in or out, no second chances."

"Damn it, man, you spend so much time toying with the outsiders that you think I'm as green as they are! I know why you'd want to give her *the routine*: Because as long as she keeps hoping, even when she's staring at the world's biggest dead end, she'll be thinking about *all* the possibilities for getting past it." There was a freight of dreadful meaning in the way he said *all*.

The second man chuckled lasciviously. "Come on, like *you* never let one of the pretty ones believe that sleeping with you would open the sacred doors? Oh, but I forgot: You're the Master's *good* little messenger. You're *soooo* pure, you'd never even dream of using your position for personal advancement or gain."

"No, I would not." The reply was stiff and severe. "And not because I'm some paragon of virtue. *He* would hear of it. Oh, he might allow me one slip, two, a dozen, a score— Who can tell where his gracious charity toward a fallible follower ends? But it *would* end; believe it. And the consequences . . ."

A dismissive sound—a sudden expulsion of breath between lips tightly pressed together—answered the first man's cautionary words. "You worry too much. He may be the Master, but if you want me to believe he's got uncanny knowledge and powers, you can go pound sand down a rat hole; it'll accomplish more. Brother, you'd better learn to save *that* crap for the rookies." He gave my arm a tender, repulsive squeeze and added: "Isn't that right, sweetheart?"

I uttered an unthinking cry of revulsion and jerked away from him so sharply that I staggered off-balance. I would have fallen if the first man hadn't grabbed me and set me more steadily on my feet.

"Easy, easy," he murmured. "Don't worry, no one's going to take advantage of you. You're under the Master's protection. Now be a little more careful about how you walk. You're too valuable to go breaking your neck on us."

"Not yet, anyway," the other said, and he followed up this sally with a gurgling laugh that made the short hairs on my arms rise up. The dread was too much to bear. Chills shook my limbs; my knees buckled and I dropped to the ground. My collapse took the first man by surprise; he lost his sustaining hold on my arms and let me fall.

I expected to feel the icy, unforgiving impact of bare stone slabs under my palms and knees. Instead, they encountered a soft, silky carpet so finely woven that my lurching footsteps hadn't even dragged against the delicate pile. I gasped, shocked to find a thing of such luxury here, in the bowels of the ancient office building where I had come so blithely, so willingly.

That was my third mistake: there wasn't enough air inside the hood to let me draw so deep a breath. My senses reeled, then fled. As I plunged into oblivion, I thought I heard one of my guards exclaim a mild obscenity, but I would never know for sure.

Visions swam up out of the blackness engulfing me, taunting memories. Once again I was the simple, thoughtless girl whose heart admired *them*, the golden souls, the favored ones. Others claimed that *they* were like the rest of us, but I knew otherwise.

How else to account for the adulation of their swarms of devoted adherents? For the most part, these people had neither the physical attractions, the athletic prowess, nor the ostentatious displays of wealth that usually evoked such fervent idolization.

How else to explain their intellectual domination of lesser beings, their astonishing ability to destroy their luckless adversaries with a few well-chosen words of power? Their triumphs were legendary, and many a devoted hanger-on took the deepest pleasure in recounting, decades later, having been present to witness such unequal combats.

And then there were the whispers, the hints, the covert rumors of how the elite among these people—the Master's own, the select of the select, chosen of the chosen—not only enjoyed the benefits of earthly renown, but would in due time know the ultimate gift: Immortality.

The first time I heard such a rumor, I laughed it off. The second time, I refused to believe it, rejecting it as a sacrilegious joke in the poorest of taste. The third, I began to doubt my own adamant adherence to what I thought were the dictates of simple common sense. At last I opened my eyes and beheld evidence as irrefutable as it was unthinkable: Death had no meaning for these people. Indeed, the so-called "dead" walked among us. I had felt their presence and been affected by their influence as much and more than that of our so-called *real* leaders, the puppets who postured and chattered in the chambers of Congress or from the tawdry stage of the Oval Office.

I wanted that power. I hungered for it. I wanted that chance to win eternal life, eternal influence. I was willing to do whatever it took to achieve it.

Now see where it had brought me.

A cool breeze caressed my cheek. My eyelids fluttered, then opened to a muted amber glow. I felt a cushion of scented softness beneath me and gazed up at a ceiling painted by the hand of genius. The scene above my head was an idyll straight out of Classical mythology, a verdant mountainside where satyrs, fauns, gods, and goddesses danced. But in one corner of the painting, just out of sight of the heedlessly frolicking throng, I saw a lone figure of gaunt, intent aspect. Cloaked and crouching, he watched the merrymakers, a malicious, knowing smile playing over his thin lips.

I knew that look. I had seen that look before, on the faces of the men who had brought me here and on the faces of their colleagues as well: It was pity. The gods frolicked, but their joy was a fragile, hollow thing, their powers a joke. The *true* power lay elsewhere and they, poor fools, would never know.

"No!" I cried, tossing my head to one side and closing my eyes tightly. The ghost of mocking laughter filled my ears, together with those sly, hurtful words of so-called "encouragement" that had been my bane from the first day I determined to make myself one of the chosen:

Just keep at it; it's only a matter of time.

You're really doing everything right. I'm sure you'll succeed any day now.

You can't waste your time obsessing over things that aren't in your power anymore. Keep busy. You'll hear something when there's something for you to hear.

Hey, don't feel bad: We all had to pay our dues. It comes with the territory.

Look, we both know you're better than a whole lot

of the people who've succeeded already. You'll get your turn before you know it.

No, really, just keep working. It'll happen for you. Trust me.

"My dear, are you all right?" A gentle hand touched my cheek and a deep, compelling voice thrilled in my ears. I opened my eyes once more and gazed up into the sharply-drawn, handsome face of a silver-haired gentleman. His eyes, the color of a winter's dusk, regarded me with genuine concern and compassion.

"Y—yes," I faltered, laying one hand to my damp brow. "I—I think so." I tried to sit up, but the room spun around me. Candles burned everywhere, and their fat, crimson bodies traced smears of blood and light across my dazzled vision. It was too much for me; I sank back into the welcoming contours of the plush chaise longue upon which I had awakened. The tawny cushion offered up the scent of lavender and crushed roses.

"I—I'm sorry, sir," I said, my lips dry. I knew to whom I spoke. Could it be any other? "O great Master, if my weakness has offended you, I beg of you, forgive me!"

The Master sat back and smiled, his long, graceful hands folded in his lap. He was clothed from neck to ankles in a robe of midnight blue, the collar secured by a silver pin shaped like a brace of lions *couchant*, with glinting sapphire eyes. Nobility and benevolence clung to him, along with a bittersweet aroma that was oddly evocative. Where had I smelled that before? Every cell in my brain clamored that it had been a recent experience, one that would be stunningly self-evident if only I could call it forth from the fogs of treacherous memory.

Then it hit me: the hood. The hood had contained exactly such a smell, and that smell was—

"Chocolate?" The Master picked up a small, golden

box from the little table at his elbow and offered it to me. "I sometimes find it to be a better restorative than liquor."

Chocolate, the famed elixir of the brethren, the eternal bean whose transfiguring power was second to none, not even its baselessly proud cousin, coffee! Wordlessly, I plucked out the first bonbon that my fingers touched, without my usual dithering over such choices. I was rewarded for my maturity with a mouthful of smooth, delectable rum truffle. It could have been the hated and shunned orange cream just as easily. In my overwrought state, I decided that I had just received a divine sign, an auspicious omen. I sat up again, more slowly this time, and rejoiced to find that my balance was restored, my vision steady. O blessed confectionary panacea!

The Master seemed to understand that I was myself again. All at once his air of sympathy transformed into a brisk, professional attitude.

"Welcome, child," he said. "I trust you comprehend the full significance of your presence here?"

I slipped from the chaise longue and knelt at his feet, my head bowed before him with the utmost deference. "I have been brought here, O Master, for you to determine whether or not I am worthy of the sublime favor, the grand blessing of membership among the chosen brethren."

I heard him utter a short, dry laugh. I didn't dare look up to see whether he was regarding me with contempt for such a toadyish response. Inwardly, I berated and abused myself for having expressed myself so feebly. How could I now hope to be admitted to the ranks of the favored few—those beings of legendary eloquence and verbal skill—after having given such a display of my own sorry way with words? I fought valiantly to hold back hot tears of disappointment.

To my surprise, the next speech from the Master's mouth was not a summary dismissal, laced lightly with scorn, but rather: "Rise, child. You do me too much honor."

I saw his hand before my face, palm upward, offering to help me to my feet. I took it and rose. He, too, stood, and his warm grip on my fingers did not slacken. When I dared to meet his eyes, I saw nothing there but kindness.

"You are only partly right," he told me. "I do not command my servants to bring me just anyone. The fires of ambition burn high and hot in you, but that is not enough. You yearn for the privileges and boons reserved for those of our clandestine brotherhood, but that is not enough."

"You have a killer rack, but that is not enough." The impious words that shattered the holy moment were spoken in a whisper so low that in ordinary circumstances they would have passed unheard, unheeded. Alas, the acoustics of this strange chamber were such that the blasphemous sally was greatly amplified. It echoed from the high, painted ceiling, snaked swiftly through the forest of gold-capitaled, green jasper pillars supporting that lofty vault, and fell like the knell of doom at the Master's feet.

His blazing eyes flashed at once to the unlucky man who had let the desire to be accounted witty supersede the discernment to be accounted wise. I knew him: He was that one of my escorts here who had spoken of manipulating me with *the routine*, and who had mocked me and my dreams. A gloating demon sparked to unnatural life in my belly. I would enjoy watching this one receive his comeuppance at the Master's hand.

I did not have long to wait. The Master held my hand even more tightly, then without warning turned away so that both of our backs were toward the hasty-tongued fool.

"Child, pay close attention," he said. "This is your test: succeed, and you may call yourself one of us from this day forward. Fail, and you deserve to share that thickwit's ostracism." His fingers traced strange shapes within my palm, after which he hooked the first two fingers of his right hand onto the webbing between my thumb and forefinger. He completed his odd succession of gestures by enclosing all my fingers in his grasp and squeezing them quickly once, twice, and after a pause of no more than two seconds, a third and final time.

"There," he said, smiling. "Now teach *him*." He indicated my other escort, the man whose devotion to the Master had caused his companion so much ill-considered mirth.

I obeyed. It was such a bizarre thing, to see the look of perplexity and astonishment in that man's eyes as my hand mimicked the same motions that the Master had just taught me. I worked as swiftly as I could, and instinctively took the greatest care to conceal what I was doing from the wretch who had so foolishly provoked the Master's wrath.

I dropped the brother's hand: I was done. He looked immediately to the Master who nodded benignly and said, "Yes, that's right: A new one. It's just as well; this last one was getting a bit *too* old, and I was afraid that the uninitiated would discover it. That would not do. Now come to me, my son. Let me see whether this child has discharged her trust faithfully."

My partner crossed the floor, under the stricken eyes of his former comrade, took the Master's hand, and stealthily repeated the same series of manipulations I had just performed upon him. I held my breath and pressed a fist to my mouth, praying fervently that I had remembered every nuance of those secret hand signs and reproduced them faithfully.

The Master looked at me. He was smiling. "Welcome, child," he said for the second time, and I understood that this was no ordinary salutation, but my official reception into the ranks of the elect. I wanted to sing for joy, to seize the Master's hands and bathe them with tears of thanksgiving, but before I could make any such untoward show, I felt my every natural impulse unexpectedly dampen and subside. A Jovian calm infused every fiber of my being. Dignity set her seal upon my brow. I stood tall and inclined my head only slightly to the Master.

"Thank you, sir," I said. "I promise that in thanks for the great distinction you've given me today, I will dedicate my work and my life to bringing honor to our ranks."

"Ah, promise . . ." the Master mused, steepling his fingertips. "That, my child, was why I had you brought here in the first place. But surely you must know that there are many, many souls out there with equal or greater promise than you own. It is no easy task, determining which shall rise and which shall fall."

He sighed wearily, then his expression hardened into an icy, terrifying mask of Judgment that he brought to bear upon the gabbling dunce whose rash words became a snare for his own feet.

"You!" the Master's voice rolled like thunder through the hidden chamber. The man collapsed in a heap, face to the ground, groveling and babbling for mercy. "Save your breath. You forgot the one rule by which all of us live or die: For every one of us within the charmed order, there are a thousand clamoring to take our places. You, fool, have now been thus displaced. The word will go forth, along with the newly established secret sign

by which our brethren live and thrive: You are outcast!
Outcast! Begone, and may your error serve as a cautionary lesson to us all."

The pitiful object of the Master's wrath slowly raised
his face from the carpet. There was a feeble glimmer of
defiance in his eyes. "You can't scare me," he declared.
"And you can't displace me. Do you even know how
powerful I am, how many follow me, hanging on my
every word?" He clambered to his feet and shook a fist
in the Master's face. "All this mumbo jumbo, all the
secret handshakes, the so-called exclusionist conspirac-
ies, they're nothing but a load of hooey! It's *quality* that
counts in this world, quality and skill that get rewarded.
I don't need you or your stupid secret society! I can *still*
make it on my own! You'll see!"

He ranted on until his former comrade glided up behind him and clapped a chloroform-soaked rag to his
face. Then he crumpled.

"Well done," said the Master. He cast a long, regretful
look over the splendors of his den. "The new secret
handshake is the least of the changes that churl has
forced upon me. I shall need a new lair—I mean, a new
headquarters—as well. Too bad: I liked it here," he said
with a shrug.

My new brother and I bowed low, and in perfect ac-
cord intoned: "As you will, O Master; as you will."

I did not encounter the Master again for almost five
years after my initiation into the hidden brotherhood. I
would have regretted this more if I'd had the leisure to
do so. Instead, almost from the day of my admittance,
my life was transformed from a series of petty, exasper-
ating disappointments, to a progression of triumphs,
each greater than the last. As marvelous as my newfound success was, it did keep me busy. (It is a grand

thing to be rewarded for doing work you love, but that does not mean you will be rewarded if you do no work at all. A golden touch still requires that you touch *something*.)

Those who had scorned and dismissed me in the past now became my dearest friends. Those who formerly had neither known nor cared to learn my name now counted themselves fortunate if I knew theirs. I was acclaimed, feted, lionized, and if the monetary rewards were not all I could have wished, the salve to my ego was often enough to take the edge off that discontent.

Oh, what a heady delight, to achieve such recognition! My new brethren chuckled indulgently over my neophyte's elation, and showed their support by attending as many of the gatherings that honored me as I attended those which honored them. The halls of many a fine hotel buzzed with our knowing whispers.

It was at one such convocation that I saw the Master again, seated at the bar. He greeted me warmly and insisted I join him. As we spoke, my eye happened to light on a sorry sight: In the dimmest corner of that same bar, huddled over a lone beer, long gone flat, was the man whose exile from our ranks I'd witnessed at my own initiation. His eyes were glazed and he held forth pompously for the benefit of empty chairs that his mad fancy had populated with his former acolytes.

A discreet cough behind me diverted my attention from that dreadful spectacle. I turned to face one of my own followers, a young man in his early twenties, bashfully requesting my autograph. (His eagerness to accost me had led him to edge his way into the space between the Master and myself. Ever gracious toward the young and ingenuous, the Master took no offense at this.) As I signed the title page of my eighth novel, I saw my supplicant's gaze wander to that same shabby corner of the bar where the poor madman blustered among his phantoms.

"Say, isn't that X over there?" my fan asked. "Didn't he used to be somebody?"

"Yes," I said, a catch in my throat. "Yes, he did."

At that moment, the atmosphere in the bar tensed. An editor had come in. The tables filled with aspiring writers hummed as they fumbled for copies of their latest manuscripts, their famished eyes fixed upon the all-powerful one, their minds clearly working wildly, trying to come up with a way to obtain his favorable attention without appearing to be too pushy.

I glanced back at my fan. A sheaf of crisp, neatly printed pages had appeared in his hands as if by magic. That same ravenous, yearning look was in his eyes as once had been in mine.

"Gosh," he said. "He's coming this way! Do you think— Do you think that if I handed him my story, he'd mind? I mean, if I offered to buy him a drink first—?"

I smiled and patted his hand. "That's not the way a *real* pro does it."

"Does what?" the editor asked, taking his place beside me.

I leaned toward him. "So good to see you," I said, taking his hand and making the secret sign.

"Ah! That reminds me," he said. "That latest submission of yours, the one about the cat who coughed up a hairball that was a transdimensional portal? Loved it. I'm making it the cover story for our January issue. The check's already in the mail."

I heard a wistful sigh from my fan and saw his head droop over his precious manuscript. Perhaps it wasn't the kindest thing I could have done, but I felt that I had to do *something*.

"You mustn't feel bad," I said to him. "You have to understand, it wasn't *always* like this for me. Getting published isn't easy, but it *can* be done. You'll get your turn before you know it. After all, it's not as if we've got some secret handshake or anything." Here I laughed lightly. "No, really, just keep working. It'll happen for you. Trust me."

His sorrow turned to gratitude. He put away the manuscript and offered to buy me a drink.

Behind his back, the Master caught my eye and smiled approval.

Noblesse oblige.

Nebula Award winner Esther Friesner is the author of thirty-one novels and over one hundred short stories, in addition to being the editor of seven popular anthologies. Her works have been published in the United States, the United Kingdom, Japan, Germany, Russia, France, and Italy. She is also a published poet, a playwright, and once wrote an advice column, "Ask Auntie Esther." Her articles on fiction writing have appeared in Writer's Market and Writer's Digest Books.

Besides winning two Nebula Awards in succession for Best Short Story (1995 and 1996), she was a Nebula finalist three times and a Hugo finalist once. She received the Skylark Award from NESFA and the award for Most Promising New Fantasy Writer of 1986 from Romantic Times.

Her latest publications include a short story collection, Death and the Librarian and Other Stories, Turn the Other Chick, *fifth in the popular "Chicks in Chainmail" series that she created and edits, and the paperback edition of* E.Gods, *which she cowrote with Robert Asprin. In addition to continuing to write and publish short fiction, she has two Young Adult novels forthcoming in 2006, including* Temping Fate *and* Crown of Sparta.

Educated at Vassar College, Esther went on to receive her M.A. and Ph.D. from Yale University, where she taught Spanish for a number of years. She lives in Connecticut with her husband, two all-grown-up children, two rambunctious cats, and a fluctuating population of hamsters.

WHEN I LOOK TO THE SKY

Russell Davis

RISING TO THE surface of consciousness, my first awareness is of black. The blackness that lives behind tight closed eyelids or the strange hindbrain awareness of lucid dreams.

Then, silver. The gleam of stainless steel knives or the bright mental flare that comes from a sharp blow to the temple.

Finally, white. Untouched snow or a wedding dress worn by a virgin at the altar.

I am awake.

Aware.

I breathe. Inhale. Exhale.

My muscles spasm with cold and ache from an exertion I don't remember. They twitch and pulse with uncontrollable shivers.

Nearby, I sense movement and then a slow warmth as a thermal blanket of some kind is draped across my skin.

Voices. I can hear voices, though they are unfamiliar and the words are not clear at first.

My fingers and toes begin to tingle as my body warms.

The voices gain clarity. A female voice says, "He is awake. Do you see how patient he is? He does not struggle or open his eyes, but waits. Waits and listens and assesses."

A male voice replies, "He can hear us, yes?"

There is a noise beside my right ear. *SNAPTH!* I am reminded of fingers snapping, but the sound is not quite the same. It is that sound, with a lisp.

"Yes," the female voice says. "Did you note how his eyes, even closed, tracked to the sound?"

The salt-and-copper taste of fear fills my mouth. The sensation is rare for me, unnatural, and I push it away. I do not know where I am or how I got here. For a moment, I am not even sure *who* I am, but I vaguely remember. . . .

"You are Damon Graves," the female voice says. "And you are here because we have chosen you."

The last part of the sentence, "chosen you," reverberates and echoes in my mind.

A memory rises to the surface of my thoughts. A woman, young and pretty with dark eyes and long hair the color of a raven's wing saying, "Damon, look! That lake is the same color as your eyes!"

The lake is in Montana. The woman is dead. I remember that on that same day we shouted "I love you!" echoes through a box canyon.

I open my eyes that are the same color as that lake. Above me, a white ceiling that glows softly with some kind of hidden lighting comes into focus.

"Yes," I say. My voice is the croaking of a bullfrog. "I am Damon Graves." When I say my name, I know it is truth. I am Damon Graves. I am—

"You are an assassin," the female voice says. "And you have been chosen."

The word "chosen" echoes in my mind once more. It is important, I think.

Without moving, I let my gaze travel as much as possible. There is no form to go with the feminine voice, and the rest of the room, what I can see of it, is as white and sterile as the ceiling.

I try to sit up, but while the shivering of my muscles has subsided, they are not yet ready to move. I stop trying. "Where am I?" I ask.

"An astute question," the female voice replies. "Your current physical location is what we call a nexus sphere. It is a place that stretches across multiple dimensions, including the one known as Time. To ease your understanding, you might think of it as a bubble or pocket that *transcends* time and space as most people think of those concepts. It is a location that is, in fact, everywhere and nowhere. The center of all things. And none." Her voice *sounds* human, but some instinct tells me that she is not. Most emphatically *not*.

"How?" I ask, testing my muscles again. They are starting to respond.

"You have been identified and chosen for a task suited to your particular talents. Once you have performed this task, you will return to the nexus sphere. Then, you will be returned to where you belong."

Another memory comes. The Manhattan skyline glowing neon at night and a penthouse apartment with leather furniture and chrome lamps that cast indirect light. Below, the sounds of the city—car horns, yelling, laughing, police and ambulance sirens, fighting—rise into the air and combine with the unique watery scent of New York concrete. It is where I live, but it is not home.

"I keep getting these flashes of memory," I say. "What has happened to me?"

The male voice answers this time. "An unfortunate side effect of your journey into the nexus sphere. Your full memories will return to you in time." There is an odd, hollow sound, like a forced breath being passed over the top of an empty bottle. I realize that it is a sound not unlike laughter. The voice adds, "You ask many questions and you do not panic. Many people brought to the nexus sphere react . . . differently."

I test my muscles one more time, and this time I am able to sit up. My head spins slightly, and I reach up and pinch a nerve that sits between my eyes. The spinning goes away. "Yeah, well, in my business panic will get you killed more often than not."

The room is empty. White and sterile. Even the table and blanket are white. There is no one else in the room with me.

"Where are you?" I ask.

"We are here," the female voice says. "But we cannot allow you to perceive us. Our existence is a well-kept secret. To some select few we are a myth, a rumor, a story to tell. To most, we are not known at all."

I take a careful step off the table and test my leg muscles, stretching carefully to avoid a strain in the cold. I am without clothing, but there seems to be little point in modesty. When I finish, I wrap the blanket around my waist. "That's not much of an answer," I say. "Who are you?"

"We are individuals concerned with the fabric of history. As a group, we are sometimes referred to as the Weavers," the male voice says.

"The Weavers," I repeat. "What does that mean?"

"It means that we are concerned with the tapestry of history, ensuring that it is woven in the way it should be," the female says. There is a pause, then she adds, "Our role is to ensure that when the threads of history are snarled, they are repaired in an appropriate way so that history may go on as it is supposed to."

"And what do you want from me?" I ask.

"We have need of someone with your talents," the male says.

"So you want me to kill someone for you?"

Another pause, then the female replies, "Yes. That is accurate."

I shake my head. "You've selected the wrong assassin, then. I don't work this way."

"We do not make errors of this nature. You are the *only* candidate for this re-weaving," the female replies.

Memories of other times people have hired me for this work come to mind, and I feel my jaw clench in annoyance. "There's a first time for everything," I say. "I work anonymously. I don't know the employer, and they don't know me. My identity is secret."

"We already know your identity," the male voice says, his voice tinged with ironic humor. "The tapestry is too important for such minor concerns."

"I hear that kind of thing a lot," I say. "Killing someone is usually important—at least to the person wanting it done, and the person getting it done to."

"Still, this is a task you must complete."

"Not really," I reply. "I don't take jobs by force, I don't do pro bono work, and I don't do wet work without information." I cross my arms over my chest and lean back against the table.

Another pause and a new voice, deeper and stronger than the other male, says, "What information do you require?"

This must be, I think, the real employer. "All of it," I say. "Who the target is, why you want this person killed, detailed information about the target's location and circumstances. Oh, and then there's the matter of payment."

"You fail to understand that the payment is your return to your own place in the tapestry of history," the voice says. "We do not pay fees and we do not negotiate."

"You brought me here, remember?" I say. "That means *you* need *me*."

The female says, "We can leave you here, too." Her tone is now as cold as the room itself. The very empty room. "Forever."

I nod. "You've made your point. Who is the target and why?"

Across the room there is a strange hissing sound; on one wall, the thin outline of a doorway appears. "Step through the doorway," the first male voice says. "You will feel a moment of disorientation. All will be made clear, and the information you require will be provided."

"What's on the other side?" I ask.

"Another place, another time," the female says. "Be warned. You must mark well the place that the doorway opens and return to it, your task complete, within twenty-four of your hours. After that, the doorway will vanish and you will be trapped there. Some prisons have walls and some do not, but a prison is still a prison."

I cross the room, my eyes scanning for any sign of my employers and see nothing. Nothing but white. The other side of the doorway, wherever it leads, could not, short of death, be worse than this. I peer around the room once more, and ask, "Why me? There are others in my profession who are as good."

"When you get the details of the task, the answer to that question will reveal itself to you," the male voice that I thought was the real leader says.

I nod and pull on the door, which opens inward. The

vision that opens before is a familiar landscape. A lake with water so blue it appears almost painted. A sky that runs wide into the horizon and mountains with snow-capped peaks. It is Montana. Not where I live now, but where I lived then. It is home.

I have not been there in a long time. I step through the door and it shuts behind me. I turn to mark its location and find that I am mere inches away from an exceptionally large pine tree. There is an odd scarring on the bark and I memorize it carefully. I will remember it when I return.

At my feet is a white metal box, about one foot square and next to it, a duffel bag. A simple note with a computer-printed message in block letters reads: *OPEN ME*.

I kneel down and undo the clasps of the lid, opening it. Inside, there is another note, which reads: *CLOTHING, DETAILS, AND NECESSARY EQUIPMENT PROVIDED IN THE BAG AND THIS BOX. TODAY IS 19-AUGUST-01. REVIEW THE CONTENTS WITH CARE*.

I set the note aside and look deeper in the box. The first thing I see is a photograph. It is the woman who is dead. In the picture she is smiling and beautiful, with a plane of sunlight crossing her left shoulder like a shawl. In the photo, I am standing behind her, lost in the shadows cast by an overhang of rocks.

I remember when the photo was taken.

I remember the woman. The woman who is dead.

She is my wife.

I set the photo aside. The next item in the box is the front page of a newspaper. There is a large, bold headline that reads:

LOCAL CONGRESSIONAL CANDIDATE MISSING

POLICE SEARCH FOR HUSBAND, SUSPECT FOUL PLAY

Beneath this paper is a second one. The bold headline reads:

HISTORY MADE! IT'S MADAM PRESIDENT!

A wave of confusion washes over me as I see that the photo on each paper is of the same woman. I don't understand until my eyes take in the date on each paper. On the first newspaper, the date is August 21, 2001. On the second newspaper, the date is November 4, 2008.

In my world, the date is May 19, 2005, and the congressional candidate is no longer missing. She is the woman who is dead. She is my wife.

Beneath the second newspaper is another note. This one reads: *THE TAPESTRY OF HISTORY MUST NOT UNRAVEL. DO WHAT IS NECESSARY AND RIGHT TO RESTORE IT.*

Clarity arrives, and I understand what is necessary.

The woman who is dead, who is my wife, is *not* dead in this particular place and time. It is August 19, 2001— two days before the media finds out that she is missing and less than one day before she actually died.

Other than these items, the white metal box is empty. The other items I need will be in the duffel bag.

The target, I already understand, is the person who killed her, preventing a career that would eventually lead to the White House.

I open the duffel bag. Inside are clothes that are recognizably mine, and boots that appear well-worn and comfortable. Below them, a large frame Glock 9 mm with a silencer and four boxes of ammunition. A cross-balanced shoulder holster, and a leather coat to hide it under.

I get dressed, tying the laces of the boots and tucking them in the top.

History needs to be set to rights and I see this as a chance for redemption.

This time, I will do it right for one simple reason.

Because *I* am the target.

My wife's name is Diane. We have been married for three years, four months, and two days. She is smart, beautiful, and charismatic. She is in politics, preparing for her first run at a Congressional seat. There is little doubt that she will win. Late at night, sometimes we talk of other dreams. Dreams she has that go far beyond the House of Representatives.

She believes I am a process consultant. This is a facade I maintain, and it works well. I travel a great deal and keep unreasonable hours. She does not ask many questions because I have made it clear that my business and personal life do not cross.

In a way, the lie I have told her and so many others is true. I *do* consult on a process. That process is killing, and I am very good at it.

People who have money and power will pay someone like me to remove someone like them. They live in fear—fear of losing their power or their money or both. Fear makes people do stupid things, but this same fear is what keeps me in business. The business of wet work is complicated; there are rules upon rules and plans and whispers and secrets.

I rarely meet the real employer in person. I don't want to because what I don't know, I can't talk about. They don't meet me in person because what they don't know, they can't talk about. Financial transactions are digital, with money flowing from one blind account to another and another through various foreign banks until it is clean and untraceable.

The information provided to me, required by my years

of experience, is usually very detailed. Places, names, faces, security measures, reasons why, and so on and so forth. I am discreet and invisible, but information is power. I don't do wet work without information. I don't enter the situation without power.

Except once.

I am contacted by a contact of a contact. The job needs to be done fast. The target will be very difficult to get to if too much time passes and right now can be found close to my present location. Unguarded, alone, and on a brief sabbatical of some sort in the mountains of Montana.

The pay is exceptional and I think I will spend some of it to take my wife on a vacation after the campaign. Somewhere exotic and warm. Somewhere that she can just be herself and I can just be myself.

I take the job and get the minute amount of information available on short notice.

I move fast because speed is important. A target that alone is rare. Often, there are bodyguards and security systems and dogs to bypass before the wet work can be accomplished. I drive my truck into the mountains, following the highway and watching the clouds.

Once, I pause for gas and call my wife. She doesn't answer. The last time we spoke, she mentioned how tired she was of the campaign trail and I suggested she stop for a day or two and rest. She promises to call me when she has more time. Perhaps she has heeded my advice and is resting somewhere. I hope so.

The road leads me to a resort that has private cabins and a beautiful view of a mountain lake, not unlike the one Diane and I saw together. The target is in Cabin Four. I park the truck on an access road and approach Cabin Four on foot, from the back.

There is a sliding glass door and I open it. I can hear

the sound of water running in the bathroom. The target is in the shower. I move through the small cabin, light on my feet. I do not make any sounds and I do not touch anything.

A small hallway has two doors—one leads to the bedroom, the other to the bathroom. The water is still running. Surprise will be my ally. I will move fast and quiet.

I open the door and steam rolls out into the hall. I can see the silhouette of the target—a woman—running her hands through her hair. Her figure is attractive. I have only seconds. If I can see her, she can see me.

I pull the Glock from my holster and work the slide. It is already equipped with a silencer. The woman pauses momentarily, then resumes bathing. I take a step, another step, then open the shower door and fire three times.

THIP! THIP! THIP! Two shots to the body. One shot to the head. The last is called the "make sure" shot in my business.

The water is still running, very hot, and I wave away the steam and lean down to look at the target.

It is hard, so very hard, to hold back my scream when Diane's face comes into view.

At the bottom of the duffel bag is a car key, and at the bottom of the hill, there is a nondescript sedan parked on the side of the road. The Weavers, it seems, have thought of everything. I move down the hill and climb into the car. There is a clock on the dash.

In about four hours, I will be walking into that remote cabin and shooting my wife.

Unless I stop myself.

I shake my head as these confusing thoughts run through my mind, and I begin to understand why paradox was a problem in the time travel stories I sometimes read as a teenager. I start the car and begin driving down the road. I do not require a map or directions. The landscape of this place is forever a part of me.

Many thoughts occur to me as I drive, and I am wondering about paradox. If I kill myself in this time, will I still exist in my own time? How can two of me be here at the same time? These questions plague me as I pick up the highway and head west.

I stop once for food, paying with the cash I find in my pants pocket. The girl gives me my change and says, "Have a nice day."

I start to respond. Politeness is a habit, then I say, "Am I really here?"

Perplexed, the girl, who is perhaps sixteen, says, "I *think* so. Don't you?"

"I guess so," I say. "But it doesn't always feel like it."

"I know what you mean," she says. "Every time I have to talk to my parents."

We both grin at each other and she laughs. The sound almost makes up for the unreality of my situation. "You have a nice day, too," I say, then take my food out to the car.

The rest of my drive is uneventful, my mind filled with thoughts of time and paradox and making things right. I killed my wife and went into hiding, disappearing into a variety of false identities and never at any real risk of being found out.

But I had to live with it. Every waking minute of every day. I kept doing wet work, of course, because it was better than sitting in that Manhattan penthouse and staring at the walls. But I never rushed a job again. Never proceeded without complete information.

This time, there would be two of me, and both of us would be in a rush.

The dirt road that leads to the resort appears on my

left. I activate my turn signal and turn in. The road winds through pine trees, and I roll down the window. I have never been back here, and I breathe the scent of the mountains and the late summer air deep into my lungs.

As I go around a curve, a brief flicker in my rearview mirror catches my attention. The other me is not far behind. I must move faster. My plan is simple, but relies on arriving ahead of my other self.

Cabin Four is on the right side of the road, and I park the sedan near Cabin Three, across the road and in the shade of a large stand of pine trees. Moving quickly, I jog across the road. My other self hasn't rounded the corner yet, but I recognize the quiet rumble of the truck engine.

The front door of Cabin Four is unlocked, and I step inside. Everything now depends on Diane. Does she trust me? She does not know that in a few minutes from now, my other self will be here to kill her. My other self does not know she is the target.

I must stand between them. I hear a door shut and water begin to run. She has heeded my advice and retreated here for a break from the campaign. I move across the main room and into the hallway. Open the bathroom door just as she's about to step into the shower. Surprise marks her features and she lets out a yelp before she sees that it's me.

Standing before me, naked and beautiful and flushed, I ache for this moment to last forever. I have not touched any woman since she died and I want to take her in my arms. Time is passing and I must resist.

"What are you doing here?" she says, reaching for a towel.

"No time," I say. I grasp her arms. "Someone is coming to hurt you, Diane."

"What?" she asks. Confusion washes over her features. "I don't understand."

"I'll explain later," I say. "Get in the shower and stay there."

She begins to ask another question and I stop her with a finger placed to her lips. Quietly, I ask, "Do you trust me?"

She nods. Yes.

"Then please do as I say. Get in the shower and keep the water running. Don't come out until I say so."

Diane reads the urgency in my eyes and does not ask any more questions. The towel drops to the floor and she climbs into the shower, pausing only once to look at me. I force a smile as she shuts the sliding door of the shower.

Listening, I hear the patio door open. It leads into the kitchen and my other self is congratulating himself right now on impeccable timing. He can hear the water running.

I step behind the bathroom door and draw the Glock from my shoulder holster, then quietly work the slide. I affix the silencer, and I wait.

My other self is coming down the hallway and the silhouette of Diane's body in the shower will be an easy, inviting target.

I raise the gun to shoulder level, keeping the point up, and watch as the door handle slowly turns. My other self is about to step through the door.

I take a deep, steady breath. The door opens.

My other self steps through, pauses to appreciate the ease of this moment.

Then I shoot my other self in the head. *THIP!* *THIP! THIP!* I add two shots to the body. The last two will do for "make sure" shots. It's not the sequence that counts anyway.

The body of my other self lies on the floor, a look of shock and surprise on my face. I was not expecting to die.

I pick the towel up off the floor, toss it over the face of my other self.

"Okay, Diane," I say. She shuts off the water and opens the shower door.

"Who . . ." she starts to ask, but I put a finger to her lips.

"It doesn't matter," I say. "What matters is . . . you are safe."

"How . . ." she says, then shakes her head, trying to absorb the situation. Her political self surfaces briefly. "The press is going to have a field day."

"No," I say. "They won't. I'm going to take the body far from here and destroy it. No one need ever know about this."

"Damon, are you crazy?" she asks. "You just shot a man! There's going to be an investigation and questions, and you can't just hide a body!"

She is shaking now. A delayed reaction to death that I have seen before. I wrap her in my arms. "Shhh," I whisper in her ear. "Everything will be fine." Her body is warm next to mine, her long, dark hair dripping wet from the shower.

In a voice only I have ever heard her use, she asks, "Do you promise?"

I nod. "I promise."

I want to stay, but prudence suggests otherwise. "I've got to keep moving," I say. "I'll take care of the body and then I'll come back. We can talk more then."

"You do have some explaining to do," she says. She is still shaking a little, but calmer. I have always admired her ability to be calm under pressure. She looks at the prone body again and adds, "A *lot* of explaining to do."

"You'll get the whole story," I say. "When there's enough time. For now, go get dressed."

She wants to say more, but nods and I can't help myself. I watch her shapely form head for the bedroom.

On the floor of the bathroom there is a heavy mat with a rubberized backing. That will do for now. I roll the body of my other self onto it and wrap it in the mat, packing towels around the wounds to keep the blood spatters to a minimum. Then I lift the body and carry it to the dining room, where an area rug will serve as a more efficient disguise for the dead weight of my other self.

I wrap the body in the area rug and look outside. The sun is still shining, but it is late afternoon and I still have much to do. There is no one on the road and all is quiet. I lift up the area rug and put it over my shoulder. I am strong enough to carry it all the way to my truck and place it in the back. I slide the cover closed, then return to Cabin Four.

Diane is dressed and sitting in the dining area. "I . . . I cleaned up the bathroom," she says. Her voice is shaking again. "The towels are in the fireplace."

"Good," I say. "Burn them after I leave."

"You . . . you will be back?"

I cross the small room and kneel down, taking her into my arms. She sobs once, softly, and then stops. "Better?" I ask her.

She nods. "Come back soon, okay?"

"Before you know it," I reply. Then I kiss her lips and they are the soft surprise I have kept in my mind for the many long days since her death. "Until then, just keep me in your heart."

"Always," she says.

"Forever," I reply.

It is a silly word game we play with each other because

the whole world is before us and we are still in love. We kiss once more and say I love you.

I do not know if I have the strength to leave, but I must.

And so I do.

After wiping my prints from the nondescript sedan, I put the key in the ignition and walk away. There is a lake in Montana that matches the color of my eyes. I get in my truck and drive there. I stop long enough to admire the view, trying to see it through her eyes. Someday, I think, she will come here and remember me. I am sorry to hurt her this way.

Nearby is the box canyon where we shouted "I love you" echoes. I go there next, driving deep inside the canyon. When I reach a place where I can go no farther, I stop the truck and get out. I remove the body of my other self from the back, unwrap it from the area rug, bath mat, and towels, then hoist it on to my shoulder long enough to position it in the driver's seat. I return the other items to the back of the truck.

I open the hood and remove the hose leading to the air filter. I use it to start a siphon out of the gas tank. Working quickly, I put gasoline in the back of the truck, on the area rug, the bath mat and the towels. An empty jug in the back is filled with gas as well, and I pour it liberally in the cab of the truck. I make certain to coat the body of my other self well.

I toss the jug into the back, leaving the hose in the tank.

My other body lies slumped over the wheel. When they find this, they will think I was killed—a professional assassination to send a message to Diane, no doubt. Many people did not want her to run. Her charisma would carry her almost as far as her intelligence. They did not know how far, not yet.

I do not feel regret. I take a book of matches from my pocket that I found in the glovebox. I strike one, and it flares a point of heat. I toss it into the back and the fire starts with a faint *WHUMP!* sound.

No, I do not feel regret. I feel clean.

The job is done, and this time I did it right.

On foot, I make the long trek back to the highway. It is not long before I am able to thumb a ride with a semi hauling logs and making the long run between the mills and the woods. We speak very little and when I ask to get out, he stops and says, "Take 'er easy."

I grin up at him. "I'll take 'er any way I can get her."

"That's the spirit," he replies, then puts the truck in gear and drives away.

I climb the hill to the pine tree. The duffel bag is gone, but the box is not. Now the box is black. I kneel down and open it. Inside there is the front page of a newspaper. The headline reads:

LOCAL CONGRESSIONAL CANDIDATE HUS-BAND MISSING

POLICE SEARCH FOR CLUES, SUSPECT FOUL PLAY

The second newspaper reads:

CONGRESSIONAL CANDIDATE A WIDOW

POLICE SAY NO SUSPECT FOR MURDER OF DAMON BLAKE

The third newspaper headline says:

HISTORY MADE! IT'S MADAM PRESIDENT!

I smile and put the newspapers back in the box. I don't know how I know what to do, but I pick it up and step forward to the pine tree. The doorway appears as I do, and it opens.

Before I step through to the white room, to the nexus sphere and the Weavers, I stop and when I look to the sky, it is blue and wide and stretches to the horizon. Far away, the woman is alive. The woman is my wife and she is *not* dead.

It is enough and I am satisfied with the wet work. That is not something I have ever felt before.

Rising to the surface of consciousness, my first awareness is of black. The blackness that lives behind tight closed eyelids or the strange hindbrain awareness of lucid dreams.

Then, silver. The gleam of stainless steel knives or the bright mental flare that comes from a sharp blow to the temple.

Finally, white. Untouched snow or a wedding dress worn by a virgin at the altar.

I am awake.

Aware.

I breathe. Inhale. Exhale.

I am back in the nexus sphere and my condition, I know, is the result of stepping through the doorway.

I shiver in the cold, but open my eyes.

"You have done well," the female voice says. "Your task is accomplished. History is made right."

"Now what?" I ask. "I'm dead now, right? So how can I go back to my own time?"

The male voice, the real employer, says, "We will return you to your own place in time, but your assessment is accurate. You will be dead. Stepping through the doorway will result in a negative matter occurrence in the continuum. You will simply . . . cease to exist in that moment."

I sigh. "It was worth it."

"Much of the work the Weavers do results in that sensation," he says. "Still, there is another alternative to death."

I sit up, forcing my cold muscles to respond. "What?"

"Work for us," the female voice says.

"Wet work, you mean?" I ask. "For you?"

"People in all times and all places are often killed out of sequence," the other male voice replies. "By removing the threat to them, we can ensure that while Time may be wrinkled, it is not unraveled."

It is an interesting proposition. I do not want to die. Saving Diane has made me want to live again, but . . .

"Do I have to stay here?" I ask. "In the nexus sphere?"

The odd laughter sounds again. "No," the lead male says. "You can be anywhere, everywhere in time. Our existences—and yours, should you accept—are not constrained in the traditional ways of mortals."

"*Are* you mortals?" I ask. "Can I see you?"

"We are like mortals," the woman says. "Yet unlike them. We are more like you. Beings who have transcended death by invitation of the Weavers."

"Will you work for us?" the leader asks. "Help us keep the tapestry of history woven as it is supposed to be?"

"I want . . . I want to see you first," I say.

Suddenly, they appear before me. Two men and a woman. I recognize their faces instantly. In my world, each was famous in their own way.

"What do you say?" the woman asks. She is strikingly beautiful, with blonde hair and wide hips and lips the color of cherries. Long ago, she was an actress.

"Will you join us?" the man says. He is tall, with a Boston accent. He was in politics before he was killed in Dallas.

The leader reaches out a hand and I take it. He is overweight, with a piercing gaze and a direct voice. He, too, had been in politics. In Britain, during World War Two. "Please," he says. "There is much still to be done. There always will be."

I look at them and ask, "Are there other Weavers? Others like you?"

"Yes," the woman says. "There are many of us, though not all are as notable as we are."

I try not to stare, try not to feel anything, to focus on the import of this decision. It is a choice of death or undeath, a type of living that I have never before imagined or experienced.

"Damon Graves," the leader says, "time is passing outside the nexus sphere. We would have your answer, sir. Will you join us?"

I speak one word. "Yes."

They all smile and the nexus sphere changes colors. Now it is a rainbow and there is not one doorway, but hundreds.

"You have made, I think, a good choice," the leader says. He gestures at the doors. "Where did you want to go next?"

—for Monica, first time, last time and *every* time

Under a variety of names and in several different genres, Russell Davis has written and edited both novels and short stories. Some of his recent short fiction has appeared in the anthologies In the Shadow of Evil, Gateways, *and* Maiden, Matron, Crone. *He lives in Nevada, where he's hard at work on numerous projects, including keeping up with his kids. Visit his website at www.morningstorm books.com for more information about his work.*

THE SUNDERING STAR

Janny Wurts

THE BIRTH NAME she used to swear in as a WorldFleet recruit was Susan Amanda MacTavish. She appeared to be no one remarkable, then. Just another stick-figure teen with dishwater-blonde hair, fidgeting in line with the gangling mob of predominantly machismo applicants. Neatly dressed, her taut posture reflecting her grounder origins, she accepted the scanlink to verify honesty. Her monitored bio-signs showed routine anxiety. Nothing to flag the notice of oversight, as she filled out the induction forms with her stylishly fussy script.

The surgical mind unveiled by her psych tests brought a specialist's assignment to Cultural Liaison. There, her alert manner and linguistic fluency drew the acquisitive notice of covert intelligence. The burning ambition that insisted on making a difference brought Private S. Mac-Tavish a promotion to junior officer within the first year. Now a skinny intellectual with a military buzz-cut, and her spacer's blacks creased like honed knives, she blazed through her mid-twenties in a meteoric rise of upwardly

mobile determination. When she cracked the ranks of
the higher brass, everyone from WorldFleet's admirals
on down thought they knew her, inside and out. Their
probes had her vetted for classified status. The exhaus-
tive dossier on her private life neatly filled in her career
profile of reports and statistics.

Yet the name under which she committed high treason
was Jessian, without any surname or title.

The morning that upended the straight course of her
fate also started without undue incident. Regulations allotted all WorldFleet officers a brief recreational leave
between postings. As S. MacTavish, she leaned toward
lazy. That meant waking up in the sheets of a pleasure
house, warmed into a daze from the athletic attentions
of her past night's partner. That gorgeous, male creature
was nowhere in sight, which suited her loner's prefer-
ence. She rolled over, content. The breeze through the
window smelled of warm sea and jungle, not the gritty
industrial taint of the orbital station left behind with her
last assignment.

For the moment, spun free of her dual identity, she
was a vigorous young woman with an appetite for luxury, who rang for a sumptuous breakfast. Food raised
under sunlight, rooted in dirt, and not synthesized inside
a shipboard gel tank, or processed from municipal waste
matter. She stretched, her mouth watering in antici-
pation.

Soon enough, the house matron herself bustled in,
bearing a laden tray. She seemed the usual, grandmoth-
erly woman, whose smile was tailored for comfort; but
not today.

Crisp, without sentiment, this madam said, "Jessian."

Breath froze. MacTavish's heart skipped a beat, before racing. Fear and discipline warred, while she held
herself watchfully still. By one secret name, awarded at

oath-swearing, all sister-initiates were summoned to serve.

"You're well rested?" The house madam prattled on without pause as she placed her steaming burden on the side table. "Good. You'll need your mind sharp. WorldFleet orders will shortly dispatch you to Scathac. You'll find other instructions sent from the order tucked inside of your napkin." Hands clasped, something more than professionally reticent, the old woman finished off, shaken. "You're sent to salvage a tense situation. The first sister given this mission has failed. Our race against time is now critical."

The young officer kicked herself clear of the coverlet and snatched up the dressing robe hung by the bed. Stunned by the shocking break from strict form, she blurted, "Don't tell me our worst fear has happened?"

The old woman clamped her jaw with reproof. But she answered. "Yes."

Ugly news was given no instant to settle.

"Enjoy breakfast, sweetheart. Then be on your way. Your tab's been squared as a gift from a relative, and your officer's dispatch is already packeted from WorldFleet hub's relay. You'll be on active duty inside an hour. Even your high security clearance won't give that the balance of power is broken."

No more dared be said. The senior initiate bowed herself out, reverted to matronly character.

As Jessian, she dressed, unnerved as though hit by an ice-water dousing. Already, the horrific nightmare began. Brilliant, irascible Calum Quaide Kincaid had made no idle threat, when his private research team had been bullied by lies, and then commandeered under mandate. Before letting their break-through concepts become the snatched prize of corrupted politics, the scientist sold out. Tossed his lifework, and that of his six genius colleagues to the volatile, underdog fringes. Applied as a weapon, their explosive new leap in development would swiftly upset impossible odds. Rip apart the blood-sucking, stalemated war that had raged for decades between PanTac Trade, and two rival empires of conglomerate governments.

Shattered by dread, Jessian crossed the quaint floor tiles and snatched on her discarded clothing. The wafted fragrance of the rich food hit raw terror, and unsettled her stomach. She sat, fingers shoved through her stubble of hair, while anxiety trampled her, roughshod. *Whole worlds would see ruin*. The covenant of compassion that founded her order must intervene *now*, before entire civilizations went down in fury and flames.

"Save us all from ourselves!" Trembling, Jessian unfolded the napkin. She accessed the message embedded on flash-sheet: time and location to make her rendezvous with the sister-initiate named as her contact. She would receive no further instructions until after her drop onto Scathac.

She went, wide awake to the personal danger imposed on her WorldFleet persona; and idealistically, fatally blind to the impact her choices might stamp on the future.

Scathac was a mottled mudball from orbit, gleaming with pockets of bitter water, clouded to opal by alkali tailings. Groundside, the planet was a brutalized wasteland. Worse than back country primitive, barely more than a dusty supply depot upkept to service the enclaves of miners that canyoned its surface.

At noon, local time, the dirt streets were empty. As Cultural Branch Officer Susan MacTavish, she strode through the huddle of prefab buildings, coated and drab under powdery dust, and snagged hoary with air-feeding lichens. The verges were scattered with thorny plants.

Also rustling fauna with venomous barbs, scaled hides, and murderous teeth.

Hands protectively gloved, she snapped back her helmet's dark-tinted faceplate and squinted through UV-laced glare. The view redefined the concept for desolate: WorldFleet was raping this world for its minerals, essential for the outer skin shielding that armored all starfaring ships. The irony scalded: that each gaping scar on this savaged landscape was covetously defended as a military asset.

Noon sun drove the base residents inside. Nothing moved in the bleak, punch-cut shadows. Past the slab-sided warehouses, beyond gravel flats sculpted to ridges, the cones of a broken, volcanic range notched the heat shimmers at the horizon. Tribal folk lived there, a feat of stark resilience that defied imagination. Stymied reason, in fact, since WorldFleet brass now pitched their brightest young talent to crack their crazed pocket of local resistance. Scathac's pack of primitives actually thought they could beat a PanTac mandate of enforced eviction.

"Sane people don't commit cultural suicide!" the special-ops officer blurted aloud. *What fanatical sect would trade their lives for a forsaken, mass grave in this place?*

"Believe it, Jessian," a cautious, unaccented voice answered her explosive thought. The sisterhood contact she waited to meet emerged out of shadow, wearing a reflective jumpsuit and a grimed head cloth, apparently native. "Never underestimate the tenacity of the human spirit."

"I don't, usually." MacTavish, now Jessian, regarded her sister-initiate with a dissectingly measuring stare. "You're Adrianna?" Given a nod, she resumed with dry venom, "Even on paper, this bunch seems extreme."

"Worse, actually." The contact's anxious glance

flicked aside. "I learned the hard way. If you can't find the opening to mend my mistakes, these people will die without leaving a trace."

Jessian stiffened. "Our order would spare them?"

"That's your mission, my dear. Enjoy the party." Before hearing more questions, the sister-initiate gestured ahead. "I'll give you the gist at the Base Port's bar. That way."

Disturbed beyond *thought* that her secretive sisterhood dared to work her in parallel with WorldFleet's assigned objective, Jessian strove to sound matter-of-fact. "These oddballs refuse to relocate again. Why? They've backed down from morbid conflict, before." In fact, their erratic history had colonized other worlds, prior to this one. Choice habitats, worthy of taking a stand; not the bare, poisoned vista PanTac's combined governments had made of this scorched patch of hell.

"They've balked at the formality of refugee processing, then skirmished when WorldFleet stepped in and tried armed coercion. There were casualties. Troops hit bang in the eye with damned darts, and nary a tribal hunter in sight. No one died. But the woundings were ugly enough to force a stand down." The sisterhood contact glanced sideward, evasive. "A reactionary deadlock, except that appearances don't pierce the surface. You've read what's on file?"

"The whole lunatic theme." A matrilineal band of rugged individualists had chosen this isolate waste to save their culture from sweeping conformity. Another whacked breed of zealot, that decried mechanized technology as boogeyman. Coughing the taint of buffeting, scorched air, clogged with the harsh grit of minerals, Jessian conceded, "One has to admire these settlers for their bloody-minded persistence." For generations, the killer climate had been deterrent enough to preserve their wonked ethnic lifestyle. Until WorldFleet's imposed regime of martial law, and wartime demands overran their pioneer rights. The strategic value of Scathac's rare ores dumped their world on the hot list of enemy targets.

"I told them straight out that their lives were at risk!" More than defensive, the sister-initiate qualified, "They won't understand. Refuse to listen. Their entrenched beliefs have no place for the concept their home grounds are no longer safe."

" *'Ah'ket tens vhehico?'* " Jessian questioned, icewater cool.

A spat oath affirmed the astute guess drawn from hours of linguistic homework. "That's just what their wizened spokesman declared!" Arms crossed as though chilled, the sister-initiate ran on with the concept's translation, " 'This place is one Word, and all other Words, living, contain the whole Arc of Eternity.' "

"Well, that may have been the going truth yesterday," Jessian snapped under her breath. She dared not unveil the hideous truth: that overnight, a single, leaping advance outstripped Scathac's costly defense grids. Kincaid's weapon would be aimed here first, one blow to cripple PanTac's monopoly on the light-speed class hulls that made starships. Before the pause lagged, she masked driving worry. "I should have expected the order's involvement." Their mission protected minority cultures, and sheltered whole gaggles of at-risk children. "It's the unwarranted ferocity of *WorldFleet's* brass, scrambling, that's got me pushed to the edge."

"You're officially dispatched to shepherd these ornery tribefolk to safety? *As well?*"

Jessian's scowl gave answer enough. To task her here—a specialist sent in on classified priority to co-opt an obscure batch of nomads—hoisted a glaring red flag:

by PanTac's grasping standards, these odd, stone-age people should have been beneath contempt. Written off as an expendable casualty, along with the working class miners . . .

The hunch to the sister-initiate's shoulders all at once sagged with defeat. "You haven't guessed? Or worse, the order itself hasn't warned you?"

"Warned me? What for?" Jessian stared. "WorldFleet command handles PanTac's dirty ops without oversight. It's self-serving logic. Genocide makes the short list, for bad press."

The contact gave that glossing over short shrift. "Don't fall for appearances. No one's launching this rescue for the humanitarian spin."

Jessian stopped, speechless. "The stake's raw intelligence? *On both sides?* You're twisting my leg!"

The headcloth's weave fluttered as the sister-initiate shuddered with outright unease. "Esoteric knowledge," she whispered, afraid in the open street. "Magic. These tribefolk possess the ability to evoke the paranormal. Miners' gossip on that has run rampant for years. Strange encounters nobody wants on the record, but prospectors' probes get knocked clean out of orbit. Personnel and machinery have been wiped off the grid by inexplicable, unseen forces. I'm not the only one standing who's witnessed the eerie proof."

Save us all! Jessian snapped down her faceplate to mask her sudden alarm. Elite training and the order's strict discipline kept her outward conclusion flat calm. "Then my official assignment hasn't been driven by Pan-Tac's overweening hypocrisy."

The sister-initiate shook her head, still rattled beyond decorum. "I won't go back out there. Unless your trained talent ranks higher than mine, you'll be royally cooked if you try. I tell you, those uncanny creatures are too reclusively savage to tame."

Which surely meant *WorldFleet* desired them alive as
a clandestine research experiment, Jessian raged behind
her dark visor. Kincaid's vengeful defection made Scathac's fey tribefolk far more than a weird curiosity.
Surely, they sparked someone's desperate hope that
their mystical powers might offer a last-minute counter-
measure. The snagging crux loomed, that the sisterhood's precepts would demand her outright intervention
to spare a free people from rank exploitation.

The terrible speed of unfolding events permitted no
chance to prevaricate. Entrained in two roles, the
young woman charged to pursue an uncataloged culture paced as she dictated her needs. Up and down
base supply's dingy office, her tigerish tread shed caged
energy.

"Compass, with satellite tracking. Topographical
charts. Yes! On paper!" she snapped to the middle-aged
loser wedged behind his chipped desk. "Boots," she continued, annoyed by his raised eyebrows and posture of
inert complacency. He and his staff would be dead as
dust, if WorldFleet's intelligence failed to deliver. *Boots;*
she chided herself, inwardly driven to resume her lapsed
concentration. "Ones with miner's soles. An ore prospector's outfit and field kit."

The desk jockey rode over her, heedless of rank;
oblivious to looming ruin. "You can't be crossing this
terrain on foot!"

"Hostile, is it?" The steel glare Jessian whetted for
bureaucrats cut his protest off at the knees. "Walking.
I've said so. The tribefolk do likewise. In flimsy rope
sandals. They travel that way all their miserable lives,
and no fool's about to earn their respect, invading their
turf with a skimmer."

"Damned stupid, if you think to be messing with
them." The man rubbed his pink forehead, his jaw nes-

tled into his creased neck like a turtle. "They'll turn
your head. Spin waking nightmares or set your compass
drifting in circles." Each resentful stab at his keypad
rapped through her clockwork steps.

"Emergency rockets," she stated.

While she circled, he snapped in contempt, "Shall I
add a tent shelter? Survival rations? Wristband with a
button locator? The prospectors wear dogtags, as well
as a pin beacon lodged in their bone marrow."

"All those things. Yes, on the locator. No beacon."
Her voice sounded crisp, despite chafing dread. Her talented resource outmatched his technology. If she fell to
mishap, no party of searchers would be sifting through
Scathac's ashes to find her remains.

"Won't matter anyhow," the requisition man sniffed.
"Idiots who tangle with wandering tribefolk tend to vanish without any trace." His leering glance swept her
whipcord-lean frame, with its downplayed, even delicate,
femininity. "I'm under your orders. Ignore smart advice,
it won't be my balls strung up for getting you lost. Shall
I put you down for the hovercraft's route? That's if
you're the brass bitch to the bone, determined to leave
in the morning."

His victim smiled, a flash of bared teeth. "I leave tonight. Since I've ordered the clothes, I might as well ride
with the resupply for the miners."

"You're sweet flesh, to those sharks," came his last,
parting jab. "That crowd of roughnecks aren't gonna
balk at snatching the opportune pinch."

Jessian froze. Her slate-colored eyes kept their bite
through charged quiet. "Will they so?" Then her brazen
façade cracked. "Bring them on, let them try." Still
cheerful, she laughed. "What earthly use is a fully grown
stud who flirts like a beardless virgin?"

*   *   *

Sunset glared like a huge, bloodshot eye above blackened peaks of vertical rock. As hardened as her promise, Jessian swayed to the lurch of the next outbound crawler. She traveled masked in a working man's headcloth, jounced as the vehicle's treads scraped across scoured hardpan. Out-country, the jagged, solidified lava would have torn balloon tires to shreds. The burly miners wedged on either side offered her no harassment. Their sunken expressions reflected bored stupor, never due to her military status.

A sister-initiate sworn in for raw talent, Jessian had been schooled to project her focused power of suggestion. To uninformed senses, a person was present, but not interpreted as a female. The miners perceived what her clothing implied: another gaunt prospector, bound into the waste for a routine ground survey.

The reweaving of esoteric energy sealed Jessian inside of a tight ring of solitude. Confined by the arduous grind of the crawler, she had too much time to dwell on her endangerment, now the secret demands of the sisterhood entangled with her career. *Both factions wanted a closed, tribal culture removed to secure its survival.*

Unless she failed outright and opted for suicide, she must decide which of two powerful factions her operative choice would betray.

WorldFleet, panicked and snatching at straws to close its breached line of defense; or the sisterhood, which *also* pursued arcane practice, and whose philanthropical service to civilized humanity was already taxed to the bittermost edge. Hung at the verge of annihilating warfare, uncounted *billions* were poised to die. If Jessian openly chose for the order, the high-profile scandal of her defection would fling their hidden covenant headlong into the predatory arena of politics. An imperative, *justifiable* breach of held trust, given that reason must argue for mercy: those peaceful regimes granted the sisterhood's backing *perhaps* stood a chance to endure through the fragmenting turmoil.

Hands clenched, Jessian coughed out the alkali dust stirred by the stiffening breeze. Scathac's days were inferno; the cruel nights, yet more murderous as the temperature plunged toward the other extreme. Unlike these rough men, aware of no worse than their next brutal work shift, the young woman poised on the razor's edge wrestled her outraged nerves.

Why had *she* been given the burden of drawing humanity's line between certain death, and the imperative drive for self-determined survival?

The crawler's gears ground. Brakes squealed, and the lumbering vehicle jerked to a stop. The driver waved toward a thorn-studded ravine, that wound toward a bottle-necked canyon. "Better make camp underneath of those rim walls, before the weather beats you to shreds."

Jessian nodded, unable to speak over the concussive roar of the engines. She brushed off the miners' kindly farewells. Half-crushed by her mission, and unwilling to hazard how these separatist shamans might repel yet another outsider's invasion, she unhooked her safety belt, shouldered her gear, and stepped off into the trackless unknown. WorldFleet intelligence gave her eight days before Scathac got blown to oblivion by Kincaid's radical cohorts.

The stars blazed down, pinprick cold, on a hostile landscape veiled under darkness. Thorns, shattered rock, and piled hillocks of crushed pumice grated under Jessian's boots. She carried no light, just the phosphorescent gleam of a hand-compass, with the winking display of the locator's readout. The clank of the crawler faded away. The sweep of its headlamps vanished behind, eclipsed by the distant outcrops. Gusts roared down off the volcanic heights, bitter and burning with chill. Jessian tucked in her facecloth. Ripped her pant leg *again*, on a serrated cactus. At each step, she felt as though Scathac itself rejected her trespassing presence. Accosted by the relentless terrain, she wondered how any sentient human dared to give birth and raise children here. Did other eyes see wild beauty where hers perceived nothing but desolate rock and despair? Had she grasped the tortuous ethnic language with enough comprehension to forge understanding?

By WorldFleet's tactical directive, she must. Else wider societies than this one must perish without a last hope of reprieve.

Doubt gnawed, in the shadows. The sisterhood's covenant itself could be swayed. Before such sweeping peril, even the order's humanitarian ethics might fail to sustain their firm character. Crisis could ruthlessly pressure the option to bolster their overstretched resource. Jessian quashed her fretting. Reined in the paranoia that outraced current fact as she stumbled atop the next rise. These tribefolks' safe harbor must be won, first. Already, her lungs burned. Chalk grit rasped her throat. That asshole at base could have been right to mock her decision to hike. She might wander for days and find no one. Only cold ashes and the stripped bones of killed game, left in long abandoned encampments. These tortuous mazes of crooked ravines could swallow a tribal band whole, even without any arcane tricks to mask themselves from discovery.

"I'll find them," she muttered, unwilling to quit for the whine of a haunted conscience. "I swear by my willing oath to the order, no innocents will die in our war zone!"

Yet more likely these savage, inimical hermits would

lurk in concealment like wraiths, laughing as she blundered about, grumbling and circling thorn plants. The image raised a bark of grim laughter. Bad odds were her business. She'd handle these stubborn reclusives with the ball-busting self-assurance that always had landed her back on her uncertain feet.

The gusts strengthened. Pelted by whipped gravel, Jessian reached the sheltered cleft of the rim rocks before she became buffeted to a standstill. Despite tired calves and an ache in her chest, brought on by clogged air and exertion, she chose not to camp. The fissure cut the brunt of the elements, and every lost minute mattered. She could sleep well enough through the heat of the day. The gale shrieked above the narrow, slot canyons, raking off dust like fine powder. Whipped into gyres, the fine particles built charge, flinging off static electricity.

Jessian pushed forward under flickering storm light. She tested each step, and listened, as well, trained senses enhanced through her talent.

No warning foreran the jolting fall, as the hardpack gave way underneath her. Ripped off balance, she plunged downward, stung by tumbling gravel, until she slammed into a hidden crevice. Lodged in the cleft, knocked breathless, with one ankle twisted to agony, she spat inhaled grit. Her first thought was the button on the locator beacon, strapped to the wrist pinned beneath her. She wrestled to move, but could not shift position. Her shoulders stayed wedged. Fear was not an option. Forced to survey the extent of her setback, she noticed the woven lattice of plant fiber, burst through by her passing weight.

She had not come to grief, except by design. Worse, the scale of this trap was too large to be fashioned for Scathac's undersized game animals. The desert tribes had defended their ground, despite all her specialized skills.

Jessian cursed. Still dazed with shock, she measured her difficulty. Bodies dropped into a crack in the earth might be lost, but not due to the practice of lethal magic. Since the reclusive hunters who had darted armed troops were unlikely to rescue their victims, she was left with a straightforward predicament she'd have to solve on her own.

Her presumption proved flawed. A wave of sucking dizziness swept her. Too late, she fought back, as her mind became clouded. Hazed out of her senses, she slipped into dreams that spun her under as if she were drowning. . . .

The veil ripped away with no ripple of warning. Jessian wakened, awash in harsh sunlight. The lancing pain of too much sudden brilliance bedazzled her eyes and fevered her brain. She lay on her back. Her limbs were strapped straight, arms pulled overhead and tied at the wrists with rough twine. Around her, robed head to foot in black cloth, stood a band of lean warriors. Each carried a blow tube and quiver of vaned darts. Dark eyes set into creased, weathered faces watched her in expressionless quiet.

Jessian licked her parched lips. Tried a neutral phrase in their dialect.

No one answered. The ring of fixated stares never blinked. Jessian languished, clammy with sweat, and pressed to gasping tears by the strain on her swollen ankle. Handpicked WorldFleet officer, and sisterhood dedicate, she refused to succumb to faint nerves. Human principles mattered! Barbaric or not, these creatures had children and wives. Their innocent families relied upon her to secure their endangered future.

"*Hear me,*" she pleaded, then talked herself hoarse. When her voice failed her, she labored in broken sentences, forced to a rasping whisper. She kept on until the cruel exposure whirled her to senseless prostration.

She did not hear, when the eldest man standing vigil broke his enduring silence. *"She did not shout with anger,"* he pronounced with soft calm.

Across the circle, another man added, *"She did not accuse."*

"Or threaten us with reprisals," a third ventured. He mused, touched thoughtful, *"Perhaps she's not like the others, deaf of mind and without a true heart."*

"She can't walk," said a last one in musical sorrow. *"Set her free, she might suffer worse injury."*

The last spokesman bowed his hooded head. *"Dead or living, if we let her go, surely others will come to bedevil us in her place."*

Communion between them arrived at a thought, sealed into harmonious conclusion: on the chance that she might be a person of substance, she must be taken within sacred grounds, and tested for Mother Dark's wisdom.

Jessian did not feel the release of the tight cords. She stayed oblivious, as tribal hands raised her. Bundled into a borrowed robe, she stayed unconscious throughout the winding ascent that bore her deep into the mountains.

Sheltered within a closed cranny of rock, Jessian remained a prisoner. She was given strange food, and adequate water, but never a moment of privacy. Always, an escort of dartmen stood watch. However she begged or raged in frustration, her captors did not deign to answer. The days crept, without respite. Still, their sharp eyes tracked her every small move. They never relented through each passing hour, even for the embarrassment of bodily necessity. Worse, if she even dared *think* of escape, the men hissed through their teeth in sharp warning.

They were reading her mind.

Punched to shock by that surprise revelation, Jessian strained the fraught limits of her sisterhood's clandestine training. Soon enough, her innate talent confirmed: she sensed the thrusting, delicate tendrils of the tribesmen's listening awareness. If their invasive touch was unsettling, she snatched bitter comfort in irony. Unwavering, she had never abandoned the merciful purpose that brought her. Trapped and alone, racked by fear and uncertainty, she recognized that these warriors had grasped the gist of her desperate talk. Understanding peeped through their stony masks, when they thought her attention turned elsewhere.

Yet the fact a new weapon doomed their remote world failed to move their granite indifference. However she exhorted, Jessian failed to raise any human concern.

"I promise, by my sworn oath to the sisterhood, you won't be thrown over to WorldFleet's agenda!" Yet even that vow of protection evoked no stir in response.

Despair settled on her, as the seventh day dawned, shining azure light through the rock chinks.

"I don't understand," she accosted her impassive captors, still bent on her senseless imprisonment. "I offer the power to send you away. Save your people. Why should you hold out? At least give your children the life they can't have, if you force them to mass immolation!"

They had seen their last sunrise. Past nightfall, Scathac would be nothing more than a blast cloud of cinders and smoke. Now, even her resource at WorldFleet command could not launch a ninth-hour extraction. Jessian wept. She must bow to defeat. Abandon the tribes to their queer, rigid stubbornness, and try to break out on her own. If she engaged her talents, diverted her guards for a moment, a strategic bonfire set as a beacon might summon her personal rescue.

Yet the instant she focused, and shaped her projection, one of the warriors strode forward and clasped his tough hands at each side of her face.

She heard the lilt of his tribal language spoken for the first time. *"Foolish savage!"*

Her thread of intent was snatched clean away. With the ease of a toy pried from a toddler, her inborn abilities were knotted tight and then lashed to a dizzying rush of expansion. . . .

Time ran through her like water. As though from great height, she saw herself in distant miniature, set free from the caves in the mountains. Limping, exhausted, she labored down the ravine, back into open terrain. There, she watched herself punch the distress codes through her locator, which inexplicably had been returned. Yet no pod descended. Her WorldFleet superiors had deserted her, wholly absorbed by the pending chain of disaster. Abandoned, forlorn, she perched on a parapet, until Scathac's sere landscape dissolved in white flame. . . .

Her scream of horror never emerged. Whirled back into herself, Jessian heard nothing, felt nothing. Lost to sensation, she drifted until an incisive call shattered the darkness.

"Teidwar'sha, outsider! Attend us!"

The summoning lifted her back into daylight. The hour was morning. *Scathac was still whole.* Seized by the grip of a living awareness, Jessian lay on her back on rough stone, staring up at the face of a crone.

The creature's muslin veils were turned back. She wore a fringed headdress of bright, patterned yarns, and her seamed wrists jangled with fetishes. While Jessian languished, too muddled to react, the ancient cupped a slender hand at her brow, and demanded, *"Why are you here?"*

Beyond words, the charged accusation unfolded: that to tribal mores, her kind were the ones whose values were sorrowfully lacking. Shock strangled Jessian's chance to respond. The uncanny *force* of the old woman's Seeing lanced into her mind, and stripped off her mask of hypocrisy. *She posed as WorldFleet's agent, despite an oath of compassion, sworn to the order in secret.*

In a whirling juxtaposition of scenes, the remembered past became present: an impassioned sisterhood senior entreated the novice initiates: *"PanTac's trade factions chase greed without mercy, and unreconciled war threatens the roots of all civilized culture. As diplomacy fails, no recourse remains but our works of humanitarian intervention."*

Shame followed, hot and immediate. Remorseful tears followed. *All* towering pride had been sorely misplaced. Seen through the offended eyes of the crone, the rigid outlook of Jessian's convictions showed irremediable flaws. If WorldFleet's armed force, and PanTac's corrupt tyranny trafficked in exploitation, the sisterhood's meddling was ugly, blind arrogance. Through empathic vision, Jessian experienced the pain caused by the coarse thoughts of outsiders. She grasped why the tribes needed strict isolation. Exposure brought harm to the web of communion that nourished their innermost being.

What demeaning presumption *dared* deny this reclusive people the right to determine their fate for themselves? The adults would not integrate, but sicken and die, with their orphaned young left to sink into madness, ripped apart by extreme sensitivity.

"I'm sorry," gasped Jessian. "So sorry." Yet her honest guilt did nothing to right an intrusion, whose ends must unseat human dignity.

The crone arose with an herb-scented rustle of skirts. Her vehemence carried a powerful presence as she raised withered palms to the warriors. *"Who speaks for this woman, whose loyalties are scattered as wantonly as the winds?"*

And like rustling leaves, a soft voice responded. *"She has not harmed, or killed."*

Another one argued, *"Not tried to entreat us with wickedness."*

"By her heart, she stood firm for what she believed was our children's future survival."

The crone lowered her hands. *"I have heard. I have seen. If she is judged worthy, who among you will rise to stand surety?"*

The warrior who had touched her, and spoken before, stepped forth from his circle of peers. *"Biedar tribe must back her integrity, since my hand wrought the snare that entrapped her."*

A handclap from the crone sealed his pledge. *"Then on Biedar's grand oath, let the spiral of Mother Dark's mystery embrace her."*

Dry fingers brushed Jessian's feverish skin. More words reached her ears, clear as jewels. *"Sleep. Rest and dream. In due time you will be released to return to your own."*

"Too late," she murmured. The sun must go down— but the coils of tribal magic noosed tight, enfolding her into vision. . . .

As though from deep space, she gazed down once more on the mottled, brown sphere that was Scathac. The desolate hues no longer seemed drab, but possessed of a surreal beauty; as though all colors lay in the essence of form, veiled as the notes in a symphony. Then, to Jessian's horror as witness, a miniscule, metal object arced past and plunged toward the central sun. The casing that cradled the weapon was tiny. A mere fleck, to bear ruin beyond the pale of all former human achievement.

Her being cried out!

The explosion would strike all *bright harmony blind, as the disrupted star hurled its concussive shock ripping outward. Her sight became dazzled blind upon impact.*

And song *unfurled, pealing out through the thundering instant of death, and a shimmering pause that was silence.*

Somewhere, unseen, a crone spoke a word, and a circle of warriors responded. Together, they spun mighty webs of strange magic, wrought from the music of intelligent matter, and the sovereignty of their human will. Jessian felt their working touch her core self. Included, drawn in, she was pulled into the heart of their vortex. To their making, she offered her steel determination: the courage that had impelled her to risk all she had for belief, that an innocent people were jeopardized. She lent the fierce character that had sent her, alone, across Scathac's savage terrain. Yet where her life-trained talent knew nothing more than projected illusion set to deceive, these wild tribefolk wrought direct *conjury.*

Force answered.

The world split!

The vast pattern of the dream's vision doubled. At one with the masterful strength of the tribes, Jessian beheld two realities, present, writ across the blast of a wanton annihilation. *In one, Scathac's surface was wasted to ash. In the second, the planet spun on, captured inside a majestic symmetry. The moment suspended, as an undaunted, fierce people steered their home world within the gravitational embrace of an untrammeled, whole sun.*

Then all brilliance faded, and blackness returned, infused with a pristine serenity. . . .

Jessian roused with a startled cry, snapped back to wakened awareness. She lay in the mountain cranny, alone. The reclusive tribefolk had left her. Scattered above the rock cleft, she saw stars, burning untouched against darkness. Her gear lay nearby: rations, tent, emergency flares, and the wristband with her locator beacon. She sat up, her shocked talent soothed by the peculiar awareness that the crone's cavalier handling had not left her stranded and desolate. Scathac still held her own people: the miners, never informed of their peril, had also been kept alive. The WorldFleet base and its outpost were gone. But the workers, abandoned by PanTac to die, had been gathered up by the tribes' mighty act of reweaving.

In their innocence, those men would not grasp the titanic event that had happened. Their eventual rescue would pose an anomaly, since all ranked personnel, warned of impending doom, had been lost, torn apart in a blaze of destruction.

Except Jessian, who now contained an experience beyond individual cognizance. She *knew*, beyond reason, the tribefolk had withdrawn, pushed deeper in hiding than ever before. Yet their web of living awareness remained, now an inseparable part of her. Thrumming within, she still sensed a current of power to outmatch all of Kincaid's rogue research; an echoing thunder of magic to diminish forever her sisterhood's pathetic tinkering.

Trembling, afraid, she addressed the night quiet, reshaped by a newfound humility. "I promise to leave your lands and your people to abide with your secrets in solitude."

She would keep her word. Even against the inevitable debriefing incited by Scathac's irrational survival; and though willful silence must break her order's sworn oath, even cost her good name under risk of a WorldFleet court martial.

Deep in her mind, she sensed the reply, and the burden beyond her life trust. *"Reveal anything that you've* inherited through our crafting, and Biedar tribe must pursue your kind for that knowledge, unto the ending of time."

Through her combined career as an established professional novelist and her background in the trade as a cover artist, Janny Wurts has immersed herself in a lifelong ambition: to create a seamless interface between words and pictures that explores imaginative realms beyond the world we know. She has authored seventeen books, a hardbound collection of short stories, and made numerous contributions to fantasy and science fiction anthologies. Her novels and stories have been translated worldwide, with most editions in the U.S. and abroad bearing her own jacket and interior art.

Recent releases include a standalone fantasy, To Ride Hell's Chasm, and the latest volume in her "Wars of Light and Shadow" series, Traitor's Knot.

She lives in Florida with a husband, three horses, four cats, and all manner of wild things parading through the back yard.

THE EXILE'S PATH

Jihane Noskateb

Twenty-two young men and women had chosen the Exiles' path, along with Elza Ragon. They had sworn together, on the ancestral fire, three vows.

I will never betray the trust, the name, the shelter of my family had been the first, and the easiest. They had grown up together, learned together how special, how precious their family was, discovered together the pride and love that came with it. Stepping now into duty had felt like a reward.

I will never forget, I will never remember. That one had made no sense, then, but they had accepted it.

The last was the strangest, and most important: *By my choices and life, I will help bridge humanity's differences, lest anyone has to find peace in exile ever again.*

They had thought they were just words, but they swore with all their heart.

Then, Grandmother started telling them a tale. The tale of their origins.

Elza

When I came back to work, on Monday morning, nothing had changed. The cheerful, "Hello Elizabeth!" of my coworkers, the bright colors on the walls, even the pile of work Magyd had left on my chair with an ephemeral soft-screen note: "Enjoy!" —everything was as it had been.

It all felt wrong.

I remained standing before my desk, not knowing what to do with myself. The ephy note seemed to mock me, and I wanted to hurt Magyd for daring . . .

. . . *for being alive* . . .

I blinked back tears. Swallowed irrational anger and fear. This was a day like any other, for him. For so many more.

The whole world should have stopped.

I sighed against the useless thought. Put his ephy note carefully on my desk, where it was recorded and saved just as it disappeared.

My throat tightened at the sight.

I'll never forget.

Pushing the thought aside for now, I took the memorods from my chair and added them to my own database, for later treatment. Took my coffee mug from its compartment, carefully, so as not to brush the other one there, and went to the coffeemaker, in the outer room, like I did everyday. I managed to smile at my coworkers, even exchange a few pleasantries.

It left ashes in my mouth.

As I got back to my chair, I nervously checked the knot of my scarf, two scarves, really, red and yellow intertwined and wrapped around my shoulders, and twisted my dragon ring back to its proper position on my finger. Then I started with my usual to-do list of the day.

Anna was dead, and the world had not stopped.

That's life, isn't it?

I had been working for three hours without pause or thought when Juliet, our junior administrator, instant messaged me to check if I had received the secured file she wanted me to reread.

I opened my inbox with the faintest tinge of guilt at not having done so earlier.

Beyond my desk, I could see people passing by, in the outer room. A cluster had formed next to the coffee-maker. Had the news reached them already?

A soft, computer voice told me I had three messages waiting for me.

Opening the first one with a short, vocal order, I sipped cold coffee and frowned at the bitter taste.

Then I looked back at the holoscreen, frowned, cold coffee forgotten.

The mail had been sent on Friday evening.

"Dreadful Monday, isn't it?" it read. "It's still two days earlier for me though, as I type this, and I'm pre-paring for my weekend. With Roland. I'm probably late for work as you read this. So why don't you take my new mug out of your drawer, and bring some coffee to my office so when I finally decide to show up at work, we can share what happened to both of us in the mean-time? I promise I won't talk about Roland. At least not too much . . . ! Anna."

I was halfway to the coffeemaker, a mug in each hand, before I realized what I was doing.

Magyd was already there; he took one look at my face, said, slowly, "So, you've heard, too? About Anna?"

I could only nod.

Valerian, a young man from expeditions, was coming toward us. "They're sending someone to investigate," he told me eagerly.

I dropped the mugs on the nearest table and checked my scarf again. My fingers, my brain felt numb. My co-workers' voices were far away.

"He's here."

That was Celyn, the receptionist.

I turned toward her, to ask who had come, then remembered. They were sending someone to investigate Anna's death.

I started retreating toward my office. I wanted to be left alone with Anna's mail, pretend it was still Friday.

But the main door opened then. For a second I didn't believe it.

He had come back, he was here . . .

. . . *called by need* . . .

I remained, frozen, drinking in the familiar sight of this man who had been part of the family, who had been closer still. Now more of a stranger.

The thought brought me back to the present.

He isn't one of us anymore. I schooled my face, my feelings. *Hasn't been for the last ten years.*

People around me were watching him with open curiosity. Celyn was talking with him, asking if he wanted coffee or anything. Magyd was walking toward him.

He takes his coffee black, strong. No sugar, no milk. He will wrap his fingers around the mug, as if he planned on never letting go. . . .

But he had let go. He didn't even wear the marks Grandmother had taught us anymore.

Magyd was now at his side. My boss, with his small, wiry body, his pale skin and hair, looked fragile next to Lewis' taller, darker presence. Lewis' eyes were that

dark gray I still looked for in storms and dusk. His body
had grown leaner, stronger. Or maybe it was his blue-
and-silver leather Investigation Force uniform.

He's the investigator on Anna's death.

A sudden, absurd urge to laugh bubbled inside me
and it was all I could do to keep a straight face.

Lewis

She hasn't changed.

Her calm, strong face, with those almond-shaped
brown eyes hiding depths of green and gold, held an
expression I could no longer read, but I knew it like I
knew my own. Differences only enhanced her. Her face
had matured, and the lines around her mouth hinted at
smiles, laughter, at tension and focus, too. Her hair had
grown; she wore it loose, running along her bare arms,
like cool, black silk against her chocolate skin.

Her body was fuller, rounder.

Softer.

She was dressed, as she had always been, without
color and little seduction, in a large, gray pair of trousers
with a tight, black top. The only color was her scarf . . .
and it was tied with a single, right-sided knot.

A ten-year-old reflex made me check her hands.

She was wearing the dragon ring on her right hand's
middle finger, tail facing us, its head probably biting
softly in her palm.

I blinked, as if it was enough to erase the sight.

Never remember.

I turned away from her and back to the task at hand.

"My name is Lewis Second-Sanracyn." I was happy to
hear that my voice was strong and firm. "I realize that,
for most of you, this is news. Your colleague, Anna

Long-Karangel, was found dead last Saturday in her flat."

What I didn't tell them was that it had been her lover, Roland First-Sonj, who had found her. First med reports said that she had been drugged. She had not suffered, but had probably died in her sleep. The poison was a slow, if lethal, one. The cuts had been made while she was dying, or just after her death; the wound hadn't bled, and the symbol carved in her mutilated throat was easy to read.

If the macabre arrangement had been meant for First-Sonj, then it had worked admirably. The young man had tried to commit suicide, messing our death scene that much more.

I watched closely for reactions among Anna's coworkers. I had read their files earlier today, but they had been text-only, and I had yet to match data and names to faces.

Shock, sadness. One or two were looking elsewhere, as if death was contagious.

The receptionist went back to her desk. The outercom rang, and she answered with the same cool voice that had greeted me. Yet there were tears in her eyes.

Magyd Charafi, the department supervisor, had asked me to give his people time to settle in before I came and disrupted their day. Now he was walking from one to the next, with a soft word or a gesture of comfort.

I decided I liked him.

Editing only a little, I went on:

"An investigation is ongoing to determine if it was a suicide, or a murder. I will need your help. Mister Charafi will let you know if I have questions for you . . ." I paused briefly, glanced in their boss' direction. He nodded.

"I realize this is not an easy task, with the news of

your coworker's demise still fresh, but it will help us understand what happened to Anna Long-Karangel."

I finally glanced back at her. She was looking at two forgotten mugs on a table. Waiting for someone to join her?

There had been only one Elizabeth in the files. It had to be her, I realized, even though the file had an outsider's name on it, not her family name: Elizabeth First-Jandarc. She had been Anna's closest friend.

She was first on my interrogation list.

They gave me a room, at my request not far from the entrance door. I could see everyone milling around, at first nervously, then caught in the day-to-day business of work and office relationships, never quite easing back into natural patterns. Only some of them had really known Karangel, but all seemed affected by her death.

My boss had been clear. This had to be conducted quickly, and discreetly.

The deceased's lover, Roland First-Sonj, was the son of Joanne First-Sonj, one of our Lawriters. The affair hadn't been flaunted: the son was a first-waver, after all, a descendant, like I or Elza, of the first wave of humanity to leave Earth's cradle, while Anna had been a Longer.

I had looked carefully, through the files, and in the office. She had been the only Longer. The rest were evenly divided between Firsts and Seconds. And while the Seconds' ancestors had left Earth a century after the rest, they had reached the already colonized clusters before the Longships, and more importantly, with unchanged bodies.

Even though she had been obviously well-liked, Anna Long-Karangel must have stood out here, her elongated limbs and features a constant reminder of her ancestors' means of travel away from Earth.

I shuddered to think that, more than a hundred and fifty years after the last multigenerational Longship's arrival, heated discussions were still raging to know if Longers and their descendants were still human by any standard. Four generations and as many genetic mutations and adaptation enhancements during their long travel from Earth had, if you listened to some, created a different species. And thus thought our local Lawriters. They were now proposing a different legal definition of Longers.

Roland First-Sonj's mother was spearheading the proposal.

Roland himself hadn't cared, not for the political aspect, nor the racial one. In truth, he didn't seem to care about anything anymore.

I had gone back to their mansion, unannounced, earlier this morning. The Lawriter had bruises under her bloodshot eyes, but she had greeted me with steel and a warning. Roland was constantly reliving the moment when he had stepped in Anna's flat. His alibi held. But he felt responsible for her death, as if coming sooner would have changed anything. Did I want to add to his guilt by asking more questions? Did I want a gun to shove in his mouth?

A politician with a stronger sense of family. I had bowed to her, and left.

It was a habit, to go back in my mind to what I knew of a case over and over again, each time adding a piece to the whole until a clearer question emerged. And once you knew which question to ask, the answer was not far behind.

But this time, it wasn't a question that was taking form.

It was a face.
Elizabeth First-Jandarc.
Elza Ragon.
I thought I'd never see you again, when I left. . . .

Elza

He asked no question I couldn't or wouldn't answer. Nothing outside the case.

We were seated with the large, meeting table between us. We both had a mug of coffee in hand.

"When did you learn of Anna Long-Karangel's demise?"

"I received a call from the hospital, I . . ." Words caught in my mouth. "I was the first name on her contact list."

"When did you see Anna Long-Karangel for the last time?"

"On Friday," I said, my eyes on my coffee. Smoke rose, drawing patterns only I could see. "I left work at four in the afternoon, and she was still there. I went into her office . . . said good-bye . . ."

"Why did you leave at four? Is that usual?"

"No. But I had family visiting from the capital . . ."

I glanced up from my mug, but he wasn't looking at me; he was taking notes, his face registering nothing.

As if he remembered nothing of the family. *Did he forget me?*

His next questions were as impersonal as the first ones.

He got up after a while, thanked me for my cooperation. I got up too, nodded, and headed for the door.

Just before I opened it, he took my right hand in his.

Stroked my ringed finger once, in the family's silent greeting pattern.

My skin tingled still, hours later, as I made my way home.

He hadn't forgotten the family, then.

"I may have to go. There is an investigation going on at my office. The investigator said he'd be back."

"Who is in charge of the enquiry?"

Lorenz and Sofia were seated on my couch, as usual almost touching, attuned to each other in a way they didn't notice.

They were both focused on me, he with a worried frown, she with a gentleness that made me want to crawl in her lap and weep. I looked away.

"Why do you ask?"

"Maybe it's someone we can . . ."

"No!" I cried out, before Sofia could suggest manipulation or . . . or whatever else she deemed necessary, and leave for me to do. "This would only draw more attention on us. It may be time for me to leave this place anyway."

Lorenz nodded, but Sofia wouldn't let it go.

"Give me his name, let me see what I can do from Alfens. We have resources at the Investigation Force headquarters they don't have here, you know that. I'll promise I won't do anything before checking up with you." After a nudge from Lorenz and a pointed look from me, she reluctantly added, "Not before you give me your okay."

I opened my mouth to speak.

Whether Lewis could still read the marks or not, he hadn't used what he knew of the family. He wouldn't betray our oath, I felt sure of it. While they would sentence him to memory wipe, at best, send the family's

Edge to kill him at worst, if they knew he was here. Even his Investigator's badge wouldn't protect him from us. Nothing could.

Years of lies and disguised truths helped me hide my hesitation. When I reached my decision, I said: "I can't remember his name. He's a Second, though. That I remember."

"Do you know how many Seconds join the Force?"

I shrugged. "What's happened in Alfens since the last family meeting, by the way?"

"Oh, I made sure Adelopoulos' little plot was uncovered by the right journalist. I had some help from Youki, as the Desnos family promised. Now we have to . . ."

I half-listened to my sister. We had just moved to the Alfensial Provinces, at the edge of colonized space, and humanity was still so set on tearing itself apart, on every planet it planted roots on, while the families were so few and scattered. *Gardeners battling weeds*, I thought, as I watched Sofia, undaunted by the magnitude of our task, her voice strong, her gestures passionate.

In my spare room, their son slept. Lorenz went up to check on him at one point. Sofia interrupted her tale of intrigue when he came back, just long enough to take his hand in hers, intertwine their fingers.

I hadn't found someone among my brethren to share my life with. And I hadn't wanted the pain of lying in bed with lies in my mouth by choosing an outsider. Solitude had always suited me. *Since Lewis.* And, right on the heels of the familiar thought, a new one: *Until he came back.*

"So, will you?"

"What?"

"You weren't listening," Lorenz teased.

"You're tired," Sofia worried, before repeating: "Get me the name of your investigator?"

I looked at their earnest faces. They were waiting for an answer.

Lewis won't betray any of us.

I found that I could.

"Of course," I assured Sofia.

Lying to them had been easier than lying to Lewis earlier.

Anna and I met in the coffee shop near our office every morning before work, except on Mondays. Anna couldn't stand Monday, and in truth, no one could stand her either, not until after lunch and her tenth coffee anyway.

But this was Tuesday, and she hadn't come. She wouldn't. Not ever again.

How Lewis had known I would be there, I had no idea. That he had come for me became clear as soon as he sat in front of me with two cups of black, strong-scented coffees. He pushed one of the cups toward me, wrapped his long fingers around the other.

"Who's here?"

I quickly finished my lukewarm, first coffee, and reached for the one he had bought me. "Lorenz and Sofia. And before that, it was Aïsha. And before that, I was the one visiting Dmitri. We are all here for each other."

He ignored the barb, wouldn't look at me.

"Who's dead?"

I didn't pretend to be surprised. There were always deaths in the family.

"Since you disappeared, ten years ago?"

When I didn't add anything, he reluctantly nodded.

"Too many," I told him coldly.

If you wanted names, you should have stayed.

"I had to go, Elizabeth."

"Why?" I cried.

The place was almost empty, and my outburst had drawn attention to us.

What have I been thinking?

I hit the button at the side of our table, probably too hard.

A short message on the tabletop shone, telling me my account had been debited for half an hour of privacy as the force-field screen went up around us.

Lewis half-raised his face, but his hair, longer than it used to be, smoother, fell in his eyes, hiding him still.

"Would they have let me go? Would you?"

"You didn't have to disappear like that. They . . ."

". . . would have erased all my memories! Do you really think I wanted to forget!" And, with less passion, unexpected venom, he added: "Wasn't that part of the oath?"

Similar emotions rose in me. "Yes, the oath. That was it, then. You wanted to keep your memories, but forgo your duty?"

"What duty? Shape humanity into our reverse image?"

"Is that what you think we are doing?" I asked Lewis. For a second, a wild hope rose in me.

I went on, pretending that, despite our childhood stories, Grandmother's tales, everything we learned after the oaths, Lewis had just misunderstood our life's purpose.

I knew better. He was telling me he had forgotten nothing.

Lewis

"What we are doing is preserving hope, Lewis. And peace. We know what comes from humanity's tendencies to form communities . . ." Elza went on, trying to convince me. Why was it so important to her, to all of them?

I felt tired. I had come here, hoping for something else.

But I was already as caught up in it as her. "Don't you exist in a community?"

"It doesn't set us apart from them! We are part of their world, we work with them, live with them . . ."

The investigator in me asked before I could think of the consequences: "Find friends in them, like you did with Anna?"

Her gaze dropped back to her coffee.

To hide sorrow, I told myself. *That's all.*

"We have no right to choose peace for them. Peace comes with a price. They don't want to pay that price!" I told Elza, hoping she understood the warning, at least.

But all she listened to was my attack on her precious principles.

"They do not know, Lewis!"

"Yes! Exactly! They will never know if they don't learn."

"You swore, don't you remember? You swore *never again*."

"That's our family," I spat bitterly. "They never want to remember, never want to forget, never want to trust humanity to know how they are meddling in everyone's life, shaping them in our purpose!"

I had spent the previous hour in the Senate's archive room, watching the record of yesterday's session. Roland's mother had been scheduled to speak on the proposed Orealian variation.

The Orealian's constitution stated that all citizens were equal before the law, but that citizens were different from one another. In the smaller planet's case, it had to do with the differences between those who chose to live underwater and those who lived on satellites orbiting the planet's moon. First-Sonj had proposed to use this as a provisional agreement in the debate on Longers.

She hadn't been there to defend her position, though, too preoccupied with her son.

But her absence and its consequential rejection of her proposal weren't proof, and I needed proof.

I wanted not to find proof. Maybe I had misread her scarf's colors, and the way she had knotted it. Maybe they had changed the marks Grandmother taught us.

As if the Exiles knew what change was.

"Why does it have to be this way, Elza?" I cried out, frustrated beyond measure, caught between the same fight we had before I left, and my need to convince myself this case had nothing to do with the family, with her.

She's still wearing her damn scarf!

"Don't you think it's wrong that the families can't even question their right to choose for everyone else?" I tried to drown my own thoughts in words. "They commit their lives only to shaping others'! *You* won't commit, not even to . . ." *to me* "to something else, closed up in your nevermores. It's a prison, don't you see?"

Elza had changed, in ten years, had learned to calm down. *For whom?*

"You don't understand," she said, in a soft, nonjudgmental voice that hurt. She leaned forward, and I found myself inches from her. "We're not trying to shut them from their own experience. We're offering a prayer that never again will a people have to exile a part of their own in order to find peace."

She was interrupted by a soft, continuous beep.

I reached for my palmputer, hesitated for a second. Before I could switch it off, she said, "Go on. It must be important."

She was leaning back in her chair, her gaze lost on the whirling of energy of our privacy screen.

I hooked my palm to the tabletop, and started reading.

It was Anna Long-Karangel's autopsy report.

Before I could stop myself, I took her hand in mine.

She looked so calm, so far away. Did she know I'd just received the proof I needed?

"Why did you come here, Lewis?" she asked, softly, her gaze finally meeting mine.

She knows.

"Because a murder has been committed," I lied.

Her fingers traced silent words, on my palm. *Do what you have to do.*

Aloud, she urged me, her calm, resigned voice making a lie of her attempt: "Once you were one of us, you shared our goals. You swore, on the family fire . . ."

In one hand, I held the report, in the other, her fingers still caressed mine, aimlessly.

"I never betrayed it, Els. But I think you did. You all did. Generation after generation we listened to our history, and never heard the real, central point. . . ."

Common Memory

"Today, you are going to hear the story behind every tale I ever told you," Grandmother had said, on that long-ago evening, after the oaths had been sworn by the twenty-three young men and women. "Like every beginning, it starts with an ending."

Grandmother had stopped there, and they had wondered if she was all right. She seemed sad and resigned.

She hushed their concern with a familiar, impatient gesture.

"At the beginning there was no family like ours and the others you've met. It was a long, long time ago. Humanity was just starting to think of itself as one. Never before had all the people known how much of one, unique kind they were, never before had they been so connected to each other beyond their differences. And yet it came to pass that humanity fought itself like it never had before, relentlessly. You know the history of that time already, you've been taught by the families the many wars that almost destroyed this fragile awareness of being, beyond boundaries, of one race.

"By then the stars were within reach; it didn't change everything, but it changed enough."

Grandmother cleared her throat. The fire crackled in the hearth. Incense still hung in the air, even though the oath ceremony had taken place hours ago.

Elza and Lewis found each other's hands, in the semidarkness, and neither felt fear when Grandmother spoke again, in her storyteller's voice.

"The first wave of humanity left Earth, ship by ship. One of them was the *Exile*. Most launches were government approved and scientifically planned. This particular launch had been decided by politicians, prepared by scientists, but in perfect secrecy. That was the first vow. And it was kept.

"The *Exile* was the finest ship. Born of a divided country, it had benefited from the technological knowledge only a civil war could breed; it also carried all the knowledge available then in its data banks. Even records on the conflict had been added to it, every opinion, every interpretation of events. Only one piece of information was withheld from the future settlers: from which side of the conflict they came.

"For, you see, the three thousand and fifty who embarked on the *Exile* came in equal measure from both sides of the conflict. They were all volunteers. They all swore 'Nevermore,' and that was the second vow. Like the first, it was kept. For all of them, it was their only memory, upon waking in deep space. From the moment they had stepped on the ship, the rest of their memories had been erased and all they knew of their previous selves was that they had chosen to become part of the Exile tribe.

"They went to the stars as one, seeking a world to call their own.

"But during their trip, some found another goal. And that was the third oath you swore today."

Grandmother closed her eyes, briefly. When she opened them again, Lewis and Elza thought they saw tears. But Grandmother's voice was as strong as ever. "The families were born. What came after that is a tale of hide in plain sight and seek a particular path. You already know part of it. Now, if you so choose, you will learn the rest. Now, the choice is yours. Will you have your memory erased, and become part of the rest of humanity, or will you remain an exile, hidden in sight, a guardian of exiles' memories, against the future?"

None chose to have their memories erased. They were eager to learn more about the ties and purposes that bound their community together.

They would also start to understand the price of silence and protection, wrapped tightly like the strongest embrace around them, one that would turn deadly only to protect its dream—and its existence. Because to break their solemn vow would mean betraying everything they had grown up holding dear.

Elza

"It was about preserving life, first and foremost, Els. We forgot that over the generations." Lewis said softly.

The memories, the privacy screen . . . those were not enough to hold the world at bay.

He was clinging to his palmputer. He had tapped a short message before switching it off, and had taken up our conversation where he had left it.

I chose to pretend, too, for a little while longer, that it was just the two of us, and I argued back: "That's what we do: preserve life! And more! Preserve humanity's integrity!"

"By killing an innocent woman just so her lover's mother wouldn't be in the Senate to defend her proposal on differentiating the Longers before the law?"

I didn't answer.

"She might have changed her politics, upon knowing Anna better!" Lewis pressed on.

"She wouldn't have! They wanted to get married! The Lawriter said if they weren't, if Roland kept Anna as a discreet concubine, as it should be, she wouldn't oppose them, but that sterile unions were illegal!"

"Then her son would have changed . . ."

"Too late! Not certain!"

He looked at me for a long, long time. I thought I recognized that face. He was thinking deep, circling thoughts.

Yet, when he had disappeared without a word, without a trace, I had been the first surprised.

What do I know of his face, really? What of his loyalties?

He asked, very slowly, carefully, "But now . . . everyone is aware of their affair. It's all over the news, the crushed lover, ready to commit suicide because his be-

loved had been murdered by some Longer-hater, her
fragile neck so easily cut up in the symbol for 'no.' Everyone sees it as a new version of Romeo and Juliet.
They forget the union would have been a childless one,
in a time of demographic crisis."

"The possible rift is being sealed."

My voice lacked conviction. I was weary beyond words.

"But how many have you created?"

I watched him, not understanding his anger. "Do you
think I created new differences between humans . . . ?"
The thought was frightening.

"No!"

"You don't make sense, Lewis."

"I'm not talking about humanity, I'm talking about its
reality, about *humans*. How many people's hearts have
you ripped open with one death? Don't you know that
we never get over grief, we just learn to live with it?"

"I know."

Even when the dead rise up again, like you. . . .

The screen around us went down. Our half hour of
privacy was up, the tabletop informed me uselessly.

Guards, in the blue and silver of the Force, were waiting for us on the other side.

I reached for my scarf, fiddled with it while Lewis, in
a monochord voice, read me my rights.

When they took me, my scarf was completely red, tied
on the left side with two knots. My hands were empty
of rings.

*Mission accomplished—agent compromised—don't risk
a rescue.*

Lewis

The interrogation room was small and gray. A concrete
table, not quite large enough for two, one recorder, and

two chairs. Her hands, thoughtlessly stroking the place where a dragon ring had been, were mere centimeters from mine on the table. Soon, my boss would come, would demand to know how the interrogation was going, would ask for the tape I hadn't switched on yet.

She spoke before I did, before I could speak.

"I never thought you'd give me away, Lewis."

I didn't. You did.

But I didn't answer her. Because she didn't mean the murder. She was thanking me for keeping my oath, protecting the family's existence.

"Why did you do it, Elza? I thought she was your friend."

If I expected tears, I was disappointed. She was still the same girl I had grown up with. Harsher lines around the mouth deepened as she raised her chin, shadows veiled her eyes, but she faced me straight and square. "She was. The best I ever had."

"Then why? Why!"

"Not *how*, *why*?" Her voice had a faraway quality, as if she wondered out loud, but didn't expect an answer. Or didn't care anymore. "And yet it's the second one you should know the answer to."

"I know how," I told her. "We found traces of coffee in her veins. It was mixed with a slow poison. You were seen offering her a special brand of coffee, on Friday, when you left. Even Magyd heard you."

That's how you got caught. Not why.

I didn't ask her again, though. It was time to play the game.

I switched the recorder on.

She put on a good fight, as if she didn't want to speak, then, reluctantly, with a voice not her own, she painted a credible story, one of jealousy and envy.

Still the same girl. Ready to sacrifice everything for an oath. And blind enough to think I'm allowing her to do so for the sake of that oath.

Elza

I was alone in my cell, and all the others in Death's corridor were empty. In less than three days, they would fill the place with a toxic, painless gas. Roland's mother had told me it was too good for me. Roland had said nothing.

Sofia had cried, but remained true to the oath. Trying to rescue me would endanger them all.

I hadn't seen Lewis since my interrogation. But no one had come in search of my brethren, and no one had been suspicious of Sofia's visits, during the short trial. She hadn't spoken of the Investigator who was responsible for my arrest.

Everyone was safe.

When they had brought me here, this morning, I had welcomed the silence, the loneliness. I came believing this meeting with death would feel like a homecoming, after years as the knife and Edge of our family.

But death . . . my own death . . . *How can I leave the others with the burden, how can I trust them. . . .*

I stopped my thoughts, before they went any further. It was too late.

They say we shed masks before death. I hadn't realized they meant masks we didn't know from skin before shedding them.

I felt sick, trapped, but retching, giving in to the body's pain didn't stop the thoughts, the feelings.

Death crowded me, choked me, and even that was an affirmation of life.

I don't want to go!

I had slept, after hours of crying and screaming in the dark, my dignity saved only by the soundproof walls of my cell, the emptiness of the place.

Morning had come through the window just as I opened gritty, puffy eyes.

I'm almost dead. This time, the thought rang empty in my tired bones, my too-tight skin.

The words were on my lips before I was aware of it.

I repeated them, over and over, keeping through the meaningless, repetitive sound nausea and panic at bay.

Lewis

I locked the first door, and started down the long corridor that led to her cell. I stopped, the different keys in my hand, sorted through them briefly and put the others back in my vest pocket. With a trembling hand, I opened her cell. Her voice greeted me, with familiar words.

For a second, I actually wondered why I couldn't hear the others. But that had been years before, before we were told the story of the Exiles, before words pieced together the dreams and beliefs we grew up with into a net of obligations and choices that shouldn't have been ours to bear nor make.

I wanted to leave, wondered why I was pouring salt on such an old wound, and took one step forward.

The door closed silently behind me.

She didn't stop.

Those words . . . *I will never betray the trust, the name, the shelter of my tribe.*

Why was she throwing those words at me?

I will never forget, I will never remember.

She stood, repeating the oath I had broken. I waited for her to make a move, anger stopping the words I had come here to say.

When her voice died out and she was still standing by the window, I finally understood that she hadn't been aware of my presence. I turned on my heels, ready to leave.

"Lewis?"

Her voice sounded so fragile. Uncertain.

I couldn't help it. I turned back and took three, quick steps, until she was one breath away. My fists were clenched, at my sides.

Her black, long hair hung on her smooth, brown shoulders. Her face was turned toward mine.

"I had to come," I told us both.

"Thank you for what you did."

She seemed smaller somehow. Almost gone.

"You were wrong, Elza," I told her.

"We just disagree . . ."

"That's not what I meant. About me forsaking our cause. I just don't serve it the same way you do. Life . . ."

I opened my hand. The key had made a small indent mark on my palm. I could feel my flesh more tender under its light weight.

"Come with me, Els."

She closed her hand over mine. Her head nodded, once, twice, and my heart started beating again.

"I can't," was what she said. It took three more heartbeats for her words to sink in.

"Why?"

"I can't. I'm already too much of a liability for our family. If I disappear, they might follow the trail. . . ."

I didn't want to feel anymore, not anger and despair anyway.

My hands captured her face and I drowned in her.

The key fell at our feet.

Against her swollen, teasing lips, I whispered, "I missed you. So much."

"You're not alone anymore," she murmured, and I wondered how such a strange woman could read my heart so easily. Her shoulders were as smooth as I remembered them under my thumbs. Hungry for her, for the eternity of her, I captured her lips again with mine, let my hands settle on her waist until she melted into me.

Everything was new, time had stopped and started again. *Never forget. Never remember.*

Again she spoke, and brought me back to my senses.

"You don't have to live like this, alone. Come back to the family."

Alone . . .

"You don't have to die like this, Els. Come with me. . . ."

She bent down, picked up the key, and put it back in my hand.

We stood for the longest time, each lost on our side of the rift. I wondered if someone, somewhere, worked to close such rifts, as she believed she did those between communities.

In the end, it didn't matter.

In the end, Elza and I made our choices, like everybody must. And nobody ever came to rescue us from ourselves.

Jihane Noskateb lives in Paris with a black cat and enough coffee cups to fill a museum, or her sink. Her previous short story, "A Ghost Story," appeared in ReVisions *in 2004. Since then, she put a history Ph.D. on hold and found a part-time job in order to spend more time working on her stories. Apart from writing, the author's obsessions range from Greek Antiquity to SF and fantasy in all their forms. Odd beasts like Darwinism, soap operas, and French rock stars join the circus and usually end up in her stories. Recycling is, after all, important.*

You can find more about her at www.mapage. noos.fr/jihanoskateb.

THE DANCER AT THE RED DOOR

Douglas Smith

The city has a song.
Its rhythm, a million broken hearts . . .

ALEXANDER KING FIRST met the Dancer on the day the street people began to glow.

He drove to his office in downtown Toronto early that July morning in his newest toy, a vintage Jaguar XKE, dark red with black leather seats—a toy he'd always wanted, and one of which he'd already tired. He pondered this as he parked in his reserved spot beneath the building of blue glass and silvered steel that bore his name. Riding his private elevator to the penthouse executive floor, he felt a strange unease awakening with the day.

He met first with his management team to finalize the acquisition of a competitor. They sat in his office, walls hung with original Tissot drawings he'd once loved. Before signing the takeover papers, he noted both the concessions he'd won and the absence of any pleasure in reaching a goal that had consumed much of his considerable energy for seven months.

He ordered the sale of the one profitable plant in the acquisition, and the closing of the remaining operations. But it didn't bring him the rush that exercising new power normally did. He felt none of the usual thrill of moving the pieces in the game. *His* game.

With a growing disquiet, he focused on his senior staff sitting around the huge teak table. He'd picked his team early in their careers, molding them into business weapons for his corporate arsenal. It came more as confirmation than surprise that he no longer felt pride in them.

After the meeting, he had his assistant clear his calendar for the morning. She closed his large oak office door as she left. Unfolding his tall, well-exercised frame from his chair, he moved to the window to stare down absently at the busy intersection of Wellington and University thirty floors below.

His toys, his deals, his people. Not a good sign, he mused, when the surest symbols of success in your chosen life bring you no happiness whatsoever.

And with that thought, in that moment, he accepted what a secret part of him had known for some time—that he was totally, utterly tired of his world, the world he had built and in which he ruled.

The only fear King had ever known had been of finding a game he couldn't win. He had never expected to become bored by the game. But it had happened.

Well, then he needed a new game.

No. He needed the *right* game.

His reflection, steel-gray eyes under steel-gray hair, stared back but offered no answers. Brooding on his dark epiphany, he gazed at the street below, not focusing on any detail, just letting the patterns of people and traffic skitter across his eyes like a kaleidoscope of random intents. He was about to turn away when a flash of light caught his attention.

On the sidewalk across the street, a man sat against the building, a hat set out in front of him. A street person—one of the army of the homeless that posted its soldiers at every corner of the downtown core.

A street person who was on fire.

King rubbed his eyes. No, not on fire, but glowing. Glowing so brightly that he obliterated surrounding details of the building and passersby.

And no one hurrying past paid him the slightest notice.

Seized by a sudden impulse, King grabbed his suit jacket and took the elevator to street level.

The day was already hot and humid, the air sticky and stinking with exhaust fumes, something he hadn't noticed going from the cool comfort of his house to car to office. He loosened his silk tie and undid the top button of his tailored shirt as he crossed the street. Scanning the far side for the glowing man, King found him now standing. No sign of the strange light remained.

King reached the opposite sidewalk and stopped. This is ridiculous, he thought. He began to turn away, to return to his air-conditioned office and suddenly unwanted life, when he stopped again.

The man was now staring at him. And smiling.

Taken aback but curious again, King walked over. The man wore tattered clothes of competing colors of dirt and held a short-brimmed cloth hat in surprisingly clean hands. His long hair was pure white, combed and untangled. His face was lined, but as clean as his hands. Black eyes, bright and sharp, stared narrowly from above a hooked nose and under snowy eyebrows. He continued to smile at King.

"Do I know you?" King asked, uncomfortable to be conversing with someone so far beneath his own station.

The man didn't answer. Instead, he raised his left hand in a fist in front of King's face. King stepped back, thinking that the man was threatening him. But the beggar simply stood there, fist poised. The back of his raised hand bore a tattoo—a red rectangle within a black one. The red was deep and bright, so shiny that it looked wet, like a patch of blood.

Staring at the tattoo, King felt a tingle of familiarity, mixed with fear. He swallowed. Get a grip, he thought. "I asked you if you know me," he repeated.

Still not answering, the man lowered his hand and turned to stare up University Avenue.

Angered at a street person ignoring him, King started to turn away when a sound made him stop. Notes, a tune, a song. Yes, a song. He scanned the passersby, expecting to find a headset dangling from nearby ears, volume cranked to maximum. To his surprise, the song didn't change in intensity, no matter what direction he turned. He became aware then of a deep bass pounding, a dancelike rhythm slowly rising out of the pavement and trembling up his legs.

A swirl of color and movement caught his eye. He turned.

And she appeared.

The Dancer.

He called her the Dancer the moment he saw her, and the moment he saw her, he knew that she was mad. Or *he* was. She spun into view around the nearest corner, then froze for a second, en pointe as in ballet, arms raised in two graceful arcs. Then she leaped, landing to waltz through the crowd as if the sidewalk were a ballroom and each scurrying commuter her partner. And with each pirouette, madness whirled around her like dead leaves caught in a forgotten winter wind.

She wore only a diaphanous gown of some strange material that changed color and shape as she whirled, sometimes concealing, sometimes revealing, sometimes seeming to disappear completely. The body it revealed was slim and lithe, with firm breasts, long arms and legs, with hair as red as rusted metal, and skin so fair and pale it seemed to glow.

He realized then that the Dancer *was* glowing, just as the old beggar had been. The glow enveloped her in a cocoon of light. In that cocoon, King caught fractured glimpses of a dark moonlit world that was not the bland sun-bright cityscape in which he now stood.

And as with the old man, no one but King seemed to notice the Dancer. People shuffled by like the undead, blinking at the sun finally rising over the towers, newspapers clutched like amulets, briefcases hanging like manacles, coffee sucked from cups as if it were their life blood. At some level, they were aware of her, as they'd move aside for her, always in step somehow, but they paid her no more attention than if she were a puddle to avoid.

Remembering the strange old man, King turned. He was gone. King caught a flash of white hair farther down the street, but then it was lost in the crowd.

And lost in the face of the Dancer as she stopped before King, a face that swept the crowds and traffic and buildings from his eyes and mind, not by its beauty, for he couldn't call her beautiful, but by its strangeness. Skin too pale, hair too red, mouth too wide. And green eyes that wandered over him as if searching for something.

But when she smiled at him with those eyes and that mouth, a hope and a fear reached inside him and twisted in opposite directions. A hope that she was real, that somehow she held the key to a door to a new life. And a fear that she *was* mad, that he was trapped in a life he suddenly hated and could never . . .

". . . escape," he whispered, before realizing it.

She laughed, a thing of cold breezes rustling barren trees on winter nights. "You wish to escape me?" she asked, smiling up at him. "So soon?" Her glow was gone, and she now wore a plain green cotton shift and white low-heeled shoes.

"No . . . no," King stammered. "Not you. My life." Embarrassed, he held out his hand. "My name is Alexander King."

In reply, the Dancer turned and spun back up the street. King stood dazed for a second, then hurried to catch up. He found that he had to almost trot to stay beside her.

"So you wish to escape life?" she asked, spinning as they went, still ignored by everyone but King. "Do you seek death, then?"

"No. I . . . I wish to escape *my* life. My world." Despite the crush of commuters, he felt as if he were alone with this strange woman. They reached the corner of University and King Street.

"Then you seek another world?" she asked, whirling around him as they waited for the traffic light.

He grimaced. "I'm not sure. Yes. Something new. Different."

The light changed. The Dancer crossed, weaving through the crowd, sometimes even hooking the arm of someone she passed and spinning around with them as if in a square dance.

And still no one paid her any notice.

King followed her to the stairs leading down to the subway. She seemed to float down the steps, while King, feeling quite dazed, almost slipped hurrying to catch her.

Waltzing up to the ticket booth, she raised her arms, spun twice, then leaped gracefully over the turnstiles. The staffer in the booth paid her no attention. Swearing, King dug into his pocket for change. By the time he'd paid and reached the subway platform, the Dancer was boarding a northbound train. He jumped on just as the doors closed.

Apparently indifferent to whether he had followed, the Dancer wove through the crowded car, each swaying step melding with the rattling rhythm of the train. Despite the number of people standing, she found an empty seat at the rear.

King jostled his way to the back and sat down beside her. The train's air conditioning was losing the battle against the heat and humidity, and the air was heavy with the stink of commuter sweat and boredom. But here in the closeness, he could smell her scent—delicate, bittersweet, reminiscent of a night-blooming flower he couldn't recall. He started to ask her name, but then stopped, suddenly not wanting to know, not wanting something as elemental as this creature to be labeled with the mundane. To him, she would remain the Dancer.

"This city has a song," she said suddenly.

He stared at her. She *was* mad, totally disconnected from reality. He should get off at the next stop and go back.

But back to what? King himself *wanted* to disconnect from his own reality, to find a new one. He wanted the Dancer to be real, so he didn't have to return to his old life.

The train pulled into the next station, Osgoode. He sighed. He stayed.

As the train left Osgoode, he turned back to her. Her smile froze him for a second. God, she *was* beautiful.

How could he have thought otherwise before? He felt a tightening in his crotch. Well, another reason to stay.

"Fine, you've dragged me this far," he said. "I'll play a bit longer. What song?"

She raised an eyebrow. "Can't you hear it? It's deafening to me."

Mad. He shook his head in reply.

She stared at the passengers. "A million broken hearts beat its rhythm. Whispered lies, unheeded cries scribble its lyrics on walls, their meaning lost in the babble, in the magnitude of the choir. Melody . . . No." She laughed, a bitter sound. "No. There is no melody."

She watched the dark tunnel walls flashing by the car's window. "And in a minor key." She smiled. "Yes. Definitely a minor key."

The train pulled into the next station, St. Patrick. People shuffled off, jostling with those getting on. The train pulled out again. The Dancer stared at the passengers. So did King. A different crowd now, but with the same air of futility.

"Do you hear it now?" she asked again. "The song?"

Still King didn't reply. He had no answers for this odd creature. He had hoped that she would provide *him* with answers—that, in all her strangeness, *she* was the answer.

Finally, he replied with a question, the only question that seemed to matter.

"Can you help me?" he asked, embarrassed by the desperation in his voice.

In reply, she raised a hand, palm toward her face. King stared at the mark on the back of her hand, the same mark the old man had carried—a blood-red rectangle within a larger black one.

"Find the Red Door," she whispered.

As King stared at the symbol, the words "the Red Door" resonated in some secret chamber in his memory, and a cold dread grew in his gut, dread of the place the words were taking him.

The train slowed. The Dancer rose in one flowing movement, no superfluous motion, her body seemingly freed from gravity and inertia, oblivious to the lurching of the subway. King remained seated, gripped by the sudden terror spawned by the symbol on her hand. Unable even to speak, he watched her walk to the door.

The train stopped.

Finally, King forced a word out. "How?" he rasped.

She turned back, surprise on her face, as if she'd already forgotten him.

"Listen for the song," she said. "At the end of day, follow the song." The doors opened, and with one last look back, she was gone.

Finally shaking free of his fear, King jumped up, but the doors had closed, and the train was moving again. His face pressed to the window, he caught a glimpse of the Dancer alone on a dark empty platform, gazing after him sadly. Then his car entered the tunnel, and he was left with nothing but the memory of her face, her smell, and their strange conversation.

And of the terror of the red symbol that was slowly fading like a nightmare retreating before the dawn, replaced by a fear that he'd never see the Dancer again.

He jumped off at the next stop, Queen's Park, ran across the platform and onto a southbound train that was just leaving. The train seemed to crawl along as he prayed that he'd catch the Dancer before she disappeared.

The train pulled into the next station. King jumped off. And froze, staring at the station name on the pale green tiled walls.

St. Patrick.

The Dancer had left him at the stop after St. Patrick.

King had got off at the next stop, Queen's Park, and taken a train south one stop to this station.

Two stops northbound, one stop southbound.

He shook his head. Impossible. He must have missed a stop coming south, lost in his thoughts.

King didn't travel the subway much, avoiding mixing with the masses, so perhaps his memory of the stations was wrong. A nearby pillar displayed the subway map. Finding St. Andrew where they had entered, he ran a finger up the University line. St. Andrew, then Osgoode, St. Patrick—and Queen's Park.

King swallowed. The Dancer had left him at a station that didn't exist.

He stood staring at the sign. Trains came and left. People pushed by him. He ignored them. For the second time that day, King felt afraid.

An urge to flee overwhelmed him. A southbound train pulled in. Near panic, he shoved his way inside. He sat down heavily, legs shaking, heart pounding, as the train pulled out.

His pride saved him. What if one of his people saw him? Or a competitor? With the same iron will that had built his empire, King forced calm on himself.

He leaned back, his fear slowly dying with each rattle of the rushing train. By the time he got off at St. Andrew, his terror had faded to a pale ghost that finally vanished completely in the sunlight and commonplace bustle on the street, leaving him with only anger at his display of fear.

And anger at the Dancer. At being toyed with, then abandoned.

Rejected.

And King wasn't a man who handled rejection well. He headed back to his office, thinking darkly of the Dancer. As he did, every detail of their short time together, every movement she'd made, every word she'd spoken, every look she'd cast his way, rushed back as if he had just lived them again. In that moment, he desired the Dancer more than he'd ever desired anything in his life. And what King desired, he acquired.

He'd found his new game.

> *The city has a song.*
> *Its lyrics, whispered lies and unheeded cries,*
> *Their meaning lost, in the babble,*
> *In the magnitude of the choir.*

Back in his office, King closed his door. It wasn't simply lust for the Dancer that drove him. She had shown him a secret world, one hiding behind the everyday, a dance step left of reality, a half beat off the rhythm of his now unwanted life. That strange creature was the key to the door to that world.

Sitting at his desk, he removed a cherry wood box from a drawer. Inside were business cards acquired over the years. He began flipping through them. He rarely consulted these anymore, relying on electronic lists. But the red symbol had awakened a memory.

U, V, W. He was nearing the back of the box. X, Y, Z.

King sat back, disappointed. It wasn't there.

Yet he remembered holding the card in his hand. In that memory, torchlight reflected off black walls, black ceiling, black floor.

Black.

His eyes returned to the box. At the very back, a small black triangle peeked above the divider behind the 'Z's. With shaking hands, King grasped the corner of the hidden card and removed it.

The card was expensive stock, completely black in a

matte finish that gave back no reflection at any angle. He turned it over.

On the same black background, a blood-red rectangle stared at him. No lettering. No name or address. No phone or e-mail. Just the same red symbol that the old man and Dancer bore on the back of their hands. But unlike the black, the red was shiny, so shiny it looked wet, so shiny that if he . . .

He touched it. Gasping, he dropped the card on the desk.

The red had felt . . . sticky.

He looked at his finger. Nothing. King swallowed. Angry with himself, he picked up the card and ran his finger over the red.

And remembered.

Fragments from an evening, not so long ago. King's table at his private club. Dinner with a woman lawyer representing a company King wished to acquire. Negotiations. Success. Sipping a sweet dessert wine. Pleased at closing the deal. And so quickly, so easily.

The lawyer mentioning that her client belonged to an even more exclusive dinner club. King, stung by the discovery of a club he'd never been invited to join, pressing her for details. The lawyer finally offering to take King there.

Then his memories of that evening got . . . fuzzy . . .

A cavernous room . . . torch light . . . black shiny surfaces everywhere . . . incense mixing with smells of roasting meat. A man talking to him . . . a powerful man . . . speaking of mysteries . . . of things King had never imagined existed in this city . . . a strange society . . . a world of power hiding beneath the mundane, alongside the everyday, behind . . .

Behind the Red Door.

His hand shaking, King dropped the card on his desk. He swallowed.

The Red Door was a private club. *Very* private. And he'd been there.

Why couldn't he remember more of that evening? And why were the fragments he could recall tinged with the same fear he'd felt in the subway?

Of course. He nodded to himself.

Power. There was power here. King understood power. He moved with the powerful. He was one of them. He could sense power and knew to fear it, especially one hidden, one *he* didn't hold.

Well, one he didn't hold *yet*. He slipped the card into a pocket. He *would* find the Red Door. He *would* be admitted to this club.

But how?

The Dancer. She was his key. What had she said, just before she'd left the train?

Follow the song. At the end of day.

The song.

It was then that King realized that he couldn't recall a single note from the strange song that had accompanied the Dancer's appearance. He summoned his memories of her, hoping they would recall the song to him. Her face, her mouth, her smell, the curve of her breasts and hips.

As those pieces came together, the first hint of the song returned—the beat he had felt rising up from the sidewalk. He remembered her body swaying to that rhythm. As he did, a few notes returned to him, then more, until finally the entire song pounded in his skull with all its original clarity and force.

Afraid to lose the song again, King played it in his head the rest of the day, even tapping its rhythm during meetings he led with detached interest. Late that evening, he rode the elevator to street level, still humming the song.

Follow the song, at the end of day, she had said.

Standing on the sidewalk and following a hunch, he faced north up University. His eyes settled on the subway entrance. The music flared louder in his head.

Smiling, he headed for the station and boarded a northbound train. At St. Patrick, he stood. The next station would be the phantom stop where the Dancer had left. Confident that the song was leading him to a secret path, he moved toward the doors.

Then he felt it—the fear that had seized him just before the Dancer had disappeared.

Shaking and weak, King grabbed at a pole. He sank into a seat, unable to move.

The train emerged from the tunnel into a dimly lit cavern. As his fear grew in his gut, the song began to fade. The cavern flickered in and out of existence, replaced intermittently by gray tunnel walls.

Anger saved him. He was losing his chance to enter a secret circle of power. Perhaps his only chance. What if he could never recall the song again? All because of some foolish fear.

King focused on the song, pulling it back into his head. As its music grew louder, his fear faded, and the cavern outside the train returned.

The train stopped. King gripped the pole beside his seat and pulled himself up on still trembling legs. The doors slid open with a venomous hiss.

No other passenger made any move to leave. King seemed to be the only person aware that the train had stopped at a station that wasn't supposed to exist.

The alarm signaling that the doors were about to close sounded, not the normal ding-dong chiming, but rather a deep ominous gong. As the doors began to slide together, King took a deep breath and stepped onto the platform. The doors closed behind him, and before he had time to regret his decision, the train was gone.

He looked around.

This "station" was a huge domed cavern, carved from a stone as black and shiny as obsidian, flickering redly under sputtering torches set in high sconces. It smelled of dampness and smoke. The platform was now a pier of blackened timbers that creaked under his feet. A gurgling sound made him turn.

Where the subway tracks should have lain, a dark river now flowed, thick and murky. Something large passed by just under its surface. King jumped back from the edge.

Seeing no other path, he set out along the pier. Still inside the huge cavern, the pier followed the river for what seemed miles. As he walked, King felt as if downtown Toronto was falling behind him by more than just the length of his strides. Finally, the dank smells of the cavern gave way to fresh sea air, and King stepped out onto a mist-shrouded beach of blue sand bordering an inky lake.

Beneath a full moon glaring crimson in a strange starless sky, a huge pyramid of rough-hewn black stone loomed over the entire scene. It looked to be a mix of Mayan and Incan, and something King couldn't place. Beyond the pyramid lay a dark jungle, lush with huge exotic plants shining black in the moonlight and rustling in a wind unfelt by King.

As King's eyes fell on the pyramid, the song flared louder in his head. Somewhat reassured, he set out for the structure, weaving his way between large blue crystal spheres that lay scattered on the sand, something black and spiny throbbing inside of each.

Broad steps led up to the pyramid's summit. King began to climb. Three hundred steps later, he stood at the top, sweat-soaked. Before him squatted a boxlike building, barren of any markings save a single door, set in the center of the wall facing King.

The Red Door.

Trembling from the climb and expectation, King approached it. The Door shone ruddy and glistening in the moonlight. King hesitated, then raised his hand and knocked.

The sound boomed back at him, startling him with its volume. The echoes continued for several breaths, reverberating from the dark pyramid, until finally fading like the last heartbeats of some great dying beast.

A peephole opened in the Door. Eyes peered out at King, midnight black floating in bloodshot whites.

His hand shaking, King reached into his pocket and held up the black-and-red card.

The eyes narrowed. The peephole closed.

Then . . . nothing happened.

King stood there, near to panic. Should he run? Should he knock again?

As he was about to flee down the steps, metal screamed against metal and a heavy bolt slid back.

The Red Door opened slowly inward, revealing only darkness.

King stepped forward into a low-ceilinged corridor slanting downwards and lit by torches. He was alone, yet he saw no place where the doorman could have gone. He set out down the passageway.

A strange script covered the walls. Whenever his gaze fell on it, the song in his head suddenly incorporated tortured cries within its music. After that, he kept his eyes ahead, away from the walls. As he descended deeper into the pyramid, the dripping of water added a dismal back beat to his echoing footsteps.

Finally, he heard voices and laughter ahead of him. And music, not the song that still played in his head, but a strange discordant melody. The corridor ended, and he stepped out.

He gasped, remembering. He'd been here before.

The city has a song.
Its melody—no. There is no melody.
And in a minor key. Definitely, a minor key.

King stood at the top of a broad carpeted staircase above a huge ballroom. The room was cavernous, fifty yards wide by a hundred long with a vaulted ceiling, carved from the shiny black rock. Torches set in high sconces washed the scene in a bloody glow. A large oval dance floor, capable of holding a hundred people at least, dominated the room.

The dance floor was empty, but at scores of tables surrounding it, men in tuxedos or tails and women in formal evening gowns talked and laughed, ate and drank. All wore masks—some simple eye coverings, others ornate and grotesque. Smoke from the torches mixed with the fumes from incense burners lining the dance floor.

Heavy red curtains covered the wall at the far end. Two attendants dressed as footmen stood at each end of the curtains beside draw ropes.

Although many people glanced up at King, no one paid him any particular attention. Deciding it best to act as if he belonged, he straightened his tie, buttoned his jacket, and descended the steps.

A man separated himself from the crowd and approached. He wore the formal attire of a Victorian gentleman and a boar's head mask. He removed the mask. Long white hair. Black eyes, bright and sharp. A hooked nose under snowy eyebrows.

The street person who had appeared to be on fire.

King swallowed, again shaken by the strangeness of it all.

But the man smiled and extended a hand. "Mr. King! Delighted that you have found us once again. Might I inquire how you managed it?" The man had a cultured English accent.

"The Dancer," King mumbled, looking around in near panic. "The song . . ."

The man's smile broadened. "Ah, yes," he said, apparently pleased with this answer. "I recall your affinity with the Song from your first visit. Come. Join me."

Taking King's arm, the man guided him the length of the room to where the tables and the polished hardwood of the dance floor ended twenty yards from the red curtains. The remaining space consisted of a raised dais of rough black stone. A pattern of concentric circles was carved into the dais, with spokes radiating outwards from the innermost circle. Below the dais where each spoke ended, a golden goblet stood.

King's host motioned him to a table in front of the dais. They sat. A woman dressed only in a loincloth and a leopard-head mask brought red wine and a steaming roast with a large carving knife. King's host offered him a cigar, lit one himself, and leaned back.

"My name is Beroald," he said, with the same air that King used when giving his own name. This was a powerful man. But a street person?

"You know me?" King asked.

Beroald puffed on his cigar. "We met on your first visit."

King nodded. He *had* been here before. "What is this place? A private club?"

Beroald laughed, a dry throaty sound. King tried to guess his age but failed. "We consider ourselves more of a society. The Society of the Red Door. But like a private club, a society with its privileges."

King's fear of this strange place disappeared. This was what he had come for. He leaned forward. "Such as?"

Beroald smiled. "Watch." He clapped his hands.

Four musicians dressed as medieval minstrels wound their way through the tables. With another jolt of surprise, King recognized them as squeegee kids who accosted him for money whenever he stopped at a light near his office. Two carried mandolins, one a saxophone, and the last a set of bongos. Taking chairs just below the dais, they set up to play.

Beroald clapped again.

The curtains drew back, revealing a dark opening in the black stone wall, like the mouth of a cave. In that mouth, King could feel, more than see, something moving, watching.

"And finally . . ." Beroald said, nodding back toward the front of the room.

King turned to look. At the top of the carpeted staircase stood a figure.

The Dancer.

She wore the ever-changing diaphanous gown from that morning, a morning from a lifetime ago. As the Dancer descended the stairs, the torches on the walls died, and the flames in the burners surrounding the dance floor leaped higher, casting the tables into shadow. The Dancer spun the length of the floor, past King and Beroald, to stand silently before the dark opening, eyes unfocused.

She raised her hands above her head, and the squeegee band began to play the now familiar song. At the first note, the opening quivered like a black membrane, then vomited a thick fog. Inside the dark mist, a misshapen form skittered into the room.

The Dancer began to dance. And glow. Her glow grew with each spin she made, each leap she took, until it lit the room and, finally, penetrated the dark mist.

And King could see the thing that had emerged from the opening.

•

The creature moved on six multijointed legs set below a body resembling the carapace of a huge beetle, black and shiny. Dark scales protected a short neck and a bulbous head. Long pincers extended from each side of a slitlike mouth writhing in a horrible parody of a human face. The thing measured at least ten feet from its head to the end of a barbed tail.

Red multifaceted eyes took in the diners. Suddenly, it scrambled forward.

King jumped up, ready to flee, but Beroald put a hand on his arm. "Watch," he said.

The Dancer spun closer. The creature turned toward her. It stopped. The music played, and the Dancer danced. As she moved, the thing stood transfixed, swaying, red eyes locked on her, hypnotized by the spell she wove with her body.

The two curtain attendants, each holding long knives, approached the beast. The nearest drew his arm back, poised to strike.

The Dancer slipped.

It was a small thing, a muscle twitch out of rhythm with the song, but King felt it, as if the dance were a living thing and had skipped a heartbeat.

It was enough to free the creature from the Dancer's spell. Wheeling on the nearest knife wielder, the thing severed the man's head with a snap of its pincers, then turned toward the diners. People screamed and jumped up, King and Beroald included.

The Dancer leaped between them, in control of her every movement again. The beast froze, captured by her dancing once more. The second attendant closed on the creature, and with a smooth precise motion, slipped his blade between the scales around the beast's throat. The creature spasmed once, then slumped to the floor.

Thick blood spewed from the wound, a red so dark it

seemed black. It flowed along the channels carved in the stone into the goblets set around the dais. When it stopped, the table attendants collected the goblets and began circulating among the tables.

As they did, the Dancer ran the length of the room, up the staircase and disappeared through a side archway. Beroald glared after her, then motioned for King to sit again.

King sat, trembling, trying again to control an urge to flee. The leopard-headed woman poured some of the blood into Beroald's and King's glasses. Beroald raised his and took a deep drink.

King stared at him in disgust. Beroald smiled, blood glistening on his lips. He leaned forward. "Do you recall anything of your first visit?"

King shook his head, not trusting himself to speak.

"How you felt afterward? The state of your health?"

The sweet smell of the blood reached King then. And he remembered. A host of minor ailments disappearing, a burst of energy for the next week. He looked at his glass, then at Beroald.

Beroald smiled. "The secret of the Red Door, Mr. King. The privilege that I spoke of."

King swallowed. "Immortality?" he asked, not believing what he was asking.

Beroald shrugged. "Who knows? A cure for all known ills and a very long life, to that I can attest."

"What I just saw . . ."

"A ritual, but a practical one. The creatures beyond that black portal may be killed solely by a thrust through a solitary and minute gap in their armor, a strike so precise that it can be executed only if the creature is immobile. The Dancer performs that function for us." Beroald paused. "Preferably more reliably than tonight."

A red-faced man with long white sideburns leaned

over from an adjacent table. "Three times this month, Beroald. Three times!"

"I'm dealing with it, Shelby," Beroald replied, his voice icy. The other man paled and turned back to his own table.

Smiling again, Beroald raised his glass in a toast. "To our health, Mr. King. Quite literally."

King looked at the glass of blood before him, struggling to assimilate all he'd just witnessed and learned.

"The efficacy of the blood," Beroald continued, "lasts but a short while."

Immortality, King thought. He raised his glass. He drank.

Sweetness. Heat. Then . . .

A dam bursting inside him . . . a hidden lake released . . . his being flooded with rivers of vitality . . . freed from every bodily pain.

King gasped. He felt wonderful. He felt strong. He felt . . .

Powerful.

He laughed, and Beroald joined him. They roared with laughter, slapping each other on the back. At last, King sat back, wiping away tears of laughter, sipping the rest of the blood, reveling in his newfound vigor. Finally, he asked the question that he feared to raise, but for which he now had to have an answer.

"Beroald, will you accept me as a member here?"

Beroald smiled. "As I said, the Society of the Red Door is not a club. None of us may give or deny admittance. We are each here simply because we found a path to the Door, and can find it again whenever we desire."

King's hopes leapt. "Then I can return?"

Beroald's smile disappeared. "I fear not."

King felt a surge of fear and anger. "Why not? I found a path."

Beroald waved a hand in a dismissive gesture. "Ah, but could you find it again? The Song led you tonight. But the Song plays for one soul and one soul only—the Dancer."

"Yet it played for me," King argued.

Beroald frowned. "No doubt your unprecedented exposure to our lady today fooled the Song into accepting you tonight. Indeed, you still reek of her." Beroald wrinkled his nose, and King wondered at this remark. "But, I assure you, it will not play for you again."

King turned to where the Dancer had disappeared. "Why does it play only for her?"

Beroald shrugged again. "Who knows? The Song will pass to another only upon her death, which is happily unlikely, given her access to the elixir." Beroald rose. "Now I must pay my respects to some friends. It has been a pleasure." Shaking King's hand, he moved to another table.

Oblivious to conversations around him, King sat there stunned, imagining his freshly won vitality draining out of him with every heartbeat. To discover immortality and then to lose it . . .

No! He would *not* let this happen. He belonged here, among the elite, the powerful. There must be a way.

In front of him, the carving knife still lay beside the roast. King stared at the knife. He picked it up. The blade was sharp, slicing through the bloody meat easily. When no one was watching, he wiped the knife clean with his napkin and carefully slid it up his sleeve. He sat there trembling for a moment, then he rose.

Walking the length of the room, he climbed the stairs and went through the alcove where the Dancer had disappeared. He found himself on an outdoor terrace, halfway up the pyramid.

Beside a low stone wall at the terrace's edge, staring

up at the red moon and the strange starless sky, stood the Dancer. He touched her elbow. She cried out and drew away, staring at him with wild, clouded eyes. Then a look of recognition danced over her face.

"You came," she whispered.

She flew into his arms, kissing him hard, twining her fingers in his hair, forcing his mouth onto hers. She pulled back. "Free me," she whispered.

"What?"

"Take me away from here. Never to return," she pleaded.

King shook his head. "Are you mad? The Red Door offers freedom from death."

She laughed bitterly. "This place offers many things, but freedom is not among them."

King pushed her away. "I wish to return here, not leave."

The Dancer looked at him, her shoulders slumping. "You will not free me?"

He ignored her. "Can you teach me to find the path to this place?"

"I don't know the way," she said, her voice a dead thing. "I know only the Song."

"Then teach me the Song."

She stared silently at the dark jungle below. Then she straightened, as if reaching a decision. She turned back to him. "I cannot teach it, but I can give it to you."

"How?"

She stroked the outline of the knife under his sleeve. He stiffened. Drawing out the knife, she pushed its grip into his now shaking hand, its tip resting beneath her sternum.

"Free me, as you planned," she said, looking up into his eyes.

The Song will pass to another only upon her death.

"Freedom for me. Immortality for you," she said softly, pressing closer to him until the tip of the knife cut through her thin gown and into her pale flesh.

"Free me," she said again. A patch of blood blossomed around the wound.

Immortality. Only upon her death.

"Free me!" she cried.

Immortality.

With a sob, King stepped forward, thrusting the blade up and into the Dancer. She spasmed, and her head jerked backward. Blood gushed from her chest, soaking her once-beautiful gown and King's hands and shirt. Crying out, he pushed her from him, and she slumped to the cold stone, no longer something elemental, just a dead thing.

What had he done? King stumbled away from her in horror.

And the Song exploded in him.

Before, it had often been so faint he could barely hear it. Now it pounded in his skull, filled his entire being. His very heartbeat seemed to match its rhythm. Beneath the music, he heard a chanting, whispers born in hidden places, words strange and sinister, rasped in cruel guttural tones from throats not human. A paralyzing cold crept into King's limbs. They felt numb, no longer under his control. His legs began to twitch. His arms jerked.

He began to dance.

He twirled around the terrace, leaping over the corpse of the Dancer, his toes drawing patterns in her blood. He kept dancing, unable to stop, even when Beroald entered.

Beroald looked down at the body of the Dancer. He smiled. He spoke.

> *"These are fools that wish to die!*
> *Is't not fine to dance and sing*

When the bells of death do ring?"

He turned to King and laughed. "She had become . . . unreliable, as you saw tonight. She would have killed herself, but the Song would not allow it. Any of us would have killed her, but again, there was the Song. On the death of a Dancer, it inhabits the *nearest* person. And none of us wish to know the Song that intimately." He looked at King who was still spinning around the terrace. "That is, none of us who know its true nature."

Inside, the band began to play again, the same music that now pounded incessantly in his head, the Song that King, to his horror, knew would never stop playing for him.

"Mr. King," Beroald said with a smile, "I believe they're playing your song."

King felt himself pulled by invisible hands as strange strings strummed the night air. He began a tarantella, his steps matching the rhythm of tambourines and castanets from the band. Glowing as if on fire, he spun down the great staircase, across the dance floor, and onto the stone dais.

Alexander King danced that night, danced for the patrons of that strange society, danced for the things behind the black portal, danced and danced.

As he would every night until his death, puppet to the Song, Dancer at the Red Door.

For the city has a song, and it plays in a minor key.

Douglas Smith is a Toronto writer whose stories have appeared in over sixty professional magazines and anthologies in twenty-five countries and twenty-one languages, including Interzone, The Third Alternative, Amazing Stories, Cicada, On Spec, Oceans of the Mind, Prairie Fire, *and* The Mammoth Book of Best New Horror, *as well as anthologies from DAW, Penguin/Roc, and others. He has been interviewed in the national magazine,* Saturday Night, *and his work has been studied in an "SF in Literature" course at the University of Washington.*

Doug was a John W. Campbell Award finalist for best new writer in 2001 and since then has twice won the Canadian Aurora Award for best speculative short fiction. Doug is an eleven-time finalist for the Aurora and has had several honorable mentions in The Year's Best Fantasy & Horror.

Doug is currently working on his first novel based on his award-winning short story, "Spirit Dance." His web site is www.smithwriter.com. He lives in Unionville, Ontario, with his wife and younger of two sons, and works in downtown Toronto where he is still searching for that phantom subway stop.

ABOUT THE EDITORS

Julie E. Czerneda is not a member of a secret society. Really. She doesn't know *those* people. They just happen to visit. When not practicing her secret handshake, Julie is a fulltime author and editor. Her tenth science fiction novel from DAW, *Regeneration*, Species Imperative #3 came out in 2006. Next comes a prequel to her Trade Pact Universe series, *Reap the Wild Wind*, out in July 2007. Her anthology *Space Inc.* won the Prix Aurora Award (Canada's Hugo). Julie has conspired with other editors before Jana, namely Isaac Szpindel (*ReVisions* from DAW) and Genevieve Kierans (*Mythspring* from Red Deer Press). Otherwise, she works alone and in . . . the shadows . . . editing the science fiction anthology series Tales from the Wonder Zone (next title *Polaris*) and Realms of Wonder, original fantasy. Oh, the secret handshake? When she gets it right, Jana's promised to let her help take over the , . . well, she can't tell you. You understand.

Jana Paniccia is not a member of a secret society either, though some may have their suspicions. After all, she's lived in six cities on three continents, once worked for the Deputy Prime Minister of Canada and for the Ontario Ministers of Energy and Finance, has an MBA in International Business, and is presently working for an international advisory services firm. In her covert writing life, her stories have appeared in the anthologies *Summoned to Destiny*, *Women of War*, *Children of Magic* and *Fantasy Gone Wrong*. Instead of world domination, she decided to branch out into editing—after all, it's pretty darned close.

Julie E. Czerneda

Web Shifters

"A great adventure following an engaging character across a divertingly varied series of worlds."—*Locus*

Esen is a shapeshifter, one of the last of an ancient race. Only one Human knows her true nature—but those who suspect are determined to destroy her!

BEHOLDER'S EYE
0-88677-818-2
CHANGING VISION
0-88677-815-8
HIDDEN IN SIGHT
0-7564-0139-9

Also by Julie E. Czerneda:
IN THE COMPANY OF OTHERS
0-88677-999-7
"An exhilarating science fiction thriller"
—*Romantic Times*

To Order Call: 1-800-788-6262